D1531973

TWO BLANKETS

A NOVEL OF THE WEST

TWO BLANKETS · BOOK ONE

TWO BLANKETS

A NOVEL OF THE WEST

R.L. ADARE

TIREE
PRESS

an imprint of

OGHMA CREATIVE MEDIA

OGHMA
CREATIVE MEDIA

Tiree Press
An imprint of Oghma Creative Media, Inc.
2401 Beth Lane, Bentonville, Arkansas 72712

Library of Congress Cataloging-in-Publication Data

Names: Adare, R.L., author.
Title: Two Blankets/R.L. Adare | Two Blankets #1
Description: First Edition. | Bentonville: Tiree, 2019.
Identifiers: LCCN: 2019936813 | ISBN: 978-1-63373-518-7 (hardcover) |
ISBN: 978-1-63373-519-4 (trade paperback) | ISBN: 978-1-63373-520-0 (eBook)
Subjects: BISAC: FICTION/Native American & Aboriginall | FICTION/Westerns |
FICTION/Coming of Age
LC record available at: https://lccn.loc.gov/2019936813

Tiree Press trade paperback edition July, 2019

Cover art by Venessa Cerasale
Cover & Interior Design by Casey W. Cowan
Editing by Dennis Doty

I dedicate this novel to my wife of thirty-five years, Iris.
I wish I had listened to you sooner.

ACKNOWLEDGEMENTS

M Y THANKS FOR this book go to my publisher, Oghma Creative Media, the inestimable Casey Cowan, and to my editor, Dennis Doty. Most especially, I want to thank my beta readers, Kathy Trueman and Kerri O'Donnell, whose patience and hard work was inexhaustible.

GLOSSARY

CAYUSE
Liksiyu: Name the Cayuse called themselves.

NEZ PERCE
ashwaníya: slave in Sahaptin (Nez Perce).

k'alas: raccoons.

máamin: Appaloosa horse.

Nch'i-wána: The great river, The Columbia River.

Nimi'ipuu: The Real People, the Nez Perce.

CHINOOK JARGON OR TRADE LANGUAGE
busi: pudendum.

ch-lai: pounded sun dried salmon.

chee whit: new one, whit meaning one.

camas: a starchy bulb eaten by many different tribes and the white pioneers, creates gaseous condition when undercooked.

cultus: weak, useless, small, frequently used in the negative as in cultus whiteman, useless white man, but used also as a positive as in cultus potlatch, a free gift.

cultus tilikum: common people.

dentalium: shell used as jewelry as well as used as a money trade item.

hyas talapus: wolf, apparently meaning Prairie Wolf, a coyote, mythical wolf being.

kloochma: female animal.

leloo: wolf.

lemolo: crazy.

mamook: to do, but also an obscenity for copulate as in "to do someone."

mistshimus: slave.

moosum: to sleep, also used to mean copulate as in "to sleep with someone," not an obscenity.

mowitch: deer, venison.

nika: mine.

potlatch: gift, gift giving ceremony.

quamash: synonym for camas, a bulb eaten for its starch, leads to gas when undercooked.

tatoosh: breasts.

tenass tilikums: children, children's.

tenino: vulva, pudenda.

Tyee: local clan leader of Chinook, they had no overall chief.

Wimahl: the Columbia River, the great river.

wootlat: penis.

whit: used as a suffix meaning "one who is." Not exactly a pronoun; used as, chee whit ("new one"), and klee whit ("laughing one").

whiteman(s): used as a referent to Caucasians.

TWO BLANKETS

A NOVEL OF THE WEST

THE RAID

CHAPTER I
EARLY SEPTEMBER, 1850

WHITE MOUSE WOKE well before dawn needing to make water. She looked about the reed mat covered longhouse that contained most of her immediate and extended family. Her younger sister and brother slept under the same hide. She extricated herself from her sister's arm and slipped from under the soft hide. The little fire had burned down to coals. As warm as the late summer had been, no fire was needed for warmth, only for cooking. She slipped her doeskin dress over her head and slid her feet into her knee length moccasins without lacing them up. All were asleep as she crept softly, across the open space. The sleeping spaces of her father, Creeping Wolf Clarkson, her older brother Elk, and older male cousins were empty. They had all gone to The Dalles for the annual trading. Grandfather, Three Blue Beads, snored in his accustomed summer sleeping place near the mat covered opening. He said he slept there to protect them. White Mouse suspected, since in winter he slept in the warmest place near the back of the hut, it was because he could catch the light breeze off the river on his face. She stepped over him as quietly as her namesake and through the small doorway.

She paced along the hut, away from the *Nch'i-wána*, the Big River, the Columbia, as the white man called it, back toward the forest edge. The moon, near full as it skimmed the ridgetop to the south, cast every stone and leaf in sharp relief.

It was unusually quiet despite the rush of water from *Nch'i-wána*. White Mouse shook her head to clear it. Perhaps it was only the grogginess of sleep clouding her senses and calling her back to bed. Tomorrow, they would go back to the river and fish the salmon, the old men with their spears, women, and children of her own age assisting, gutting the fish and moving them to the smoking racks. White Mouse glanced to the smoke shed. The breeze must have partially opened the door.

Long moon-cast shadows crept along the forest edge, sharply outlining the boundary of the riverside meadow and the blackened forest. She squatted to pee. It was so quiet. Yes, the *Nch'i-wána* still hurried to the sea, and it made no secret about it, but that sound was always in the background and had been all ten summers of her life. This was different. She opened herself to listening as grandmother Hawk Wing taught her.

Open yourself, not just your ears. Hear with your whole self.

What do you hear?

The answer was—nothing. There was no chirrup of the cricket, no skittering of nocturnal foragers nor the quieter rustle of the predator. No sound of the k'alas, the raccoons, digging in the midden pile for their midnight meal. There, just there, was the rustle of the horses and the quietened neigh of one of them. Something was amiss. She could feel it.

A hand, a large hand, clasped over her mouth and dragged her back into the brush and trees. She twisted. The arm and hand only tightened their grasp. She saw the flash of white and dark spots as an Appaloosa horse, a *máamin*, was led from the corral, a gag of buckskin tied about her mouth. She was taken up and thrown over a warrior's shoulder, and they began to move, in a silent walk at first, then at a ground-eating lope. White Mouse noticed they kept to the shadows on the border of the grass that fronted the *Nch'i-wána*. Any ten-year-old could track them, yet these were warriors, albeit young ones.

They turned up a stream and ran in the middle of it, masking their tracks. Still, a tracker would know they had to come this way. About a mile up they cut across a sandbank and entered a tributary leading off to the east. A half mile up this stream, they exited onto a shale bank and traveled some hundred paces up onto a rocky path. Carefully backtracking, they reentered the tributary where they had exited it. Downstream they went, cautious not to disturb any rocks. When they reached the original stream, they turned back upstream. At a slow walk, now wading in the deepest parts of the creek, they made their way another eight hundred paces until they came upon another stream entering from the west. They entered and took some little time to look over their path. This stream they followed step by careful step until they reached another shaly beach. They exited, and leaving one warrior to follow and hide their meager tracks, proceeded upward, ever upward. At last, they reached a rock track that led out of the canyon of the *Nch'i-wána* and took up their ground eating lope once again.

By the time the sun crested the horizon, they were out of the deep canyon and traveling at the pace White Mouse knew a warrior could keep up all day long. She could see, now, that there were three of them. The young man who carried her wore his hair long, had his face painted, and wore chest armor made from hardened elk hide, stiffened with cedar bark. So, these were Chinook. All three had the peculiar flattened heads of the Chinook and their noses pierced with bone as well. These warriors were high caste.

They traveled across the plateau most of the day, passing her from one to another without even a pause. Finally, in a grove of trees, they dumped her down. They ate a bit of *ch-lai*, dried salmon jerky, and rested until evening. Tying her across the Appaloosa colt's back, they proceeded once again.

This routine, travel hard, a short rest, then travel hard, continued for another two days and nights before they began the steep descent into the canyon of *Nch'i-wána*.

With the ululation of the young and triumphant, they entered their own camp. In contrast with the camp of the Nez Perce, this was much more permanent. Longhouses, one sizable enough to hold one hundred Chinook, were built on log frames and planked in cedar. They strutted through the village up to the *Tyee's* longhouse.

The *Tyee* sat in the sun before the totem that served as entrance, wearing a stern countenance. His flattened forehead wrinkled from his many summers, and his hair grayed at the temples. No clothing graced his body save a short cape across his shoulders. He looked upon his young warriors with anger in his eyes.

"See, what we have brought you, *Tyee* Running Blade," the eldest said.

"I see that you have brought me troubles, Drifting Smoke, perhaps many troubles."

"We have only raided a Nez Perce camp on the other side of The Dalles."

"During the truce of the trading?"

"Ha—that only applies to the trading place itself. This was a day's travel upriver from the trading place."

"That is a question to be debated by elders. But assuming it is true, what have you brought?"

Drifting Smoke gestured to his companions who stood masking the colt. Fox Tail carried White Mouse forward and dumped her to the ground.

"So, you brave warriors of the Chinook managed to capture a nine or ten-year-old girl. Anything else?"

Drifting Smoke gestured again, and Fox Tail and Fire Start brought forth the Appaloosa colt. "Yes," he said, "We have stolen this horse, this pride of the Nez Perce, just as our ancestors did."

Tyee Running Blade stood. "Do you know what you have done?"

"We have brought pride to our village and our nation."

"Look about you and tell me what you see."

"I see what I have always seen, the village and people within it, our people."

"How many longhouses?"

Drifting Smoke counted. "Large and small I count seven."

"How many of our people would those seven longhouses hold?"

"Maybe two hundred?"

"How many do they hold now clasped and protected from all the things that threaten them?"

"I don't know exactly—eighty?"

"I will tell you. Eighty-seven to be exact, including those that came from two other villages, one upriver and the other downriver. Those villages also held another two hundred and fifty Chinook at one time. But after the *cultus* whiteman's disease ran through us like a knife through salmon, our three villages of four hundred and fifty have been reduced to just eighty-seven souls."

"So, it was a brave deed for us to raid the Nez Perce," Drifting Smoke said.

"The Nez Perce are now the strongest nation along the *Wimahl*, the Columbia. They were hurt by the diseases, but not as we were. They still number three or four thousand. You have insulted our ally, our richest trading partner, and now our strongest possible enemy."

"We left a back trail that led toward the Cayuse lands."

"The Cayuse and the Nez Perce are like a brother and sister under the same sleeping furs in the depths of winter. The brother knows when she bleeds, and she knows that he farts in his sleep. They are so intertwined now, there is nothing the one does without the other knowing."

"Surely they will not miss one little girl and one horse."

"The girl we can hide here, and they may not seek retribution. The horse is a different matter. I once saw a Nez Perce at The Dalles turn down six hundred dollars for an Appaloosa when you can buy a normal horse for fifteen dollars. None but a Nez Perce may own one."

"So, we have endangered and shamed our village," Drifting Smoke said. "I led these warrior boys. I will stand the punishment, *Tyee*."

"I was young once. I remember the old times when we Chinook stood no insult to our honor, the old times when we took a toll on every canoe that wanted to pass our village. Now the boats pass us by. These are not those days, Drifting Smoke, no longer. We must either kill the Nez Perce horse and bury the hide or—" he broke off, thinking.

"What if I was to take the horse to Portland and sell him to a *cultus* whiteman? All Indians look the same to them and the Nez Perce would never know who stole him."

"Drifting Smoke, in spite of what you have done, you recovered and thought well just now. Take the colt, cover him with a blanket, and make good time. Let no one see you as a Chinook beyond this tribe. Go to Spalding's Stable up the Willamette about two miles from Portland. He is a greedy man who I met once when I went to Portland to trade. Wear *cultus* whiteman's clothing, remove your piercing, cover your proud, broad forehead with a hat, and with any luck, this storm will pass us by. Go now. And be quick."

Drifting Smoke led the Appaloosa away.

"You two, come forward. If I hear that you have even whispered of this event in your sleep, you will be cleaning salmon with the women and children until this time next year. Not a word of the horse or the girl."

"Yes, *Tyee*. Not a word."

"Get going then. Clean that paint off your faces, and put that armor back before your fathers find you have taken it," *Tyee* Running Blade said. "Now, let us see what problems Drifting Smoke has brought me. Get her to her feet and ungag her."

Since she was a girl prisoner, one of the women lifted her by the hair to an upright stance and removed the leather strap about her head. White Mouse straightened her back and looked straight at *Tyee* Running Blade. He looked back at her, the sunlight glinting off the straight narrow bone that pierced his septum and extended to the corners of his mouth.

"Second wife, Bears-Many-Children, remove her clothing. No slave has a right to such property."

Bears-Many-Children, dressed in a cedar grass skirt and several strands of glass beads dangling between her naked breasts, stripped White Mouse's doeskin dress and moccasins from her body. She pulled back into the group of onlookers admiring her new possessions.

"So, little child, do you understand the Chinook Jargon, the trade speech?"

"I talk little English. I am *Nimi'ipuu*, Nez Perce. No Chinook." She spat in the dust before the *Tyee*.

The *Tyee* gestured. "Second wife, switch her."

Bears-Many-Children picked up a reed switch and began beating her about the shoulders and on her bare legs. Tears formed in White Mouse's eyes as she collapsed to her knees.

"Stand her. Now, child, do you understand. What you were before, now, you are nothing, *mistshimus*, slave to the Chinook. You are only property. Do you understand Chinook Jargon?"

"I am *Nimi'ipuu*. No *mistshimus*. No Chinook," White Mouse said.

Tyee Running Blade signaled the whipping to continue. After several repetitions of this circle of dialogue, he said, "Enough for today, a day when I wish for long gone times when I would just kill you and bury your body beneath the post of a new longhouse. For now, I must consider the needs of the kin group and work you instead. Take her and cut her hair. She has no right to own such hair. Put her to work on the lowest job. She is yours to work, second wife, Bears-Many-Children. Work her and work her hard."

RESISTANCE

CHAPTER 2
EARLY SEPTEMBER, 1850

WHITE MOUSE WAS switched off to a hut where women were smoking salmon. Bears-Many-Children took up a flint knife and began hacking off White Mouse's waist length hair. Two other women joined in with their own knives.

They do this for pleasure, just to shame me? She realized, when two of them fought over the same hank of hair, pulling it first toward one, then to the other, that they wanted her hair as property.

"So proud the Chinook," she said in her own language, "that they will fight over the hair of a child slave." She grabbed up the flint blade of the nearest, Bears-Many-Children, who was so startled she just let it go. "Let me show you how a *Nimi'ipuu*, one of the True People, regards the *cultus* Chinook."

She scraped the blade across her scalp from forehead to nape of neck blooding the flint and removing a huge hank of hair which she dropped in the dirt. She grasped another large section over her left ear and shaved it off and tossed it down. Bears-Many-Children and her sisters sat and stared at her as one would toward the insane. White Mouse sang out in the *Nimi'ipuu* language, a song of Coyote and how Porcupine got his quills.

"When Coyote saw how long and thick Porcupine's fur was, he was envious. He thought 'What a nice pillow Porcupine's fur would make.'"

White Mouse danced a few steps, stopped and rough shaved off another strip, dropping it in the trodden dirt beneath her feet. Blood streamed down the whole left side of her scalp now. She began her dancing and singing again.

"When Porcupine was asleep, Coyote snuck up on him and holding him down between his teeth, shaved off all his hair and made off with it in a bundle. Porcupine crawled—bloody—into a hole."

White mouse shaved off another large hank and dropped it over the salmon the women had been cleaning.

"Coyote found he only had half the amount he needed to make his soft fur pillow. So, he waited awhile for Porcupine to grow new fur, and then went back to the hole."

White Mouse scraped off the last of her hair, dropping it to the ground.

"Coyote called to Porcupine, 'Come out, little Porcupine so we may be friends again.'

"Porcupine said, 'We were never friends. You just want me to come out so you may shave my fur again.'

"Coyote became angry and said, 'Come out, or I shall dig you out and have the last of your fur for my pillow.'

"Porcupine said, 'You will not like it, for I have been in this hole so long my hair has hardened into spikes.'

"Coyote began digging at the hole, 'Very well, I gave you a chance to cooperate. Now, I shall take what I want.' He dug, and he dug, and when the hole was wide enough, Coyote stuck his head in to bite Porcupine.

"He withdrew it quickly, his nose spiked with quills.

"Porcupine said, 'I told you that you would not like my new hair.'"

White Mouse was finished. Blood coated her hands and dripped down her face. Small random patches of short black hair remained on her shaven and bloody scalp, the hair scattered about amidst the salmon scales. She dropped the flint blade onto the ground.

"I am *Nimi'ipuu*. No slave. No *mistshimus*. No Chinook." White Mouse said. She spoke very clearly in Chinook Jargon, "Now I will be Girl-With-No-Name. Beat me again, Bears-Many-Children, if you wish."

Girl-With-No-Name wandered the camp. She was obviously mad, for who but a mad person would do such a thing. All those who saw her moved out of her path. All, except some of the young children who followed her. She walked aimless along the river bank, past the cedar canoes of *Tyee* and the lesser nobility. When she walked by the fishing place where men stood upon the rocks and speared the fish, and her blood dripped a few drops into the water, the fishermen stood away from their spears. The blood of a mad girl upon their rocks and the pools of the sacred fishing spot was a bad omen. She did not care. She was Girl-With-No-Name.

Two of the more daring boys threw small stones at her, but when she turned toward them they ran away. She approached the women carrying the salmon to the smoking shed. They backed away.

Are they all so afraid of me that they will let me leave the village?

She began walking more purposefully yet still with an aimless step up-river. In ten minutes, she came to the last of the longhouses, small and abandoned. In another half hour, the forest side closed in, a cliff side that dropped straight into the river.

"*Ayieee. Aiyiee,*" she heard behind her. Two boys, about sixteen jogged up.

"So, our little mad girl thinks to walk back to the Nez Perce, does she?" Fire Start asked.

"But the cliff has stopped her," said Fox Tail. "Nothing for it but to carry her back."

He grabbed her and tossed her onto his back. Off they ran, laughing, back to the village. They dropped her to her feet before Bears-Many-Children.

"It seems you have lost something, kin-mother."

The cane came down hard on her legs, nearly buckling her over.

"Sit," Bears-Many-Children said.

The cane came down again, and again. She dropped to the ground.

"Clean fish," Bears-Many-Children said. "Worthless *mistshimus* do not even have right to name herself. A name is property. You are property."

Girl-With-No-Name reached for the flint knife to clean the salmon.

"No knife for you, *mistshimus*," Bears-Many-Children said in Chinook Jargon handing the flint to her neighbor. "She cuts. I know you speak the Chinook Jargon, the trade tongue. Language is property. You no speak. You only listen. This is way in true Chinook tribe. *Mistshimus* do work they can, low work for stupid slaves. The common people, the round-heads with small names, like Bone Knife, do what they can. Bone Knife is very good with knife."

Bone Knife smiled at the mention of her name and demonstrated. With one quick slice starting from the anus of the fish up to the fins she opened up the salmon, and the guts half-spilled out.

"I have big name, important name. I watch, see you do job right. *Mistshimus* clean with fingers. No deserve knife."

So, passed the afternoon. White Mouse, Girl-With-No-Name, realized she could only take so many beatings. Now the cuts on her scalp just hurt and her legs hurt from the switching. If she were to get away from these Chinook dogs, she would have to make better plans, and she needed her strength. She cleaned the guts from the salmon that fed them all. This was something she knew, and she could do it and dream at the same time.

She remembered her own tribe's summer camp on the *Nch'i-wána*, three days travel away. How could two tribes be so different? Here these Chinook lived lives in one of three groups—noble, commoner, or slave. The slaves did the worst work. The commoners performed medium skilled tasks, and the nobles were regarded as great if they owned a lot of property, including slaves. Only the nobles could own slaves or own most property. A tool, a name, a song, were considered property and jealously guarded.

Girl-with-No-Name remembered her own tribe, the *Nimi'ipuu*, who shared the work and the joys. True, there were the elders and chiefs whose words were regarded, but even they could be challenged and argued with. Everyone had a right to go on a vision quest to find their guardian spirit and their true name, the name spoken only to intimate friends when they became adults. The *Nimi'ipuu* had slaves too, usually prisoners taken in war, but frequently these were eventually adopted into a kin group. Seldom were they killed.

Are they looking for me, my family and my tribe? There were only the women, children, and the old in the summer camp when she was taken. Most of the warriors and some of the women, too, were at The Dalles for the yearly trading.

Will they let the stealing of a *Nimi'ipuu* horse, an Appaloosa, go unchallenged? She had never heard of this happening before. For one Nez Perce to steal an Appaloosa from another tribe, might be worth two or three coup feathers. For a Chinook to steal one was a great insult, perhaps a cause for war.

I have not seen the Appaloosa here, so no one may find I am here.

The Chinook, unlike the *Nimi'ipuu*, had few horses, and Girl-With-No-Name had seen no trace.

As the evening mealtime approached, she was shifted from gutting fish to cleaning and fetching in the cooking area. This tribe took their meals communally, and so, with the fourteen other *mistshimus*, there was much to do. Even among the slaves, she could see the same competition for the better job. As the newest and the worst slave, she had earned the lowest job. To her fell the pounding of camas into flour and the cleaning of the pickle-weed, or sea beans as some called them, for boiling. She scooped up a handful of dirt and added it to the camas flour. The pickleweed, the Chinook must have traded for. Girl-With-No-Name knew of it and that it only grew in salt marshes. The Chinook were great traders. One had to credit that to them.

A large fire was built of alder. Bone Knife demonstrated the proper method to cook the salmon.

"Lay each cut of salmon on these hardwood sticks. See, each stick de-barked and same length, the length of a man's leg," she said and waited for Girl-With-No-Name to nod. "Push the stick through skin and flesh, and out through the skin on other side." She waited until Girl-With-No-Name nod-ded understanding again. "Put the end of stick in the dirt. Two hand widths from salmon to dirt." She measured with her hand and looked up to judge Girl-With-No-Name was following. "Two hand widths. Now you try."

Girl-With-No-Name threaded the salmon fillet on the skewer, pushed it into the ground and measured out two hand widths from the ground.

"No, no. Yours too close to ground. Two hand widths. Two."

Girl-With-No-Name measured with her hand. She was two fingers shy.

"Your hands too small. Use my hand width, not yours," Bone Knife said. The fillets were lined up almost exactly the length of a woman's leg from the fire. Finally, the noble woman in charge judged the commoners' work to be acceptable.

The camas flour Girl-With-No-Name pounded was shaped into cakes by two common women who chatted happily as they worked. They placed them on hot stones from the bed of growing coals and baked them.

The two women took a waterproof basket, about as tall as a man's forearm, and filled it with water. They pulled several stones from the hottest part of the fire with sticks like tongs, blew off the ash and dropped them into the basket. When the water was boiling, they dropped in the pickleweed. The noble woman judged the time by singing a counting song. She ordered the water poured out, the pickleweed placed on shallow carved bowls of cedar, and carried to the feast.

After they had brought the salmon fillets and the camas cakes in, the slaves retired to the cooking area, where they fell upon pieces of blackened salmon that had dropped to the ground, broken camas cakes, and the few limp pickleweed stalks they could find.

I do not like this fighting for food, but I must eat.

She growled like an angry wolverine and bared her teeth. One woman holding a coveted whole fillet that was merely burned dropped it and backed away. Her blood-streaked face and reputation earned her two half-cakes of camas and a handful of pickleweed. Girl-With-No-Name settled back in a corner against the cooking shed to eat.

That night, Bears-Many-Children tied her to a stake in the cooking area with a long damp rawhide strip and went off to her longhouse to sleep. Other slaves slept wherever they could find cover or comfort. Girl-With-No-Name worried at the knot for a good hour before she gave that up. The harder she worked the knot, the tighter it became. The stake was as thick as her wrist and stuck out of the ground the length of a man's forearm. She started rocking it back and forth, back and forth. After a period, she was able to push it almost to the ground on either side, like working a rotten tooth loose. Finally, it just snapped, and she pulled it out. The stake was as long as a man's leg. She would have to carry it.

She looked at the moon and gauged it about midnight. She padded through the camp upriver. Knowing, now, she couldn't just walk the bank, she would have to work back up the creek they had come down when they brought her here. Past the midden pile and the last empty houses, she came upon the creek. Now she began to run. It was awkward carrying the stake, but freedom beckoned. She ran up the creek until her breath came in great gulps and saw in the dim light the path up toward the rim.

She was barefoot, and her feet hurt working up the rocky path, but now she approached that state of, I don't care. I don't care. I don't care. Every step she repeated this chant until she reached the edge where canyon turned to grassy tableland.

She rested a half hour and then began to run. All she knew was to run eastward. Keeping the moon on her right, she ran away from it.

The dawn was approaching. There was no place to hide and looking back she could see her back trail that a six-year-old could follow. She kept running.

Maybe they will just let me go. She did not believe it. *Tyee* Running Blade did not look like a man to just let things go.

At what she gauged to be ten o'clock, she could hear her pursuers at a distance. She was, oh, so tired, but she pushed herself to run.

A hand before midday, they were close enough that she could see them, and they were loping along laughing. It was the same two who had caught her the last time, likely the two young men from the raid. She stumbled and dropped the stake. It tripped her, and she fell. She picked it back up and ran on.

At midday they caught her, and she collapsed onto the ground. One of the boys, Fire Stick, pulled a bone knife from his belt and cut the stake loose.

"Burr-Up-My-Ass," Fire Stick said, "pick her up and let's go."

Fox Tail picked her up and threw her over his shoulder. They headed back to camp at an easy lope. She was exhausted, but they were not even winded, and they carried on a suggestive conversation about a certain girl they liked most of the way back.

"So, do you think your little fire stick is enough to set Quivering Deer's basket boiling, or will she quench it and send you running for flint and tinder to light it back up again?" Fox Tail asked.

"Ha. You can ask her, Burr-Up-My-Ass, when you are trapped in her wet thatch, burrowing up after I am done with her."

At mid-afternoon, they entered the camp and dumped her before *Tyee* Running Blade. The sun gleamed off his high forehead.

ESCAPE ATTEMPT

CHAPTER 3
EARLY SEPTEMBER, 1850

"STAND HER," *TYEE* Running Blade said.

Fox Tail stood her up.

"First wife, Swimming Salmon, beat her."

Swimming Salmon, who had numerous chains of glass beads across her bare breasts, a choker made of dentalium shells about her neck, and beaded anklets, stepped forward. Her arms were decorated with tattoos of salmon swimming upstream toward her shoulders. About her hips, she wore only a broad belt of shells and whiteman's beads in several rows. She was a stern-faced heavy-set woman with graying hair braided tight and set off with shells. The tight braids stressed her wide sloped forehead. Her broad nose was also pierced with a bone curved down to meet her full lips. She set to her task and beat Girl-With-No-Name until she collapsed.

"This is your first warning. If you are foolish, you will get a second. The third will mean your death. Swimming Salmon, see what you can do with her."

Swimming Salmon stepped forward, her beads and breasts swaying. She whispered to the *Tyee*. He nodded and produced two keys which he handed to Swimming Salmon. She grabbed Girl-With-No-Name by the ear and led her to a storage shed. Ducking within, she soon emerged with a long chain of pounded iron links and two brass padlocks. One end she fastened around the ankle of Girl-With-No-Name. She tested it by pulling hard. It only scraped the ankle and would not come off. The other end she fastened about a piece of oak firewood a hand's length thick and as long as a man's leg. Again, she tested it and found it could not be removed. Smiling, she placed the keys on a thong and hung it about her neck.

"You will find, *mistshimus*, I am not as agreeable as second wife. It is why I am first among women here. Go find work among the slaves. If you do not find work, I will beat them, and they will beat you. You are beneath my punishment." Swimming Salmon tossed her hair and the beads danced.

Girl-With-No-Name picked up her anchor and walked to the salmon smoking shed. She settled next to the slaves cleaning salmon and began gutting them. The women and girls showed no animosity toward her and none toward their Chinook entitled masters either. They accepted their station and chatted and joked about everyday life. After an hour of cleaning, she moved to the cooking station and began pounding flour. Although she had frightened them yesterday, today they seemed to hold no memory of it.

Maybe that is their secret to acceptance of this sort of life, live only right now and don't think about yesterday or tomorrow. I cannot live that way.

She ground the camas root into flour. Later, when the entitled and common folk had been served, she fought over her share and a bit more. She knew she would have to have food if she were to make an escape attempt again.

Later that evening when the titled and related common folk had settled into the longhouse to sleep, and the slaves slept huddled together, their bodies warming each other near the fire pit, Girl-With-No-Name picked up her log and wandered toward the upriver edge of the camp. Along the way, she picked up a couple pieces of rawhide and some thong. Here, past the midden pile of fish guts and bones, stood a couple of smaller pit houses long abandoned. The farther longhouse had fallen in on itself with only one plank wall still standing, but the nearer was still mostly intact. Inside it was dark, but some moonlight passed through spaces where the bark roof had collapsed. Near the back was a pile of rubble and old boards. Worming her way into it, she found a small space where she could curl up and sleep.

The next day when she started working, Swimming Salmon unchained the oak log and chained her to a similar sized alder log. She said nothing and walked away. Girl-With-No-Name tested the chain. Still no give to it, but at least the log was lighter. As before, she went through the day, always on the lookout for a piece of camas cake or leather. Toward evening she was walking past an area used by the flint knappers. She found a broken but usable knife blade, hid it under a rock, and continued her work day. That evening she frightened off a slave from an almost whole burned salmon fillet and took that and her newly found knife back to her burrow.

With care not to disturb anything, she snuck back beneath the pile of debris. There was little light in the building and even less back here, but she could work by feel. She had enough rawhide to cover the bottoms of her feet, not real moccasins but at least some protection. Girl-With-No-Name augured holes into the rawhide and strapped them on her feet. She needed more thongs and resolved to look for some on the morrow. She also needed a bag to carry her supplies.

The next morning when Swimming Salmon found her, she was working with two other slaves tanning hides. As usual, she had the worst job, but now she did not care. The two other *mistshimus* girls paid her no attention at all. Swimming Salmon simply grabbed her by the ear and led her off. Girl-With-No-Name went without protest. She wanted to show Swimming Salmon how compliant she was. At the campfire, she unlocked the chain and relocked it about a birch log. It was still awkward but was a little lighter than the alder one had been.

I still cannot remove the chain, but this is a green log. If I can just slip the bark, I may get the chain off.

That meant tonight she must go and begin the first part of her escape plan. She carried the log back to the leather working area. The other two *mistshimus* girls were gone to the preparation of the midday meal or some other task. She looked about, and no one seemed to be near except for a couple of dogs. Checking within the cedar planked shed, she saw near the back a pile of old leather scraps. Digging under the stack, she found several pieces that would work for her "sandals" as well as an old discarded leather bag. She took these and slipped back out. Now, she needed to hide her precious finds. Girl-With-No-Name put the straps into the bag and hid it in the shed beneath an old log.

She went back to work. Girl-With-No-Name laced a hide to the stretching frame, a vertical rectangular frame of poles lashed together. The hide had holes punched in it already. They wouldn't let her have that tool. She laced the hide to the frame along the top edge with damp rawhide thongs, and then laced the bottom edge, followed by the right and left.

She worked most of the day like this then fought over what extra food she could garner. She managed to "accidentally" burn two salmon fillets and break four camas cakes which, through growling and mad antics, she claimed for herself. Later that night, she retrieved her bag, and placing her food within it, made her way back to her sleeping place. Now her time was limited. She took out her broken flint knife and slit the birch bark. Next, she cut around the whole log just next to the chain. Wedging the knife in between the bark and log she managed to peel the bark loose. Soon, it was done. Now, the chain. She worked the chain, link by link down onto the debarked area. When the chain was off the bark, there was a good finger's width of play in it. It was still a tough job getting the chain off, but by first sliding one side two finger widths, then the other side, she managed it. She hid all her supplies back under the debris. It was close to midnight now, and she only had 'til dawn.

Carrying the log, the bark, and the end of the chain, she jogged quickly to the creek and up the creek to the path leading to the plains above. They would assume she would come this way, so there was no reason to hide her trail. When she reached the top, she saw that her previous path, as well as the one followed by the boys, was still clearly delineated.

That is good. If the old path was grown over or not clear, that would spoil all my plans.

She began to run, sometimes straight along the path, sometimes a bit alongside, trying to simulate a panicked ten-year-old girl. When the moon had moved a mere handspan across the sky, she flopped down. She broke up the pieces of birch bark, trying to make sure no cut edges showed, and scattered them around. The log she tossed off to one side. Now she ran another mile or so as before, as if a panicked girl was just trying to get away. Finally, she stopped and looked back. Her meandering path appeared real enough. Now came the important and tricky part. She walked back, attempting wherever possible to place her footprint in one of the other returning footprints. When she got back to the path down to the creek, she was even more careful not to leave any trace of her return. She drank deeply from the stream and pissed. This would be the last opportunity for either at least until tomorrow night. She followed the stream to the Chinook camp. She glanced over at the river and the canoes. Pulled up on the beach at the end was a derelict. She diverted and pushed it into the water. It leaked a little. She grabbed a paddle from one of the larger canoes and laid it inside, then pushed the canoe out into the current.

Maybe that will give them something else to think about.

The main path through the camp passed by her hiding hut. It was filled with footprints. When she reached the abandoned hut, she backed in, brushing aside any footprints she could see in the graying light of predawn. Once within, she did the same over to her burrow beneath the debris. She had to make it look as abandoned as it had before she discovered it. Satisfied, she crept in and lay down to sleep. All she could do now was wait.

Tyee Running Blade was not having a very good day. He longed to sit in the sun and dream of the days when the Chinook were a strong people, and he could just kill the little irritation.

"So, first wife, your charge has escaped you?"

"She is mad, that one. She was responding as a slave should. Then she just disappeared."

"So, you let a ten-year-old girl escape you?"

Swimming Salmon bowed her head. "Yes, *Tyee*, I did."

"Question the other *mistshimus* and the round-heads she worked with. Find out anything you can. Remind the *mistshimus* that they will be beaten because the girl has run."

"Yes, *Tyee*." Upon leaving she said, "She should be killed and be done with it."

"Fire Stick, Fox Tail, you see the irritation you have brought upon us with your rash action. Go up the creek and see if she went that way. She cannot have traveled fast with the log chained around her leg."

"Yes, *Tyee*." They were off on the run. No one wanted to be around *Tyee* Running Blade when he was in this sort of a mood.

They reached the path up to the plateau in a half hour, and in another half-hour of quick and hard climbing were on top. Before them lay their former path.

"She came this way. You can see her footprints, and she was running," Fox Tail said.

"You couldn't find a hole in a bush, Fox Tail. Let's just get her back. This game isn't fun anymore."

They ran side by side up the path and by the time the sun was halfway to its apex, they arrived at the point where the *mistshimus* had sat down. Fox Tail held up his hand, and they looked over the scene.

He picked up the bark scraps. "She must've tried to scrape the bark off so she could loose the chain."

"Over here, Fire Stick. The log." Fox Tail retrieved the sapling.

"This must have taken at least a couple hours. So, we are close," Fire Stick said. "You pick up all the bark, every piece mind you, and return to *Tyee* Running Blade with the bark and the log. He will want to know. Then come back. This is no time to be nosing about that round-head girl you like. I will continue running her down. If I catch her, I will bring her back."

Fox Tail gathered the birch bark and the log and turned about jogging toward camp. Fire Stick loped down the path toward Nez Perce lands. He was confident he would soon catch her up and return her to camp. In another quarter hour, he reached the point where she had doubled back. He did not notice it at first. He was not tracking, just following. Fox Tail slowed to a walk and stopped. Looking back, the track was straight, no more meandering. Forward was the same, the path of three warriors loping single file, not the path of a panicked girl. Squatting down he found the large footprints of Drifting Smoke and a little further on the smaller footprints of himself and Fox Tail as well as the hoof prints of the Appaloosa colt. Footprints of the girl but only one set, the last time they had come this way.

She has fooled us, this sly little girl. She didn't come this way.

Turning about he began to run in earnest back to the camp. The *Tyee* needed to know about this development. He reached the pathway down just about the time Fox Tail crested onto the plateau.

"Where is the girl?" Fox Tail asked.

"She didn't go that way, the little ferret. Search about carefully toward the river and the other way too. See if you can find any sign. We know she came up here. I am going to tell the *Tyee*."

Fire Stick sprinted off and thereafter down the creek. When he reached the camp, everyone was talking about the girl, like meat bees buzzing over a fresh corpse. An elder and several common people were discussing something important near the canoes. He ran up to the *Tyee* and fell upon one knee.

"Many pardons, *Tyee*. I followed the *mistshimus* girl's trail until it met up with the track from the last time. I saw her footprints from when we chased her as well as our own fainter tracks from the raid. Nothing fresh. I am no tracker, but I do not believe she went that way. I left Fox Tail on the plateau to search toward and away from the river."

"Rest a moment," *Tyee* Running Blade said. "What is this, Long Pipe?"

The elder from the canoes stepped forward. "One canoe is missing and a paddle. It is the old leaky canoe, but the girl may have taken it."

"I am regretting my promise to let her live. Fire Stick, take a canoe and four of the best paddlers from among the *mistshimus*. Go upriver to the trading place at The Dalles. Fetch back the tracker, Wolf Scent, and another warrior. Paddle fast. We need you back here by tomorrow night. Eat, get supplies for two days, *ch-lai* as well, and go within the hour."

"Yes, *Tyee* Running Blade, I go." Fire Stick loped off to gather his supplies.

Fox Tail roamed the edge of the plateau above the canyon, careful not to disturb any sign the *mistshimus* might have left. Like Fire Stick, he was no expert tracker, but he knew the basics. He found no sign that she had gone either way. He decided to return to the *Tyee* after a fruitless two hours searching.

"*Tyee*, I have found no sign of the *mistshimus*. A tracker might find something I have missed."

"Fox Tail, I have sent Fire Stick to The Dalles for Wolf Scent," the *Tyee* said. "A canoe and paddle are missing. It's possible she may have taken the canoe downriver, though that seems foolish to me. I want you to take a canoe with two *mistshimus* paddlers and two round-head fighters. Search for the canoe or any evidence she went downriver. Take supplies for two days. If you do not find anything in a day, then return here."

"I will eat and go, *Tyee* Running Blade," Fox Tail said.

"This girl is a pestilence," Running Blade said. "There is nothing worse than a smart *mistshimus*."

It was difficult for Girl-With-No-Name to sleep with the activity percolating through the camp. Each new discovery about her brought with it new talk and a flurry of activity. With her ear against the cracks between the planks, she did hear of the sending for the tracker at The Dalles and the search for the missing canoe. She finished making her sandals and packed her parfleche bag. She ate and slept.

As night crept on, she crawled from her burrow with her bag, her sandals slung over her shoulder, and her knife. The chain she muffled as well as she could. Peeking out the door, she saw no one. She slipped along the moon shadowed side of the building. Still, there was no one in sight. Now, there was nothing for it but to begin her escape. The most difficult thing for her was not to run, to maintain a steady walking pace toward the creek. She reached the creek and glanced about. Still no one about, so she turned up the creek and began walking. About halfway up she drank deeply, then squatted and pissed in the creek. When she reached the wooded edge, she began a slow trot, hoping her footprints would blend in with those of the many who had passed here in the last few days.

My real worry right now is whether the *Tyee* has someone up here watching the path.

It appeared not. She reached the plateau and attempted to blend her footprints in with those left behind by Fox Tail in the tall grass. It was all she could do. Every handspan of time taken now, that delayed pursuit by two handspans, was a gain. She might gain a couple of handspans of sun time here if she were lucky. So, she proceeded away from the river staying in Fox Tail's trail. After a short while, his trail stopped and turned about. This was the end of Fox Tail's explorations. She backtracked fifty paces to a point where she had seen a deer trail cutting across the plain. This would have to be her way. She put on her sandals and laced them up tight. Now all she could do was run.

For the first three hundred paces, she stepped lightly and as unobtrusively as possible as she followed the deer trail. She knew any tracker would likely see it. Then she opened up her stride and ran. She knew not to sprint no matter how much she wanted to. *Nimi'ipuu* territory was at least three days run from here. She had to set a pace she could maintain. It was nigh on midnight now. So, she had nearly half the night to get out of sight of anyone looking. She hoped to make nearly as good time as a war party, given her size, and could run like this all night. At dawn, she would sleep a short while, then rise and run again. The chain irritated, but for now, she would put up with the pain.

She ran only until she found herself short on breath, then walked, ran, and walked again. Eventually, she lost the deer trail and then she just ran east, keeping the moon on her right. When the early pre-dawn light lit the sky, she collapsed into the shoulder-high grass. She curled up and slept as best she could. After a short nap, she sat up and ate some salmon and a half a cake. She was not worried about running out of food. Water was another issue. She had found nothing to carry water in and could only hope to come across the occasional stream. She checked the chain on her ankle. The leather she had put there to pad it was holding, but her skin chafed anyway. She gathered up her parfleche and chain and began jogging toward the sun.

Back in the camp, there was nothing the *Tyee* could do except wait. Every hour that passed, the *mistshimus* bitch was farther away, and he did not even know which way she had gone. He noticed all were avoiding him, and he did not blame them. He wished he could avoid himself as well. Alas, he could not. He was *Tyee*, and the responsibility was his. The Bent Creek Clan depended on his judgment. He went over all the steps he had taken, and all seemed logical. Still, he felt like he was missing something.

THE LONG CHASE

CHAPTER 4
SEPTEMBER, 1850

WOLF SCENTS ARRIVED at dusk along with an exhausted four paddlers, Fire Stick, and a second warrior, Great Bear. He jogged up to the *Tyee's* longhouse and entered through the portal in the totem that stood in front of it. Great Bear followed with their gear.

"*Tyee* Running Blade, I come as you called," Wolf Scents said. "We paddled all night to get here."

Tyee Running Blade explained the circumstances of the raid, his decision to sell the horse and the *mistshimus's* previous escape attempt. He also told about the canoe and sending Fox Tail in search downriver.

"Stealing a canoe and setting off downriver does not make sense to me," said Wolf Scents, "but she is a Nez Perce. They often do things that make no sense. I have brought Great Bear. He can track as well and is a good runner. Let me talk to the last to see her. Likely we cannot start the hunt until tomorrow before dawn, and she will have a day-and-a-half lead, but perhaps we will find out more on where to begin."

"She is only a ten-year-old *mistshimus* girl," said the *Tyee*.

"Who has escaped twice and evaded capture for forty-eight hours altogether," Wolf Scents said. "We are old friends, Running Blade. The Nez Perce are an odd people, but they are a sly and brave people as well. Let us not discount her abilities. The mouse is small, even insignificant, but it will still eat all your camas cakes."

Tyee Running Blade grasped Wolf Scents by the shoulder. "You are right, friend. Let us get to the bottom of this basket. We will go to the salmon cooking area. She was last seen there."

At the cook fire, the slaves remembered little in actual detail.

"Did she work hard?" asked Wolf Scents. "Did she do anything odd? Where did she sleep?"

All agreed she worked hard. "She fought for food like she was demon possessed." The others nodded. "I think she slept that way," one said, pointing upriver. "The *mistshimus* girl did not sleep with us." All agreed on this point.

"So, we know a little more. She avoided the other *mistshimus* and perhaps slept upriver." Wolf Scents said.

"I don't give a *cultus* whiteman's damn about where she slept. Where is she now?"

"Patience, friend. Let us see what we can see." Wolf Scents bent down. "See here, the tracks of a small foot. They do not follow the others on the common path to deliver the food." He followed the footprints. "It looks like they passed this way more than once." They followed the trace past the midden pile.

"Did you have those huts searched?" Wolf Scents asked pointing to the abandoned huts.

"No, what fool hides in his enemies camp?" the *Tyee* said.

"A little mouse, perhaps." There seemed to be no tracks anyone could follow on this portion of the path, as this route was frequently used. "Here, look here." Wolf Scents said.

"I see nothing, just a clean threshold."

Great Bear had caught up to them. "Perhaps a little too clean?"

"Exactly what I thought. Good eye, Great Bear. It has been brushed clear."

They entered. "Do you smell that?" Great Bear said. "I smell salmon."

"Everything smells like salmon in this village, but I get your point. This hut has been abandoned for three summers. No reason for it to smell like fresh cooked salmon," the *Tyee* said.

"This was the little *mistshimus* mouse's lair," Wolf Scents said, "and I would bet my wife that is where she holed up."

Great Bear moved to the pile of debris and started moving old planks. "No one who knew your wife would take that bet." Soon he had her hiding spot exposed. "Ah, see the cut bark? The little mouse had a knife. Here are leather scraps as well."

"All right," Wolf Scents said, "we will start our search on the plateau tomorrow at first light. This is what happened, I think. She collected food and a knife. She probably has foot coverings as well. The night before she disappeared she slipped the bark on the birch log and carried it up and laid the false trail. Probably cut the canoe loose at the same time. Likely, when Fox Tail comes back, if he is lucky, he will have found the canoe, but no trace of the girl. She hid here until last night before making her run. To-morrow we will start our search. It is a good three day run for a warrior to Nez Perce territory. With luck, we may catch her up. This is only a ten-year-old *mistshimus* girl after all, even if she is Nez Perce. I will need Great Bear and two other warriors. Now let us eat and rest. We meet at the top at the first gray light."

They climbed out of the ravine at first light. Fox Tail's riverward trail yielded no trace. Wolf Scents began his search in the other direction, and soon found a trace of something.

"See here, a small footprint set right into Fox Tail's barefoot print. Let us pursue this." He searched on hands and knees. Ten paces farther on he found another. "Here, her print overlaps his." Another twenty paces. "And here are two small prints. She definitely came this way."

He straightened up, and stooped over, began moving quickly over White Mouse's occasional footprints. Every twenty or thirty paces he would say, "and another," or "here are two." Now, he stood up, and soon they were at the end of Fox Tail's trail.

"You can see here she has doubled back." With care, they worked their way back to the almost invisible deer trail. Following on the side of this, they soon found unmistakable evidence of her passage.

"Now, we have her path. We just have to catch her. Great Bear, take Fire Stick and run ahead. Run quick pace, then stop after a quarter day and rest. We will run slower and pass you while you rest. Go now."

Thus, began the chase. Great Bear and Fire Stick ran at a fast pace for a quarter day along the side of White Mouse's trail. When the sun reached its zenith, they lay down to eat and sleep. Wolf Scents and his companion, Hawk Talon, ran at a more leisurely lope, a pace that could still outstrip a horse on a long run. At little past midday, they caught up to and passed Great Bear, who lay snoring. They continued for another two hands of the sun, then lay down for their own rest.

Wolf Scents could see no slackening in the *mistshimus* girl's stride or pace. Yet they were men. She was only a ten-year-old girl. The terrain had to take its toll eventually as they ran up each sloping hill and down into the troughs. Only time would tell if they caught her. They had the advantage of speed and number. She had a strong head start.

White Mouse kept on running. She also knew to stick to the loping stride that ate up the miles. She might be small and only ten, but she knew the ways of the prairie. She ran as straight as possible, but the hillsides rose on her right. She knew the *Nch'i-wána* was off to her left some miles and knew she did not want to get too close, lest she get caught by the steepening hillsides near Celilo Falls. So, she tried to crest the shallow hills and run to the left of the steeper ones. She still had not passed the track from the raid, so she assumed it must still lie some distance on her left.

She came across a small creek and stopped a short time to drink, eat a camas cake, and drink again. It relieved her to find water. That had been her greatest fear. It was nearing sundown and she vowed to keep running until dark, then sleep until moonrise.

They continued in this way, prey and predator for two days. Gradually, White Mouse began to tire more easily. The chain cut into her ankle. Her sandal-moccasins began to disintegrate. She was nearing the end of her food supply as well and had no time to search for any. She had climbed up to the plateau above Celilo Falls and was somewhere near Cayuse territory, the *Liksiyu* as they called themselves. They were a similar tribe to the Nez Perce in lifestyle. A couple miles past the great Celilo Falls on the *Nch'i-wána*, she began the steeper descent into the Deschutes canyon. It took her some little time to find a ford where she managed to cross. It was beginning to get dark, but she needed to climb out of this canyon before it got so dark she couldn't see. She scrambled up the far side and climbed the two-hundred paces or so to the rim. She knew she was in Cayuse territory now, no longer Chinook. That somehow made her feel better.

She ate the last of her salmon and camas cake and lay down to rest.

At the rise of the moon, she got up and began to walk east into Cayuse territory. She knew she could now be no more than a day's journey from Nez Perce lands. Presumably, the Chinook would not follow her there. All she could do was hope. The moon was only up for six hours before it became too dark to see. She lay down again to wait for the predawn light.

Wolf Scents reached the Deschutes River at just about the same time. They rested on the edge of the canyon, not daring a descent in the dark. He knew they were close, less than twelve hours behind the *mistshimus*. She was slowing. His four men were fresh and rested. He also knew they would be in Cayuse lands beyond the Deschutes. While their numbers had been reduced by half by the measles epidemic three years before and further reduced by the war with the U.S Government in the ensuing years over the Whitman massacre, they were not particularly friendly to the Chinook.

All he could do was take sustenance, drink and lay down to rest until first light.

He and Hawk Talon woke before first light and began the descent. Hawk Talon lost his footing in the darkness and tumbled fifty feet down the slope. When Wolf Scents reached him Hawk Talon was gripping his ankle.

"By all the *cultus* whiteman's gods, I have run three days and then fallen and sprained my ankle in the last half day of the chase," Hawk Talon said.

"It is my responsibility, friend," Wolf Scents said. "We could easily have waited another hour. This is the long chase. I forgot that."

"I will wait here and send Great Bear on at a run. He and Fire Stick can be no more than a couple hours behind us. Go. Go now and catch the little *mistshimus* bitch who has twisted my ankle."

"You will have your chance at her when we return. I go now." Wolf Scents began looking for the spot where White Mouse had forded. When he found it, he could see across the river where she had climbed out of the canyon. He only hoped that Great Bear caught up with him soon. He did not fancy meeting a Nez Perce band on horseback in Cayuse territory. Cayuse and Nez Perce had long intermarried and were almost one tribe now, since the Cayuse war.

He climbed out of the canyon and found the spot where White Mouse had slept only a half day before. Her path out showed she was walking now, at least part of the time. He began a fast lope, sensing the end of the chase. The sun had climbed above the trees when Great Bear caught him up, and they slowed for Great Bear to catch his breath.

"Win or lose, this will be the last day of the chase," Wolf Scents said. "We dare not enter Nez Perce lands chasing a Nez Perce girl. We would be lucky to exit that situation as slaves with our balls still attached."

"More likely, only our balls would be sent back as a gift to *Tyee* Running Blade," Great Bear said. "I would like mine to stay with my living body. *Tyee* or not, this fiasco of the Nez Perce *mistshimus* was not our making. So, let us go catch her and return to the longhouse and *mamook* our wives, eh?"

"Let us catch her up and go home. I dislike this prairie country." Wolf Scents turned and began the long chase once again.

Great Bear surged by him, "Come on old man. Let us run." The final pursuit began.

White Mouse started working her way northeast. She had not passed their original raid path. If she could find that, she would know just where her village lay. She jogged now for fifteen minutes and walked for fifteen. It was all she could do. At the sun's zenith as she crested one of the long slopes she paused to look back. Across a wide depression and at the top of the next hill she could see two men running along her track. She turned about and started running in earnest.

At mid-afternoon she looked back. Now the men had closed half the gap and were clearly visible now. She ran. The sun moved another hand down the sky. She crossed the raid track and turned up it. She knew she was close, but so were the men chasing her. As the sun began to lower toward the horizon, they were no more than ten hundred paces behind her. Her leg where the chain wrapped her ankle ached with every step. One sandal was long gone, the other still hung on by a couple of straps. She bent and took the time to cut it away and ran for her life.

As evening approached, they were only two or three hundred running strides behind her. She ran as fast as she could, but with a growing sense of futility. She was not going to make it. They would catch her.

"No. I am White Mouse of the *Nimi'ipuu*. I do not give up. I will not be *mistshimus* to these dogs."

She could hear the "keeii" of their calls as they redoubled their speed and the adrenaline of the chase overtook them. A few moments later, she could hear the breath of one behind her. She cut right, and he missed his grip on her. However, the second tackled her to the ground.

He put his hand over her mouth as she struggled beneath his naked sweat soaked body. His weight pinned her to the earth, and all she could do was kick her legs.

"You have led us on a very fine chase, little *mistshimus* bitch, but it is over now."

For some reason, he was whispering, and his hand over her mouth was clamped down like a tight gag.

Two horsemen approached. Wolf Scents straightened from his crouch and mastered his breath. He stepped forward twenty paces.

"Good evening, brother *Nimi'ipuu*," Wolf Scents said. He saw that they were young warriors, perhaps fourteen or fifteen summers, but warriors still.

"Chinook. What are you doing here on Cayuse lands?"

"I could ask you the same question brother *Nimi'ipuu*, but I shall not. We are on our way to visit my nephew, in the Cayuse village."

"You have overpassed it. Their summer camp is down the last stream you crossed. Who is your nephew?"

"What is that to you?" Immediately, Wolf Scents knew this was a mistake.

"The Cayuse are our true brothers," one on an Appaloosa said. "They ride with us, they hunt the buffalo with us, they marry our sisters."

"They do not run naked through the fields," the other said, laughing.

"My apologies. I did not mean to offend," said Wolf Scents. "We are tired and would just like to make the village before nightfall."

"Who is your nephew?"

"Ah," Wolf Scents said, "He is one who survived the *cultus* whiteman's disease three years ago. He itches all the time, and his kin now call him Scratchy Brother."

The boys looked at each other and then at the pile in the tall grass that was Great Bear lying atop White Mouse, her legs flailing. "I think we may have heard of him," one said. The other nodded agreement.

Girl-With-No-Name twisted under Great Bear. She managed a subdued "mmph" before he clamped his lips over hers in a less than friendly kiss.

"What is your friend doing?" Appaloosa boy asked his spear glinting in the late sun.

"Well," said Wolf Scents chuckling, "my friend Great Bear needs to *mamook* a woman twice a day, every day." He sat down in the grass. "Once in the afternoon and once in the night. You are men. You know how it is."

Great Bear grunted and humped against White Mouse, whose legs just flailed more, adding to the impression.

"Chinook are no better than animals," the other boy said in Nez Perce.

"I agree. It is disgusting, but he is a big man, and he says he has his needs. Sit down with me, and we will wait until he is finished. It will only be a half hour or so." Wolf Scents stretched out making himself comfortable.

"Let us be away from them," Appaloosa boy said in Nez Perce, "before I puke." To Wolf Scents, he said, "Finish your business here quickly and be on your way." Before Wolf Scents could answer, he wheeled his horse and galloped back the way they had come.

Great Bear said, "I swear could feel his lance up my ass. My balls shriveled and slipped up inside my body. I don't think they have dropped yet."

"Gag her quickly," Wolf Scents said, "and let us be away from here."

When they reached Hawk Talon and Fire Start's camp on the Deschutes River the next day, they found a tranquil scene awaiting them. Fire Start was roasting the haunch of a black-tailed deer he had brought down. Hawk Talon had his sore leg up on a stump and looked quite comfortable chewing a piece of the sizzling venison.

"Ho, so you managed without me after all," Hawk Talon said.

"It was close, but Great Bear's impression of elk rutting sold the story finally. A piece of that mowitch, Fire Stick, if you would. I've had enough *ch-lai* for a few months." Wolf Scents told the story of bringing down the *mistshimus*. "It was close. If those boys had been experienced warriors, I don't think even Great Bear's farts could have saved us. Between his grunts as he pretended to *mamook* the *mistshimus* girl and his farts, they just wanted to get away from us."

"I do not fart when I *mamook*," Great Bear said.

"It was that one great salmon smelling fart that finally did it," Wolf Scents said chewing down on the venison. "It was as if Great Bear had eaten a dozen undercooked camas bulbs. The quamash boiled in his gut and came out in a great explosion like a whiteman's cannon ball. I was sitting twenty paces away, and it almost knocked me over. Must've parched every piece of green grass for ten paces. All the grass was flat and dried as *ch-lai*. One moment he was on top of the *mistshimus* keeping her quiet, the next he was in the open, and her legs were flailing. Likely, she thought she was dying."

The others laughed, and Great Bear knew a good story was building. There was no point in denying it now.

"The two boy warriors of the Nez Perce were surprised at the explosion, and one of the Nez Perce's horse neighed and reared. I suspect he smelled the fart roiling up from Great Bear. That was when they decided to take their horses and gallop at a dead run. You saved us this day, Great Bear, you and your camas bulb farts."

Great Bear laughed too. Wolf Scents had told a story that he knew he would hear a few more times over the winter fires. He took a piece of venison from Fire Stick.

"Tomorrow," Wolf Scents said, "I want you, Fire Stick, to accompany Hawk Talon down the Deschutes River to Celilo Falls. Let us be away from these *Liksiyu* lands. He can rest there until I rejoin him for the trading. You can stay with him, Fire Stick. No talk of the *mistshimus*." He looked over his shoulder in disgust at the girl who had caused so much trouble. "No talk at all. We will take her back overland. As much as I would like a nice canoe ride back to the village, we must take the more difficult way."

When they deposited Girl-With-No-Name back before the *Tyee*, two days later, the memory of the chase was long gone, replaced only with the difficulty of carrying a tied-up bundle of angry, frustrated girl who pissed on Great Bear and bit Wolf Scents on the neck.

"*Tyee* Running Blade, we have brought you back your little *mistshimus*," Wolf Scents said. "It was the long chase, and it was a close thing. We met up with two young Nez Perce warriors right at the end. Great Bear imitated an elk rutting for them, and they rode away. She is a disgusting little bitch, *Tyee*. I would recommend killing her."

"Thank you for your effort and your counsel, Wolf Scents. If I had not spoken aloud my word on this, I would have killed her already. I look forward to the day I may kill her since my word on this is now fulfilled."

Girl-With-No-Name looked at the *Tyee* with hate in her eyes and fear as well. So, the dogs will not kill me. What will they do to me now?

"Now, I shall keep my promise. Assemble the *mistshimus*."

The Bent Creek Clan's fourteen *mistshimus* were herded to the forefront. They looked confused and accepting to Girl-With-No-Name. None looked at the *Tyee* but instead hung their heads.

"You who were here heard me speak. Those that were not were informed. All *mistshimus* shall be punished for allowing one to run." He looked to the women nobles standing before him. "It shall be your privilege to beat them. Cane them to the ground."

Seven women stepped forward led by Swimming Salmon and Bears-Many-Children. All bore canes or switches which they applied forcefully to the *mistshimus*, man, woman, and child. Amidst much crying, they beat the *mistshimus* to the ground until they were curled up writhing in pain.

Finally, after several minutes, the *Tyee* said, "Enough."

The noble women of the clan stepped back dignified and responsible.

"Stand, all *mistshimus*."

They stood.

"Form the fisherman's line."

Girl-With-No-Name saw that now the *mistshimus* seemed eager as they formed two lines ten running strides long and two strides apart.

"Give them canes and switches."

The *mistshimus* were handed the canes and switches they were beaten with. Additional ones were passed out.

"Bring the *mistshimus* prisoner forward." Girl-With-No-Name was dragged up and stood before the *Tyee*. "Remove her gag and tie her feet."

Her gag was cut loose, and her bare feet tied two handspans apart. Her arms were still bound behind her back. The *Tyee* stood and stepped before her. His hand shot out, and he grasped her tightly about the throat. "This fulfills my vow not to kill you. The next time you come before me for any punishment your life is forfeit. I shall take pleasure in this deed."

He set her down and prodded her toward the waiting two lines of *mistshimus* who began a slow and ominous chant.

"The salmon swims upstream seeking to evade the fisherman. Beat the salmon into the nets."

He pushed her, and she stumbled toward the left side. A boy, not more than six, cracked his cane across her back and again across her legs.

"*Ayiee*," he shouted.

"*Ayiee*," the rest of the *mistshimus* repeated.

Girl-With-No-Name caromed to the right where she was met with a switch across her chest. She bent over and was caned across the back.

Each blow was accompanied by a cry from the giver, "*Ayiee*," and a repeat from the other *mistshimus*. She knew enough now to try to avoid falling for if she fell they would not stop beating her. Step by shortened step she made her slow progress toward the end of the line. Each switching, each caning wrought a cry from her deepest self.

The cry out of "*Ayiee*" and echoing "*Ayiees*" intensified as she neared the end. A blood frenzy had taken over the *mistshimus*. The chanting continued as well but intensified. She fell to her knees and then upon her face.

"*Ayiee*," cried the beating *mistshimus*.

"*Ayiee*," repeated the others.

She had only a long pace to go. She wormed her way along on her stomach, pushing the ground with her toes. One short step to go.

"*Ayiee*" came the cry and "*Ayiee*" the repeat, but Girl-With-No-Name no longer heard them. Time seemed to slow to a pause. She knew the caning continued. She felt the blows and knew in her mind that they hurt, but some part of her had stopped feeling. She only knew the distance she must travel. Her whole being fixed upon that fact.

Finally, there was silence, and the canes and switches no longer rained down. She lay there curled in a fetal ball whimpering. Still some part of her, some tiny hard place deep inside spoke, "I am *Nimi'ipuu*. I am *Nimi'ipuu*. I am *Nimi'ipuu*."

"The punishment is ended," the *Tyee* said. "Who among you noble Chinook will take responsibility for this *mistshimus?*"

The gossiping immediately ceased, and the women took a subconscious step away from Girl-With-No-Name.

"There is none among the brave and noble Chinook women who will take on this one ten-year-old *mistshimus* girl? Not a single Chinook who is not afraid?" *Tyee* Running Blade's voice took on a disgusted tone.

The women only looked at each other. None wanted this problem on their hands.

"Perhaps we Chinook deserved the *cultus* whiteman's disease."

"I will take her." A woman stepped forward. She was a round-head, but she carried herself with the same high self-regard as the others.

"Of all of you, only Stinging Nettle has courage." He waved. "Come forward, Stinging Nettle."

The woman of about thirty years, well-formed of breast and buttocks— Running Blade noticed—and holding her head high, stepped up before him. She wore no jewelry aside from a necklace of wolves' teeth long enough to brush her nipples. Her hair was still black as a moonless night and fell to her waist.

"I will take the *mistshimus* girl. You know I lost my husband and two girls to the *cultus* whiteman's pox five summers ago. Though my blood is as noble as any here, no Chinook man of this clan will have me, because I am a round-head. When any are sick, I heal them, yet very few will speak to me. My clan did not flatten the heads of their children, so I am lowest of the noble born. I do not take offense at this. I merely speak of it as truth."

Running Blade said, "I recognize the truth in your speech, Stinging Nettle. I take some courage that at least one woman here is strong enough to step up to this task I set you. It will be a hard test."

He signaled and Girl-With-No-Name had her binding cut and was brought forth.

"You have a *mistshimus* who serves you, Stinging Nettle?"

"I do." She gestured with a hand and a girl of twelve stepped to her side.

"From this time forward I am binding these two together. Whatever fate falls upon one shall fall upon the other."

A leather strap was bound tightly about Girl-With-No-Name's waist and about the other *mistshimus* girl's waist as well. They were tied together with another piece of leather about three strides long.

"Know this, if this wretched *mistshimus* should attempt another escape I shall kill first your *mistshimus*, Stinging Nettle. After that, I shall kill this one."

"I accept your terms, *Tyee*."

Tyee Running Blade said, "Swimming Salmon, the keys which failed you?"

Swimming Salmon brought forth the keys from the thong about her neck. Running Blade unlocked the padlock about Girl-With-No-Name's ankle.

"Listen well, little Nez Perce *mistshimus*. I have heard the Nez Perce are a proud and honorable people. If you have any pride or honor within you, you will not allow an innocent to suffer for your actions. Do you understand?"

"I am *Nimi'ipuu*, of The Real People. No *Nimi'ipuu* would do such a thing. Girl-With-No-Name will not dishonor her people."

"Go then, Stinging Nettle," *Tyee* Running Blade said, "and take this *mistshimus* from my sight."

Stinging Nettle inclined her head and led her two *mistshimus* away. The whispering among the women began almost immediately.

"Go, all of you," the *Tyee* said, "I wish a little peace in my life before I die."

STINGING NETTLE

CHAPTER 5
SEPTEMBER TO OCTOBER, 1850

THE NEXT FEW weeks passed in a blur of apathy for Girl-With-No-Name. The bruises and cuts from her beating healed slowly, but within a week her body was mostly a large multi-colored discoloration. It was not that Stinging Nettle treated her badly, for she did not. As far as Girl-With-No-Name could tell, she treated both her *mistshimus* much the same. She was neither cruel to them nor was she sympathetic. Her other slave, she called *mistshimus* Nika which meant "my slave." Sometimes she would call her Nika when she was feeling generous. Girl-With-No-Name she called variously, *chee whit* which meant new one, *lemolo mistshimus*, crazy slave, or some combination thereof. In any case, it did not matter to Girl-With-No-Name. Rooted in this horrible place both by her honor and by her age, she had made her best attempt at escape only to be caught. She had been close, so close, but that did not matter anymore. Now, she was only *chee whit* when Stinging Nettle was feeling charitable and *lemolo mistshimus* when she was not.

To Girl-With-No-Name it made no difference. If she was told to do a particular task she did it. She took no pride in her work, but she attempted to do it well because she did not want *mistshimus* Nika to be punished. She did the work, dull-eyed, and when she was done with that task, sat or stood and waited for the next order. Once, when she had been ordered by Stinging Nettle to grind camas into flour, she ground it until she was finished. When *mistshimus* Nika made the cakes and moved to the fire pit to place the cakes on to bake, Girl-With-No-Name followed in the same apathetic state.

Why? Because Stinging Nettle did not tell me to make cakes. Only to grind the flour.

Even the name which she had taken in a moment of stubbornness, Girl-With-No-Name, was not hers to take. Names were property to these people, and *mistshimus* did not own names. The girl leashed to her could be called *mistshimus* Nika, or sometimes just Nika, because Stinging Nettle owned that expression to use as a slave name. Nika had no right to it herself.

She still sometimes forgot her apathy, usually when she was on the edges of sleep. Then she would mumble, "I am *Nimi'ipuu*. I am Girl-With-No-Name." Those times were becoming more and more infrequent as one week turned into a month. White Mouse burrowed deep into her hidden place. If she came out to feed or just to look around it was when Girl-With-No-Name, and now increasingly *chee whit*, was not present to witness. White Mouse had to be cautious. In her paws, she carried the seed that had been a viable person. This was not a seed to be eaten. Not yet anyway. This was a seed to be hidden away in the vining tree that grew in the dark places. It had to be protected. It had to be remembered. Perhaps there would come a time when it could be brought out into the sunlight to grow. But not yet. Not yet.

Her bindings with Nika created a strange relationship. Girl-With-No-Name thought of her as Chatter because the girl talked incessantly about anything and everything, whether it be the consistency of the camas flour they were grinding, the salmon they were preparing for the evening meal, or the herbs that they ground and then steeped for Stinging Nettle. When they went to the damp areas of the creek to dig the roots of the Bleeding Heart, Nika spoke of its incredible sedative and analgesic qualities. She was always earnest in her speech and seemed to have no animosity toward anyone.

One day in early Fall, when they were scraping hides, Girl-With-No-Name having finally been allowed a bone scraper, Nika was chattering about the quality of this nice hide, and how it might tan out, and what it might be used for, Nika's moon cycle began for the first time. Of course, she was in wonder about this development as well.

"See, *chee whit*, I bleed. It is so exciting. I will be a woman now," Nika said.

Girl-With-No-Name turned toward Nika, and the dull look that protected her was sparked by the earnest surprise in Nika's eyes. Nika's enthusiasm penetrated even Girl-With-No-Name's depth of solitude. The response came forth that was not apathy or self-pity.

"I see, Nika. The blood of the woman now flows from you. I am happy—" Was happy even a word she could say? For Nika, she decided it was. "I am happy for you and respect you for this."

"Thank you, *chee whit*. You are ever kind to me."

To Girl-With-No-Name, this statement seemed an impossibility, but she sensed that Nika believed in it. "We must tell Stinging Nettle."

"Yes. Let us go, and tell her now. I hope she will be happy for me. I hope she will not be disappointed that I have to go to the moon cycle hut for cleansing and cannot work. I hope...."

Girl-With-No-Name stopped listening. Too much hope was not something she could afford.

Stinging Nettle was sufficiently pleased for Nika's sake, though Girl-With-No-Name could detect a bit of irritation. Not only would she lose the labor of Nika for the cleansing period, but Girl-With-No-Name would also be virtually useless to her as well. This wasn't something she could bring to the *Tyee's* attention. She removed the short strap that bound them and tied them together instead with a rope of some twenty paces.

"You," she said directly to Girl-With-No-Name, "*chee whit*, cannot enter the moon cycle hut. Yet the *Tyee* has decreed you shall be bound to Nika. It is such a bother, yet it is what it is."

She led Nika to the moon cycle hut, and two other round-head women took her inside. Girl-With-No-Name settled herself along one planked side of the small building and waited. It seemed the one thing she was getting very good at doing, waiting until someone came with a task for her to do.

"I will bring you some tasks to perform here while you wait for Nika. You should have enough rope to perform your own daily eliminations. Do so as far from the hut as possible and bury your spoor."

Girl-With-No-Name looked up at Stinging Nettle.

"Do you hear me, *chee whit*? Nika may be *mistshimus*, but even to *mistshimus* this week is significant for her. I am titled, but I know this. She has been *mistshimus* Nika to me for six summers. I may not be allowed to show it, but I take pride in Nika." Stinging Nettle picked up the rope. "You through this rope are now blood-bound to Nika. Do not spoil this week for her."

"I hear, and I understand," Girl-With-No-Name said. "I will take care for my blood sister. My honor as a *Nimi'ipuu*. I will not soil her week of becoming a woman with petty acts."

"I accept your pledge. If you should violate it, I will slit your throat and let your body rot on the midden pile." Stinging Nettle turned to go. The last Girl-With-No-Name heard her say was, "My *mistshimus* Nika." There was a note of affection to her voice that no one was meant to hear.

The several days that followed were filled with routine tasks, discomfort, and boredom, all of which seemed to be bellwethers of her new condition. When Nika emerged from the moon cycle hut, she was greeted only by Girl-With-No-Name, and she seemed not to be disturbed that Stinging Nettle was not there.

How strange these Chinook are. Among the *Nimi'ipuu*, even the emergence of a slave from the moon cycle hut as a woman was an important event for the tribe.

That Stinging Nettle cared was obvious. That she could not or was not allowed to show it was equally obvious. In any case, Nika put her arms around Girl-With-No-Name and hugged her with some tears in her eyes.

"I knew you would be here for me, *chee whit*. Thank you, my blood sister."

A MONTH LATER, Nika had her courses again, and again Girl-With-No-Name spent several days on the long rope outside the moon cycle hut. It inconvenienced Stinging Nettle. Girl-With-No-Name did not care. It seemed to bond Nika even more to her, which she did not care about either. She cared only that no one bothered her or beat her. Any tasks that were brought to her she did to the best of her ability, and then she dismissed the memory.

Perhaps she was falling into that state she had observed earlier among the *mistshimus*. If that was true, then she did not care about that either.

There was an air of excitement about Stinging Nettle's hut when they returned. She was planning some gathering expedition upriver to begin the next day. They spent most of that day loading one of the smaller canoes with supplies and some trading goods. Nika, at least, was very excited. She had gone with Stinging Nettle before on this gathering and spent no little time telling Girl-With-No-Name about it.

"We will paddle upriver to the base of the cascade, then portage the canoe around the first rapids. After that we get back in and paddle to the next and the next. Finally, we have to carry the canoe around Celilo Falls themselves."

She went on like this most of the day until Girl-With-No-Name had the whole trip memorized.

Why would Stinging Nettle be taking me upriver? It could not be possible they were thinking of returning me to my tribe.

Despite her attempts not to raise any hopes, and the Chinook never evidenced that they considered such a thing, the little spark burned. Eventually, Girl-With-No-Name buried this spark deep and fast, and it bothered her no more.

The next day, they arrived at the cascade. The *Nch'i-wána* boiled over the rocks, throwing spray high into the air, and frothed white all the way across its two bowshots' width at this location. They unloaded the canoe and, leaving one round-head warrior to guard their supplies, portaged their canoe around the first of the cascades. At times, they had to lift the canoe with ropes and other times lower it. By mid-afternoon, they had passed this obstacle, and the four paddlers returned for their supplies.

The paddle upriver to The Dalles on the morrow was a one-day affair with four *mistshimus* paddlers, two round-head warriors, Stinging Nettle, and herself. It was pretty along the great river, and the current was no match for their paddlers and the lightweight Chinook cedar canoe. The paddlers sang to match strokes, and an air of peace settled over Girl-With-No-Name.

By evening they had reached the whiteman's village of The Dalles and the larger native trading area. They did not stop, perhaps to avoid any contact with the *Nimi'ipuu* who traded there but continued on past before pulling up the canoe to a grassy bank and their camp for the night.

The following day, they paddled a short distance upstream to the Narrows. Again, they unloaded the canoe and left one round-head to guard the supplies. On this section, Nika and Girl-With-No-Name took a place carrying the canoe. They climbed up a steep path alongside the river until they were some twenty-five paces above the rushing water.

Looking down upon the river Girl-With-No-Name was amazed. I never knew that the great *Nch'i-wána*, which in some places is so wide you can barely see the other side, ever could pass through such a narrow space. Even I could shoot an arrow across the river here.

Preceding Stinging Nettle were Girl-With-No-Name under the canoe's stern end and then Nika leashed together again with the short tether. They walked beneath their burden, sometimes veering away beneath the trees and sometimes closing to the very verge of the hurrying *Nch'i-wána*. Neither the relative peace and shade of the trees nor the rush of the river stopped Nika's chatter. The bank began rising steeply on their right as their path narrowed.

Girl-With-No-Name plodded along watching her feet, occasionally casting a glance to the river churning below.

"*Chee whit*, look at that. I have never seen the *Wimahl*, hurry like that. Like hungry dogs chasing a rabbit." Nika half turned to Girl-With-No-Name and said, "I am so glad you are my friend, now that I am a wom—"

One moment she was there chattering away. The next she was sliding over the edge. The lashing brought her up short, and she looked up at Girl-With-No-Name with gratefulness and hope in her eyes. It was that look that Girl-With-No-Name would see in her dreams. She braced herself against the weight of Nika. She was holding, holding, but the canoe was beginning to tip.

"We are going to lose the canoe," Stinging Nettle said, her knife slashed down, and the tether was cut.

Girl-With-No-Name watched as a wide-eyed Nika fell to the rocks below, her body broken but still alive, the *Nch'i-wána* rushing past on both sides of the boulder where she lay. There was blood there, and a leg bone pierced the skin. The still living *mistshimus* girl who only moments before had been saying, "I am so glad you are my friend, now that I am a wom—" had her life cut short before she could even complete her sentence.

Stinging Nettle said to Girl-With-No-Name, "Move on, *mistshimus* Nika. It is done. Move on."

As she began walking ahead, she replayed the scene again and again. Nika's incessant chatter which Girl-With-No-Name only half listened to, her turn, and last sentence, and then she was gone over the edge. The look of gratitude when she was brought up short on the tether.

Those weren't her last words. Her last words when she looked up and saw the knife coming down to cut her loose were "Live for me." Then she was gone. She walked on with tears streaming. Why did she have to say that? Why?

She didn't notice when the portage over the Long Narrows ended, and the canoe was set down. She just sat down with it. She did not notice as the *mistshimus* paddlers hiked back to bring their supplies up nor the setting up of camp for the night. The next day she got in the canoe, and they paddled up a little distance to the Short Narrows. She got out of the canoe when told to, picked up her end when told to, walked when told to. The visage before her was truly astounding—the rushing river, the red rocks carved by thousands of years, the crisp blue sky overhead, and the rocky path beneath her feet.

Why did she have to say, "Live for me?" Why?

They loaded and paddled up the now calm river toward Celilo Falls. Her eyes took in the panorama, and it truly was astounding. The wide horseshoe bend of the falls dropped twenty paces into the water below. As falls went, it was not so high, but the sheer volume of water passing over it was impressive. They made camp on the north side, and after eating, fell into a tired sleep.

For Girl-With-No-Name it was not so much a sleep as a waking dream. Always the same, a replaying of Nika's last moments ending with that look of hope, then recognition, and her last words, "Live for me."

She woke once during the night, then fell back asleep. She could swear that her head was in Stinging Nettle's lap, and she was stroking her hair saying, "Nika, Nika, oh, Nika." Later she tried to reconcile this with the Stinging Nettle she knew in waking hours and knew it must have been a dream.

They portaged up the north side of the falls. The fishing platforms were abandoned now, the tribes either gone to their winter camps or some to collect huckleberries. They had left behind great stacks of baskets of dried, pounded salmon, each as heavy as a man could carry. The baskets were stacked in tight groups of seven, with five more on top, all covered with reed mats tightly bound. Everywhere were the remnants of this year's salmon harvest—an immense quantity of bones, scales, and skin. Everywhere skittered vermin living off the leavings. Fleas hopped about as plentiful as the salmon in spawn. The *mistshimus* continually slapped them off their legs. They finally set down the canoe and ate a meal before returning to the bottom of the Falls for their supplies. They loaded the canoe and crossed the peaceful river, which roared downstream to the south side. They made camp there, and round-head warriors and *mistshimus* alike talked away into the night around a communal campfire. The hard part was done. Now they could paddle easily to their destination.

Girl-With-No-Name didn't wonder why they were here. Presumably, they were to collect herbs for Stinging Nettle's supply, or perhaps foodstuffs. She did notice, in a peripheral way, that the climate and terrain were different here. It was drier and much less forested once you got away from the river valley. Once, this was home, or at least across the river lay her tribe's summer camp, but she might as well be a lifetime from it with that span of glassy water that separated her now. She was beginning to think she would never see it again.

As the evening gave way to night, she lay down where she sat to sleep. Nika's eyes, and her last words to her and her alone, haunted her.

Live for me. Afterwards, she fell to the rocks below and lay broken.

The next morning, all in the camp were excited. They loaded the canoe and proceeded to paddle across to the south side of the *Nch'i-wána*. The river that had flowed past her all of her life, had in fact been a part of her life, now was her curse. She could no more get away from it than stop breathing. Since Nika's fall and her parting death wish, "Live for me," she could not even find a way to stop her breath. In some way, she had taken Nika's words to her heart, past her *mistshimus* Nika self that she occupied for Stinging Nettle.

Now that Nika was gone, she was Nika, past the *chee whit* or *lemolo whit* self that others of the Chinook called her, past even Girl-With-No-Name, her own name of defiance. Nika's words fell like a seed through the sieves of herself down into the lower hidden portions. Down below the leaves and trunks to the tangled roots where White Mouse made her lair.

For some reason, White Mouse darted out from one of her hidden places and caught this brilliant green seed, put it in the pocket of her cheek, and scampered back into hiding with it. It was deposited there along with the other seeds, carefully hidden in the dry burrows. Now the emerald "Live for me" seed lay alongside the "*Nimi'ipuu*" seed and others of her ten-year-old memory. Deep at the bottom of the pile lay the "Hope" seed, the one that could not be exposed to the light.

They paddled along for a half day. The smell of the land was different here, more prairie and less forest. To Girl-With-No-Name, these were Umatilla lands. All the summer villages were abandoned. They passed through Cayuse lands, and again the summer village was long abandoned. Since the Cayuse war and the whiteman's disease, the Cayuse had diminished in numbers. Girl-With-No-Name knew of several who had joined with the *Nimi'ipuu* for as many summers as her lifetime. Many more had died in the war following the Whitman killings. There is something about the aroma of a place, more than its sight, which stirred memories. As they paddled nearer the shore, these memories in Girl-With-No-Name began to surface.

She tried to repress them. She knew that they only bode pain in her new station in life, but they surfaced anyway. The chasing of butterflies along the bank with her brother Elk Clarksonson, Elk the Son-of-Son-of-the-Clark.

"Hurry, little Mouse, you are too slow to catch butterflies," Elk said, though in truth he was only three paces ahead of her. The young warrior, three years her senior, ran along the banks of the *Nch'i-wána* only a memory of distance from this spot where she paddled with her Chinook owners. They ran happy and carefree, just this last summer, the boy now a man, but the man forgotten for the moment as they chased the yellow swallowtails.

"Run, White Mouse. How do you ever expect to be a mother of a *Clarksonsonson* the way you run?" At that moment, she remembered passing him in a burst of pumping ten-summer-old legs and them falling together on the grassy banks.

"Ha. I will be a grandmother of a Son-of-the-Clark before you ever even find a *Nimi'ipuu* girl who will take a chance with that little thing you've got down there."

For that period of time, they were both just children. Now it was just a memory—and a fading one. It was true that The Clark, son of William Clark was her great-grandfather. The Clark still lived with the *Nimi'ipuu* though not with her clan. He lived and was honored, as she would have been honored.

They paddled around a little bend and Girl-With-No-Name inhaled sharply. The bank along the *Nch'i-wána* appeared more and more familiar to Girl-With-No-Name in an unsubstantiated way, more the way a countryside will feel like home even though you have not been to exactly that spot before. This was home.

There was the spot she had fallen with Elk Clarksonson in their chase of the butterflies. There, farther on, was the midden pile. There were the depressions in the soil where it was dug out before putting up frames and reed mats. Now it was all gone.

The canoe ground up on the bank. Girl-With-No-Name leaped out and ran to the spot where her family's hut had been, where her grandfather, Three Blue Beads, had lain snoring guarding the doorway the last time she had been here. There, where her sister's arm had tangled in the bed skin over her. She remembered quietly pushing Soft-as-Doe-Skin's arm off her so as not to wake her and walking ever so quietly out, stepping over grandfather's snoring guard.

She fell to her knees. It was gone now. True, they might come back next summer to fish again. However, Girl-With-No-Name knew her clan's movements, and they might just as easily not come back to this spot for four or five years. Next summer they might take the teepees and horses and go east across the mountains for the buffalo hunts.

It had not hit her before, but now the loss of family, clan, and tribe washed over her like the *Nch'i-wána* flooding its summer banks in the spring.

All before it was torn and tumbled—trees, brush, every kind of debris. All was lost before the *Nch'i-wána* when it was angry in the spring, and the wise man or girl knew to get to high ground.

Girl-With-No-Name knelt in the depression in the dirt that was all that remained of her family and her memories, tears streaming at her complete loss of what gave her life meaning and continuity, meaning in the present and continuity with the generations upon generations that came before.

Where was her "high ground" now? What could serve as her connection to the past and give her a reason to continue? All was lost. All was lost, except a thought occurred, dredged up from White Mouse's hidden den at the roots of the tree.

The only real thing in her life since she had been stolen had been those three words Nika had spoken.

She allowed them first to form in her heart. Live for me.

She allowed them to rise to her lips in a whisper meant only for herself and her friend Nika, "Live for me."

She rose to her feet. She turned toward Stinging Nettle. "I am *Nimi'ipuu*. I am White Mouse of the *Nimi'ipuu*. I had a friend, a true friend, Nika. I did not honor you when you lived. But I honor the look in your eyes and the words you spoke when you died. My blood sister, Nika, you said 'Live for me.' My friend, my blood sister Nika, I will live for you."

Stinging Nettle said, "Come, Nika." She held out her arm in comfort.

She looked at Stinging Nettle. Walking past the comforting arm, she stepped into the canoe and sat down. "I am ready to go now, Stinging Nettle. Thank you."

Stinging Nettle dropped her arm and resumed her position in the canoe. "Paddlers, to the other bank."

Over the next three weeks, they dug camas root on the plains above the river and biscuit root on the high rocky ground. Girl-With-No-Name knew that the biscuit root was not only a food source but also "Bear Medicine," good for respiratory problems. The *Nimi'ipuu* had always dug it in the spring, but perhaps these shores were too populated in spring for the Chinook. They collected a large basket of huckleberries. Other prairie herbs they collected as well. Finally, they had all their canoe could carry and they headed back downriver.

The portages were approximately the same except in the places they could float the canoe downriver unloaded. Girl-With-No-Name spared a glance over the edge where Nika had fallen. There was no body there. Perhaps the current had swept up and taken her, or perhaps she had dragged her broken body to the river and ended her suffering in the rushing water.

THE KISS OF STANDING BEAR

CHAPTER 6
SEPTEMBER TO NOVEMBER, 1853

THERE WAS A change that overtook Girl-With-No-Name over the next three years. It was gradual, even imperceptible at first, but eventually, even to her own inner self, it had to be accepted. She had in some way accepted the fact that she was not going to be rescued. She was not going to escape her Chinook owners. Not a physical escape at least. The odds were stacked against her and the punishment too high for failure.

This change in her attitude brought relief for Stinging Nettle and *Tyee* Running Blade. Running Blade felt glad the controversy of the captured Nez Perce girl had faded into the background now, and he could finally get some peace. Stinging Nettle took pleasure in the progress her new "Nika" had made, though in secret she still thought of her old *mistshimus* as "Nika." Such were the customs of their people. One non-person had died. That was a loss to Stinging Nettle, both in the years invested in training the girl and the loss of a functioning member of the lowest caste to the tribe. Her energy, her knowledge, and her efforts would be missed. That she was of the low caste did not diminish the loss to the tribe or to Stinging Nettle. Also, the fact that she had enjoyed the use and practical ownership of two *mistshimus* and now she had one was not lost on Stinging Nettle. Her social standing, once looking brighter with the two, was now dimmer with only one. She belonged to the titled caste, and that was how things were measured.

Always, property was the measurement. How many slaves do you control? How many canoes do you own? What is your wealth in beads, clothes, furs, and other objects that can be given away in a *potlatch*? As such, Stinging Nettle was titled but relatively poor. She had lost much when her husband and children were carried away by the *cultus* whiteman's disease. She had lost more when the stupid *mistshimus* had stepped off the cliff.

Did I make the right decision, to cut the girl loose? Could she have been saved? The imminent threat of losing the canoe overwhelmed all sense of proportion. To have lost the canoe would have ruined her, perhaps even caused her to be demoted to round-head status. Such instances were rare, but they did occasionally happen.

This new girl, this *mistshimus whit*, presents a quandary. On the surface, she is the perfect *mistshimus*. She is a quick learner, clever with her fingers, sharp at observation. And she does not talk all the time. She seems to have finally accepted her position in life and gives me no trouble, no trouble at all. Why is it that she disturbs my thoughts like this? Stinging Nettle shook her head and decided not to dwell on it. Maybe Coyote knows. I do not.

For Girl-With-No-Name, these three summers and winters passed. Whether they passed swiftly or slowly, she paid no heed. She did every task set before her and set herself to do it to the best of her ability. She observed the Chinook around her—the *mistshimus*, the round-heads, and the titled—as well as her environs. Though one couldn't tell it from observing her casually, very little passed her eyes, her nose, or her hearing that she did not pay attention to in the calm way which was becoming natural to her. Calm acceptance was becoming another layer in her shell of defenses as well as a method to pass unnoticed among the Chinook.

She learned the ways of Stinging Nettle, the way of the healer. She learned of the Bitter Cherry. Although its name suggests a food source, it was more often used as a medicinal herb. Its bark could be chewed by pregnant women to help with childbirth, or as a laxative. Its roots could be rubbed on a new mother's nipples to induce a child to nurse. Or an infusion of the rotten wood of the plant could be taken to prevent a woman from getting pregnant.

So, the three years passed. She learned, and she grew. Though she made no real friends among the *mistshimus*, they accepted her. They had no ambition, so she accepted them as well for what they were, pleasant enough companions. The round-heads were more cautious in life. Though it was not common, they could upon extreme occasions even become *mistshimus* themselves. It would take an extreme action on their part to have such a fate overcome them, such as injuring or killing a titled person, but it could happen. They, on the other hand, could never become titled, even should a titled person become enamored by a round-head. A titled man or woman might take a round-head as a lover but never as a wife or husband. Thus, they lived a somewhat secure life but always overlaid with an edge of insecurity.

Girl-With-No-Name passed through this complicated world of castes with little regard. She found a boy of some interest to her, but he was noble born and *Tyee* Running Blade's son. Known by his child's name of Little Bear, he had somehow escaped the haughtiness of his father. Upon occasion, she would pass his way on this task or the other. Perhaps it was her lack of deference that caught his attention.

One late afternoon she passed him as she finished delivering the fire-roasted salmon and camas bulbs to the *Tyee's* eating area in his longhouse. It was cold, and windswept rain bore down on the village as it often did in late spring, so all the nobles ate with the *Tyee,* and it was a jovial feast. The titled sat in a strict social order surrounding him, and all their *mistshimus* attended them. The noble children ate separately but nearby. The round-heads ate some distance away.

"Girl," said Little Bear, "bring me a portion of the salmon." For a thirteen-year-old boy, it was an exercise in his authority.

She turned about and fetched him salmon on a cedar platter which she delivered with as much grace as a twelve-year-old girl could muster.

"Girl, bring me a camas bulb."

Girl-With-No-Name retraced her steps and procured a fat, fire blackened camas bulb. She delivered it to him.

"Girl," he said again, "I am thirsty. Bring me something to drink."

She turned and bent down and poured him an earthenware cup of water from five feet away. She presented it to him.

She looked at him. "Would you have me wait upon your sleeping rugs now, Little Bear? To take a girl who has not bled yet is a crime, even if she is a *mistshimus*. But since I am *mistshimus* and you are noble born, I must obey."

His two friends, boys a year younger than Little Bear, laughed.

"Do you say thus to provoke me, girl?"

"No, sir. I am *mistshimus*. I am here to serve. In service I merely remind you of the *Tyee's* law not to take an unblooded girl to lie with you. As *mistshimus*, I would be compliant as a reed."

"I know my father's rules and the Chinook's as well."

Girl-With-No-Name noticed Stinging Nettle beckoning to her. "I am sorry, sir. My mistress beckons me for service. I must go."

"When you are blooded, perhaps I shall take you then, little *mistshimus*. Be off with you."

She removed herself and walked back to Stinging Nettle to attend her.

THIS TYPE OF meeting happened several more times over the course of the next year. Always Girl-With-No-Name was deferential to Little Bear, though not afraid or as subservient as he was used to among the born *mistshimus*. Even those bought by the Bent Creek Clan or captured from other Chinook seemed to be born to it.

When he made his manhood and went off for his vision quest, he returned with a new pride but also a somewhat different understanding. He was now Standing Bear, and Girl-With-No-Name saw in him not only a pride that was not there before but also a questioning look that was missing in most Chinook.

He caught her up one day in very early summer. She was walking along the river bank returning to Stinging Nettle. He sat in the sunlight, the light breeze streaming his ebon hair away from his flattened forehead, knapping a flint arrowhead.

"*Mistshimus* girl, come sit here beside me."

Stinging Nettle did not need her immediately, so she complied, squatting down and sitting back on her heels. "Standing Bear."

"I have been wondering. Why are you so different?"

Sensing a possible punishment Girl-With-No-Name said, "If I have offended in any way, I am sorry. I wish only to serve."

"Always you say things that get my back up. You are different than other *mistshimus* in the Bent Creek Clan. Why?"

Something about the way he asked, or something about the way he looked made her answer, "Do you want a true answer? Or a *mistshimus* answer?"

"You see, no other *mistshimus* would say such a thing. I want a true answer."

"I was born *Nimi'ipuu*. It is true that among the *Nimi'ipuu* we do have what you call *mistshimus*. Some are killed, that is true also, especially during wartime right after they are captured. Most live among the tribe and are often adopted into the tribe. They are not treated that differently than others in the tribe. Their children are not born into slavery. I do not complain. I understand I am *mistshimus* here and will likely be such until the day I die. But it is different for me than other *mistshimus* here. I hope I do not offend."

"You took a great risk by giving me a true answer. I will honor that risk. My father is very traditional and lives by the old ways even as they slip away."

Thus, began the series of very strange conversations Girl-With-No-Name had with Standing Bear. Such as she could tell, he did not report her conversations with him to his father. She was certain she would be punished for speaking out, yet she was not.

A moon later, Standing Bear had just returned from a trading expedition to the fort at The Dalles. As Girl-With-No-Name passed by an empty hut Standing Bear motioned her inside. He bade her to sit and talk with him a while.

"I will, of course, talk with you, Standing Bear," she said.

"I have just come back from the stockade at The Dalles. The *Tyee* put me in charge of some of the trading."

"That is good to hear, Standing Bear."

"But that is not what I wanted to tell you. You must promise not to repeat what I am about to tell you. I, also, am somewhat fearful of his wrath."

"I will attempt not to, but you must understand his wrath against his son will not likely kill you. With me it is different."

"I am sorry. Of course, you can make no such promise. I will hold you to none. Anyway, what I heard is that Oregon will become a state in a few years. In the United States."

"I do not know of these United States."

"It is the whiteman's tribal organization, a vast tribe spanning from ocean to ocean. They are all one and each state is like the Chinook or the *Nimi'ipuu* or Paiute and is part of it. This Oregon's northern boundary will likely be the *Wimahl*, the Great River."

"The *Nch'i-wána?*" she asked.

"Yes, that is what the *Nimi'ipuu* call it, the *Nch'i-wána*. The Oregon whitemans have already made a rule that says there can be no slaves in Oregon. That was passed by their elder council several years ago."

"But that won't affect the Chinook *mistshimus*."

"It may. Some Chinook clans have already accepted it downriver and freed the *mistshimus*. My father holds fast to the old ways, but even he feels the strength of the Chinook waning like the moon. Unlike the moon, I fear it will never wax again."

"Thank you for telling me this, Standing Bear. It gives me some strength to know I may not be *mistshimus* forever. Please don't trick me on this. I do not think I could bear being tricked on something like this." She looked at him with pleading eyes.

"I would not trick you. I like you," he said. And then he did something completely unexpected. He kissed her. It was a beginner's kiss, just a brush of the lips. Yet it was still a kiss.

Girl-With-No-Name bolted from the hut leaving a surprised and confused Standing Bear, still with his eyes closed and his lips pursed.

Why did he do that? Why would he kiss me? I am *mistshimus*. Does he want to claim me even before I am blooded? But he said he liked me. And I do like him. He is the only person among the Chinook to ever talk to me like I was a person. Yet, he is titled, and I am a low *mistshimus*.

The little White Mouse within dashed out and retrieved the seed that fell with the kiss. It was a glowing ruby red. She put it in her cheek pouch and hurried back beneath the leaves to her den. Carefully she deposited it in line with the others. She sniffed appreciatively. It was a long line beneath the roots of the tree, each seed of differing color displayed to its advantage. Someday, White Mouse hoped, these seeds would become necessary.

A few days later as Girl-With-No-Name was carrying water back to the cooking area, Standing Bear called to her.

"Girl, come here," he said. "Sit with me."

Girl-With-No-Name did not even need to weigh her options—she had none. She returned to Standing Bear and squatted back on her heels. He was beading a pouch with whiteman's beads and tiny shells. The design was interesting and non-traditional from what she knew of Chinook beadwork. It showed a canoe portaged by Chinook, but above it was a strange wagon on rails being pulled by what he intended to be a single mule.

"That is a strange design," she said.

"I know," he said, throwing it down. "I can see it in my head, but I cannot execute it. The shells are supposed to represent the old way and the whiteman's beads what is coming. It came in a dream, but my skills are too poor."

"I see the canoe. But what is this wagon above it?"

"I did not tell you the last time we talked. I saw this when I was last at The Dalles. The wagon runs on wood rails and is pulled by a mule. The rails run for several miles along the old portage path."

"What are these miles you speak of? Will you teach me?"

"You are full of questions, but it is confusing, and I will teach you. It is a whiteman's measurement. My father makes me learn the whiteman's way as well as our own. For trade." Standing Bear seemed embarrassed.

"I am sorry, but I do want to know."

"Look across the *Wimahl*. That is around a half-mile, I think."

"Ah, so it is a big measurement. So, a day's horse ride would be—?"

"Thirty to forty miles, I think, depending on the horse and the ground."

"I understand. Go on with your story."

"When they get past the cascades, the mule is unhitched from the wagon. He is hitched to a windlass, and they lower the cargo a hundred feet down a cliff on a rope to the boats waiting below."

Girl-With-No-Name interrupted again. "I am so sorry. One hundred feet?"

Standing Bear laughed, "You are very impolite—for a *mistshimus*."

"You said you would teach me. I do not mean to be impolite."

"No, you are correct. How big would you say the *Tyee's* longhouse is?"

Girl-With-No-Name stood up and squinted her eyes looking at the *Tyee's* longhouse. "I'd say, maybe twenty-five to thirty paces." She glanced back at Standing Bear.

"Your paces or mine," he said laughing.

"Now you are making fun of me."

"Yes, but it makes a difference. We have measured it and the longhouse is sixty-eight feet long."

"Hah. Your feet or mine," she said.

"Ah, so you understand. Sixty-eight U. S. government feet. And don't say, 'I didn't know the U. S. government had feet.' It is their standard."

"I can understand. Go on with your story."

"All right. They hitch the mule back up, and he either carries cargo back downriver or runs the empty cart back for another load. The whiteman built this thing. I know this is only a small beginning. There will be more and more. The Chinook are no longer needed to portage around the rapids. Soon, I fear, they will be no longer needed at all. At that time, we will go into the *cultus* whiteman's midden pile."

"Well, your beadwork could be done better by an eight-year-old girl," Girl-With-No-Name said and laughed.

Standing Bear looked at her in offense, "Do you mock me?"

"Your pardon, sir. I meant no offense." She hoped she sounded contrite. Standing Bear was title born, but sometimes in his friendliness and openness, she forgot she was still *mistshimus*. She must not forget this fact.

He looked around. "No, I am sorry. My raising got the better of me. I look, and I see things changing all about me, but no one else sees. My father will die for the old ways. The old ways will lose anyway. Not everything that he fights to maintain is bad. We have many strong traditions of living within the earth's bounds instead of just taking whatever we can take like the whiteman. But the barrier between noble and *mistshimus* is not one of those things."

"You should not speak so openly, Standing Bear," she said. "The winds of winter that whistle down the gorge and blow the great cedar to the ground do not distinguish between the brave warrior and the fool standing next to him."

"So, my father says also. He speaks, now, only of the old times when the Chinook were strong. Once we were the greatest traders on the river, now we are almost nothing. Tomorrow or the next year we will be gone."

"It is sad, Standing Bear, but we must take care talking like this. People will notice."

"I know. I am sorry. I did want to ask, why did you run away when I kissed you?"

"I would ask, why did you do it? Are you the noble Chinook claiming his *mistshimus*, sir?"

"I kissed you because I like you. I think maybe you feel the same."

"I am *mistshimus*. Feelings are property. We are not allowed feelings."

"Does the part of you that is not *mistshimus*, and I know there is such a part, feel the same? I want a true answer."

"I do—like you, Standing Bear." She looked down.

"It is enough then." He gestured her away. Girl-With-No-Name was hurt, but then she saw the two Chinook women looking over at them and gossiping. These were just round-head women, but Girl-With-No-Name knew that, in a community of eighty individuals, you did not want to be a topic of gossip.

A moon and a half later, near the end of the falling leaves salmon run, she was carting a basket of fish bones and other dinner detritus to the midden pile. The days shortened now, and the wind ran brisk out of the west. Great thunderclouds built and signified rain during the night. The Chinook were snug in their longhouses for the night with only the occasional *mistshimus* about on some service or other.

Standing Bear was on the other side of the pile, which was higher than she could see over.

She heard his whisper over the rising wind, "Girl, come here." A quick look around betokened no one observing, so she slowly picked her way around the pile.

"You called, Standing Bear. I am here."

"Come into the abandoned hut," he said. He seemed somewhat anxious and eager at the same time.

Anxious not to be caught, and eager for what?

He opened the low flap of the hut and entered first. It had not changed much since she had hidden here three summers before other than her hiding place behind the debris had been exposed.

"The midden pile is about eight feet tall and thirty feet long," she said.

"What is that?" he said.

"The midden pile. I paced it off against the *Tyee's* longhouse."

"The midden pile? Oh, you measured it. I had something else in mind."

As she straightened, he took her into his arms and kissed her firmly, if a bit awkwardly, full on the lips. This was no brushing of lips as before. This was a boy warrior's kiss, and he made the most of it. Some part of her just wanted to be close to someone, anyone. As she returned that kiss, the kiss of a boy, newly a man, and a girl, not yet a woman, she felt something within her give way. She could not lie with him, though she felt his sex rise between them proud and hard. It was not time yet for her. Still, she could kiss him. There was no law she knew of that forbade that. Her bare body pressed hard against his, and they exchanged something. Not just passion, but also a release of loneliness she felt lifting from her.

When they broke the kiss, Standing Bear was panting. "I see your spear is readied for battle, Standing Bear," she said touching his erect organ.

"Do not tease me, *mistshimus*," he said.

"I do not, truly."

"I would lay claim to you when you are blooded—"

"I am *mistshimus*," she said. "Of course, I will lie with you."

"—if you would have me."

"I am *mistshimus*. What have my wishes, if I even had any, to do with it?"

"I know they should not, yet some part of me dearly wants it to be so. When I have thought of you at times in the longhouse, my spear, as you call it, stands up to be noticed. There are girls, young women who have noticed and tittered behind a hand. They are round-heads, but I know I could have one to bed me if I wanted. When I think of that, my spear becomes a limp stalk."

"I can't imagine this," and here she stroked his organ again, "being anything other than a spear."

"I have tried to get over it and spilled my seed onto the ground when all are asleep in the longhouse late in the night."

"I would imagine Sweet-Pollen-Flower would open to you, Standing Bear."

"She is one of the women who has smiled upon me. I have tried to imagine myself with her in the long dark of the longhouse."

"She is succulent. Even I can see that."

"Yes, she is, and I begin imagining myself with her, but by the time I am finished and my seed spills from my body, it is you I am with. And not you as *mistshimus*, you as a person. That is why I wish to lay claim to you if you should want it, too. My dreams haunt me with this, and I do not want it otherwise."

She looked at him, so proud of his young manhood and so sad. "I should be proud to have you Standing Bear when I am a woman of this tribe. I am *mistshimus*, so I have no control over my body beyond that. Any titled may take me or order me to lie with a round-head or other *mistshimus*, but your claim is first. I believe only the *Tyee* has the status to overrule it."

"Thank you," he said. "I hoped it would be so."

"I must go. I will be missed. And you," she stroked his organ once more and felt the quiver beneath her touch, "should plant that spear somewhere or there will be more laughing behind the hands."

When she entered Stinging Nettle's hut, Stinging Nettle motioned her over.

"Mistress Stinging Nettle," Girl-With-No-Name said.

"There is gossip about you and Standing Bear?" She said it as a question.

"He wants to lay his claim to me after I go to the moon cycle hut."

"Ah, of course. Well, he is the son of the *Tyee*. And you said?"

For some reason, Girl-With-No-Name looked directly at Stinging Nettle, not assertively but with no deference either. "I said, I am *mistshimus*. Of course, I will lie with you."

"Take care, Nika, with Standing Bear. It is an honor for a *mistshimus* to be so chosen. He is young, but he is also the *Tyee's* only son now, after the whiteman's disease took his other sons. Do not form any attachments. I do not want to lose another *mistshimus* to foolishness."

"Yes, Stinging Nettle. I will take care."

MOON CYCLE HUT

CHAPTER 7
DECEMBER, 1853

GIRL-WITH-NO-NAME awoke doubled over with cramps. Outside it was still dark, the dawn at least two hours away, though she would be hard pressed to tell with the cloud cover and the chill wind-driven sleet. She knew what the cramps betokened. As Stinging Nettle's *mistshimus* apprentice, she had seen many women with cramps before their monthly courses began.

She put on her moccasins and cape of ragged rabbit skins. Even the *mistshimus* were allowed such luxuries as foot coverings and a tossed-off cape in the dead of the *Nch'i-wána* winter. Winters on the Columbia River could be harsh, and Girl-With-No-Name had even heard of a winter so cold that the river froze over and a person could walk the great river from bank to bank.

Thus prepared, she laid back down in a fetal position and waited for Stinging Nettle to wake up. When Stinging Nettle awoke, she called for her *mistshimus*. One look at Girl-With-No-Name and she also knew that it was the girl's time. She eased out of her sleeping furs and moved to the area where she stored her herbs.

"Take this with you. It is la. Make a tea of it. It will ease the cramps. Now go, Nika, and good fortune."

Girl-With-No-Name left Stinging Nettle's hut careful to close the door flap tight to the stinging sleet. Though she could not see it, she knew the moon would be full in two nights. She walked the distance to the moon cycle hut knowing the next time she made this walk she would be a woman. Even for *mistshimus* it was still important. She remembered she had been roped to Nika when she had made this walk. No blood sister would await her exit as a woman, but it did not matter. She would exit, and her life would be forever altered. Even as *mistshimus* she would no longer be a child. She would be a woman with a woman's elevation in status and a woman's responsibilities. This meant, of course, that she could be called upon to lie with a noble or directed to lie with a round-head or even another *mistshimus* should a noble so desire it either for entertainment, reward, or for procreation. Or profit, for that matter.

She reached the moon cycle hut and scratched on the doorway before entering. Dimly lit by a small fire, this was a realm of mystery. Though its furnishings were not remarkable, sleeping rugs on shelves along the outside and the small fire in the center with some cooking supplies and a pot for tea, this was women's territory. This was a territory Girl-With-No-Name had not entered before. Only two of the sleeping rugs were occupied. One of the women, a *mistshimus*, stirred. When she got up, she motioned Girl-With-No-Name to the fire pit.

"This your first time?" she asked in a voice pitched only for her.

"Yes, it is," Girl-With-No-Name said.

"I will help as I can, though little instruction is given to *mistshimus*."

"Thank you."

"Thanks are property. Not yours to give. Remove your cape and moccasins and drink this tea. Get in the sweat lodge. Tea and cleansing sweats. That is all I know or can offer."

Girl-With-No-Name removed her clothing and put it on a sleeping rug away from the other two. She drank of the tea, which was very bitter, and crawled into the little sweat lodge at the end of the building. The other *mistshimus* added fresh coals then closed the door flap, and she was left alone in the dark. In the corner, she saw a stack of moon cycle sails made of cattail fluff that women used. She took one and put it between her legs, laid down, and waited.

At least this was no mystery to her as it had been for *mistshimus* Nika.

Girl-With-No-Name had not thought of her in a long time. The eyes and voice that had once haunted her dreams had gradually gone silent after a year or so but now returned. This time she let them. She knew, more or less, what to expect from her moon cycle. She also knew that it would be traditional for a girl turning into a woman to go on a vision quest to seek her adult name and spirit animal. This quest *mistshimus* were not allowed. A name and a spirit animal were property to these Chinook and thus out of reach to the lowest caste. She knew she could not even ask for the time to go on a vision quest from Stinging Nettle. This period of time, however, while she was secluded in the moon cycle hut, she would be left mostly alone. Or she presumed so at least. This would be the only time she could seek her name and her spirit guide. She meant to use it as such.

The heat of the sweat lodge enveloped and cleansed her. A ritual cleansing was typical for a vision quest. The heat rolled over her, and the eyes of *mistshimus* Nika sought hers out. Her voice sang in Girl-With-No-Name's ears.

Live for me.

White Mouse scurried up the root with a seed in her cheek pouch. It was the "Nika" seed, and she knew it was important. She laid it very carefully on the highest branch of the tree where it would catch the first dawn's light. As the sun crested the horizon in Girl-With-No-Name's mind, she saw the emerald seed flash into light. She reached down into the branches of her mind and plucked it up, gazed into its green depths and put it into her own mouth and ate it. She could feel it going down, spreading roots and linking up all her memories of Nika.

The sweat rolled off her body. There was a stirring outside the sweat lodge. An irritated voice, "Well, who is in there?" It was Bears-Many-Children. "Get her out. I am not sharing the sweat lodge with a *mistshimus*."

As the door flap opened and the other *mistshimus* poked her head in, Girl-With-No-Name signaled she had heard. There was no need to distress her with this task. Girl-With-No-Name crawled out and headed for the main door.

"Oh, it is you, *lemolo mistshimus*. Do not expect any grace from me." Bears-Many-Children crawled into the sweat lodge.

Girl-With-No-Name stood outside the moon cycle hut and just let the weather surround her. She walked to the downwind side and squatted to pee. The wind and the stinging of the sleet were invigorating.

When she went back inside, she went to her pallet. In addition to the herbs provided by Stinging Nettle, she had three other small packets. She knew little about the vision quest of a woman either in the Chinook or among the *Nimi'ipuu*. She did know that among other things it was comprised of two essential parts—the cleansing and the quest itself. Other parts might be just traditions and vary by tribe. This would be her only opportunity to cleanse herself and seek her spirit guide. To that end, she had prepared three purges. With the help of these, she hoped to prepare her body to seek.

She got some water from beside the fire and an earthenware cup. Pouring the water over the herbs, she set it aside to let them diffuse into the hot water. Her skin and hair were coated with salmon oil brought out by the heat. That she would take care of through sweat baths. She had not eaten today and intended to fast through the experience. She knew that was part of the cleansing. Her tea ready, she drank it down. It was wretchedly bitter, and she knew of its effects, so she threw her cape over her shoulders and moved to the doorway. She could feel the infusion roiling in her stomach and judged it time to make a quick exit.

Everything came up in a rush as she spewed on the ground and side of the building. She bent over and heaved again and again until it seemed there was no more. Turning toward the rain, she let it wash her. As she passed back inside, she looked down and saw blood running down her leg.

So, it has begun. I will be a woman. And I will seek my spirit guide.

"Out of my way," Bears-Many-Children said pushing past Girl-With-No-Name. She crowded out through the door flap leaving it open.

Girl-With-No-Name closed it, then saw the blood on the floor of the hut. She and the other *mistshimus* began to methodically clean it up. Girl-With-No-Name looked into the sweat lodge and saw a bloody moon cycle pad on the pallet and fetched it out and placed it on the fire to burn. The other *mistshimus* looked to her and nodded in appreciation.

Bears-Many-Children reentered and headed for her sleeping rugs. "Clean up that"—then noticed the already swept floor and let it drop. She doubled over in cramped pain.

Girl-With-No-Name remembered the herbs Stinging Nettle had given her. Always Bears-Many-Children had treated her cruelly. Perhaps it was because she had been the cause of embarrassment when she was first abducted or perhaps she was just a mean woman exercising her power. The first rule of a spirit quest was to cleanse. This included the emotional as well as the physical.

"May I have her cup please?" she asked the other *mistshimus.*

The other woman handed her a metal cup. It was worn, but it was metal, a trade item, and a valuable one. She shook out a portion of the herbs Stinging Nettle had prepared for her into the cup and poured hot water over them. After a few minutes, she brought the cup to Bears-Many-Children who lay, still groaning.

"Bears-Many-Children, sit up if it would please you, and drink this potion. Stinging Nettle sent it for you," Girl-With-No-Name said.

Bears-Many-Children rose to one elbow. Pain was in her eyes. "What? Stinging Nettle?"

"Stinging Nettle sent this for your cramps. It is special tea made from spearmint, hibiscus, and ginger. It will help you."

Bears-Many-Children drank the tea down. "It is soothing." She lay back down. "Now I will have to thank Stinging Nettle." Soon she was asleep.

Girl-With-No-Name nodded a request toward the sweat lodge. The other *mistshimus* smiled a "go ahead." She crawled through the entrance and sat down.

Now, what do I do? I know nothing of what to do. I will sit still and wait.

Sitting still and waiting were things Girl-With-No-Name was quite practiced at. She felt the sweat bead up on her brow and throat. Next, it began between her thighs and below her still small breasts. She was not so practiced at not thinking of anything but attempted it. It was part of being still after all.

The reflecting pool does not think of a rock thrown upon its surface. It envelops the rock and the ripples eventually pass away. I shall be that pool.

White Mouse darted from the brush. She paused, still except for her pink ears twitching. The girl becoming a woman sat above the pool, but she was not aware of White Mouse. Not yet. She drank a little water from the pool, disturbing the reflection. When her reflection cleared, a droplet fell into the pool directly in front of her. It crystalized into a tiny seed, and White Mouse lifted it carefully out with her little paws.

Curious, this seed is about Bears-Many-Children, but it is almost clear. She put it into her cheek pouch and scampered back to her den beneath the roots. She placed the seed next to a red seed, so dark and angry it appeared like a miniature storm within and watched with amazement as they became one. The angry red softened a little, became lighter and glowed. White Mouse knew what to do then and took it up in her cheek pouch back into the branches.

Girl-With-No-Name had lost track of time and place. She sat, and she chanted a song. It was odd because it wasn't a song she had been taught. Somehow the words came unbidden, and she sang them out softly. She saw the pool and the tree, movement among the branches, but could not focus on White Mouse. She saw a glint of carmine and reached down to the branches to pluck it up.

Another seed. This time a dark carmine seed with a white glow. She ate of the seed, and it joined the emerald green one, linked up like a flickering tiny fire for a moment then settled back to form an array of two.

Girl-With-No-Name judged she had been in the sweat lodge long enough and emerged into the dim hut. Bears-Many-Children still lay softly snoring. The other *mistshimus* sat nearby beading a belt with a complicated salmon pattern. She looked up as Girl-With-No-Name closed the flap door, then back down again.

Was that a look of acknowledgment? We *mistshimus* never speak of important things, only about the task ahead. But sometimes with just a look or gesture, a lot is said. Or seems so at least. It is so little a thing that a person could always be mistaken. Perhaps the smallness of it makes it a great matter. The smallest gesture, a lifted eyebrow, a tiny smile might encompass a wide range of meanings. How did I miss this before?

Girl-With-No-Name passed out the doorway, taking a waterproof basket with her. She walked the short distance to the stream, dipped the basket, and poured the cold water over her. She did this two more times, then squatted down on the edge of the stream and let her water join the stream. A short distance beyond, it flowed into the *Nch'i-wána*. From there it would hurry on to the sea. She had never seen the sea but had heard of it, a water so great that all of the troubles of man and woman would not even ripple its surface.

Suddenly she felt cold. The sleet had stopped falling, but the wind was still brisk.

But where has the day gone? I came here this morning. I have taken two sweats and spent some little time between, and now it is night.

She shook herself like a dog and refilled the water basket. Looking down at herself she seemed clean and clear. The salmon grease and smoke had been sweated from her body. She felt a little faint from no food and wispy like smoke or mist rising from the waters.

She went inside and prepared the second purgative. When it was ready, she drank it down. The taste was foul, but she drank it to the dregs anyway. Then she drank a large amount of water and sat back on her heels and waited. An hour passed and when it came, she barely had time to get outside and squat to pee. It seemed like she was pissing her insides out and her urine had a strong odor. She went back within and prepared the third and final purge. This tasted, if anything, worse than the other two. Again, she followed it with as much water as she could drink. She did not have to wait so long this time until it felt like her intestines were twisting like snakes mating. She rushed out again and made it some distance from the hut before squatting and letting go. Her bladder let go as well. When all seemed finished, she covered her spoor with dirt and went to the creek to wash.

The moon had broken through the clouds for a few minutes and shone clear and bright on her skin. Purified for perhaps the first time in her life, certainly the clearest she had felt since she had been captured, she splashed water on her legs, nether parts and loins, and then across her whole body. The waters ran crystalline clear from her now, and she felt that same crystalline clearness within. She looked to the moon which was almost full and felt a force rise within her from the ground below. There was a skittering sound as some small creature ran from the creek toward the moon cycle hut.

Likely just some critter out checking the midden pile for tonight's leavings.

She entered the moon cycle hut and sat on her rug with the pad between her legs. It was warm in here, so very comfortable. She sat and just let her mind drift. This cycle of sit still and drift, enter the sweat lodge and sweat out the last vestiges of filth her body had absorbed in thirteen years, bleed and bathe, went on for two days.

Finally, it was night again on the third day. The rains and wind had temporarily ceased, and the evening was filled once again with the sound of the rushing river and the little sounds of nocturnal critters in their own life-and-death struggle for existence. She had given up questing for visions. She had given up thinking about anything at all. The vision quest was a thing, and she had given up on things. Now, she existed in the moment. At times she bled, and she took care of that, washing herself and disposing of the pad. With a fresh pad, she would enter the hut and sit, or go into the sweat lodge. It did not seem to matter.

All this White Mouse saw—or sensed would be a more accurate term. She had been waiting still and quiet for this moment. She knew how to move in the night undetected, and this she did, gathering all the seeds in her collection until her cheek pouches bulged, then climbing the tree as only she knew how to do, until she reached the topmost branches. Here she arrayed the seeds in such splendor of color and shape, it was as if the tree had grown them itself.

When the girl-woman looked down and saw what White Mouse had wrought there was delight in her eyes and tears too. She reached down, and White Mouse wondered which seed she would choose first.

Is it truly dear White Mouse who has brought me these wondrous seeds?

Her great soft hands passed by the seeds and to White Mouse's surprise cupped her up and raised her to the woman's shoulder. For Girl-With-No-Name was a girl no longer. White Mouse could see that and feel that as well.

You shall hide no longer in the roots, dear White Mouse. You who have protected me for so long, and I have not even known it. Clever White

Mouse to have hidden these seeds for so long a time when I knew not that I was even having these experiences. What should I do with them?

She listened as White Mouse chittered into her ear.

Put them into my cheek pouches? And protect them?

White Mouse squeaked, excited.

Girl-With-No-Name stroked White Mouse's fur. White Mouse climbed up her hair on top of her head and peeked out through the tousled hair.

I do not have cheek pouches like you do, White Mouse, but I will do as you say.

Girl-With-No-Name gathered up all the many-colored seeds and put them one by one into her cheeks. She felt as though her cheeks bulged with them as they expanded with the moisture and began to swirl within her mouth. She put her hand to one cheek and then the other. Her cheeks felt normal to her hand but within she was being suffused with color and memory.

I went on this vision quest and searched and searched for you, White Mouse.

White Mouse rolled on her back in pleasure, tangled in the hair. Girl-With-No-Name reached up and rubbed her fat belly with a fingertip.

I imagined every type of animal that might be my spirit guide—an owl, a snake, a hawk, even a cat.

White Mouse squeaked and rolled over again hiding beneath the locks. Girl-With-No-Name's hand protectively covered her.

You are silly, dear one. Never would I let any harm come to you. In my strangest dreams, I never imagined my childhood name held the secret.

White Mouse clambered down her hair to her ear and whispered.

Yes, you are right. We must keep you a secret. Among these Chinook, a spirit guide is property. They are odd that way, everything is property to them. But as we live with them, I will keep you a secret.

"Let us go to sleep now, little mouse," she said sotto voice. The other *mistshimus* looked over at the sound. She drew her ragged furs to her shoulders and lay down to sleep protectively cradling White Mouse against her small woman's breast.

White Mouse chittered.

I am happy to have found you at last, also, White Mouse, so happy.

STANDING BEAR

CHAPTER 8
DECEMBER, 1853 TO JANUARY, 1854

WHEN GIRL-WITH-NO-NAME next awakened, she was alone in the hut. Both the *mistshimus* and Bears-Many-Children were gone. She went outside to take care of her toilet, splashed some water over her face and body, and returned to the hut. It was not the time for her to leave yet. She ate some food, put some wood on the fire, and lay back down to sleep.

White Mouse tucked herself in on her neck to watch over her. Along with her courses and the moon, the beadwork of seeds was fading, but only because it was being absorbed into the girl—now woman—who White Mouse protected. Girl-With-No-Name put her hand over White Mouse and stroked her fur.

When she awoke again, she sensed it was early morning. Some little time she spent tidying the hut. She put two more small logs on the fire and looked around. She saw the metal cup of Bears-Many-Children forgotten and gathered it up to return it. Satisfied, she exited closing the flap door with care.

It was full on day now, and the sunlight glinted off whitecaps on the *Nch'i-wána* as she had never seen before. The trees along the south side of the camp reached for the sun. Girl-With-No-Name saw how every single branch grew to take advantage of the light. The smells of the camp from the rotting odor of the midden pile to the ever present smell of salmon and smoke suffused the air around her, almost overwhelming her with a sense of the dance of life and death.

She was new. She was a woman now, and she had White Mouse riding her shoulder. White Mouse chittered something, but Girl-With-No-Name did not hear, so charmed was she by her new perception of the world.

When she reached Stinging Nettle's hut, the healer looked up to greet her, took one look at her, and her face changed from greeting to warning. "Come inside the hut *mistshimus*. Now."

"Yes, Stinging Nettle," Girl-With-No-Name said. Her feet felt as though she were dancing.

Within the hut, Stinging Nettle took her by the shoulders. "Did you not listen to a thing I said?"

"Yes, Stinging Nettle. I am a woman now. I was quiet and still when I was in the hut. I gave Bears-Many-Children the tea and said it was from you. I brought back the cup she forgot." She held it out.

Stinging Nettle slapped her leaving the imprint of her hand on her face.

Girl-With-No-Name began to cry, the slap was so unexpected. "But—"

"You pursued a vision quest. I know my herb stock. You took herbs from my store and quested."

Girl-With-No-Name straightened her back. "I did."

"I am not so cruel to begrudge you that. Even *mistshimus* were allowed that in my old tribe, yet you wear it like a cape of many-painted eagle feathers. It flows about you like stars in the night sky. I do not question whether you found your spirit guide or what it is. Clearly, you did. You must bury that knowledge deep and never show anyone. Do you understand? Or do you need to be beaten until you understand?"

"I understand, Stinging Nettle."

"In the Bent Creek Clan, as traditional as it is, a Spirit Guide and a private name are considered the highest form of property. A *mistshimus* would be killed, and slowly, for the pretense of such knowledge."

"Yes, Stinging Nettle, but it is not pretense."

Stinging Nettle slapped her again. "To this clan, which believes no *mistshimus* is capable of having a Spirit Guide or a private name, to pretend such is one of the highest crimes."

The facade of dull acceptance passed over the face and body of Girl-

With-No-Name, changing her posture to the passive acceptance of her position and her face to the stupid day by day resignation of the *mistshimus*.

"Is this better, Stinging Nettle?" Girl-With-No-Name asked.

"Don't be insolent. Teach your spirit animal to be on guard. It, at least, may be smart enough to protect you. I will not tell of this to anyone, but I cannot protect you if you are found out."

"I understand," Girl-With-No-Name said, then with excitement in her voice, "I found this in the moon cycle hut. I think it belonged to Bears-Many-Children, so I bring it to you. I did not know what else to do with it."

The eager twinkle to her eyes made Stinging Nettle laugh in a grumpy "Hmmph" as she took the cup. "That was good, Nika. Now Bears-Many-Children will owe me two favors. Let us go out into the sun and grind herbs and see what the day brings."

Later in the afternoon, as Girl-With-No-Name ground herbs and Stinging Nettle sat back enjoying the brief winter sunlight, Bears-Many-Children approached.

Stinging Nettle smiled, "Bears-Many-Children, welcome," offering her a place to sit. "Perhaps, you would like some tea?"

"That would be welcome, thank you, Stinging Nettle."

"*Mistshimus* Nika, bring tea, the hibiscus."

Girl-With-No-Name rose to prepare the tea. She returned with two earthenware cups full, serving Bears-Many-Children first as guest and then Stinging Nettle. She waited.

Stinging Nettle took a sip and gestured with a flick of her fingers. "Back to your task, *mistshimus*."

Bears-Many-Children and Stinging Nettle sipped the tea a few moments savoring the sweet flower smell. Both knew it was a rarity in the middle of winter and not locally collected.

Finally, Bears-Many-Children said, "Your *mistshimus* brought me a tea of spearmint, hibiscus, and ginger in the moon cycle hut. She said it was from you. That was a kindness, Stinging Nettle. I thank you."

"No thanks are needed. I know how your cycles can be sometimes."

"Never the less, it was a favor, and I thank you for it."

"Just something between two women of the tribe. That reminds me, she brought back your metal cup. She was afraid it might have been misplaced." She handed the cup to Bears-Many-Children.

Bears-Many-Children took the cup, "I wondered where this had got off to. It seems that makes two favors I owe you."

"You owe me nothing, Bears-Many-Children." Stinging Nettle took a sip of the tea.

Bears-Many-Children pressed the cup into Stinging Nettle's hand, "Please take this then and let us call it even."

"Bears-Many-Children, you are too kind to me. I shall do as you wish. Thank you for the gift."

"The *Tyee* has need of me this afternoon, Stinging Nettle." Bears-Many-Children got to her feet and left.

Late that afternoon Girl-With-No-Name saw Standing Bear passing by. At that moment Fire Stick and Fox Tail came up to Stinging Nettle. Fire Stick poked Fox Tail in the ribs and laughed.

"Fire Stick and Fox Tail. What do two fine warriors need of me?"

"It is Burr-Up-My-Ass who—"

Fox Tail gave him a look.

"Pardon, Stinging Nettle. Fox Tail has business with you."

"Sit then, Fox Tail." Fox Tail sat, and Girl-With-No-Name knew what he was there for. She looked to Standing Bear, but he was gone.

"I would like to—that is, I—"

"Perhaps a cup of tea might help you loosen your tongue. *Mistshimus* Nika, tea, please. The spearmint."

As Girl-With-No-Name was preparing the tea, Standing Bear ran toward the *Tyee's* longhouse. The *Tyee* sat outside enjoying the sun. "My pardons father. I would lay claim to the *mistshimus* of Stinging Nettle. She has just emerged today from the moon cycle hut."

The *Tyee* digested this. "Go on."

"May I have two blankets to trade, father? There is another there with Stinging Nettle, Fox Tail, and I want to win this *mistshimus*."

"Fox Tail, eh? As I recall, he was one of the young warriors who started this mess to begin with. Yes, go on. But not two of the new ones. Good quality, but not new. No *mistshimus* is worth two new blankets."

"Thank you, *Tyee*, father." Standing Bear was dashing in to choose the blankets before the *Tyee* had finished his sentence.

So now this *mistshimus* has cost me a metal cup and two blankets. Well, at least my son prefers women. There is that.

Girl-With-No-Name prepared the tea and brought it out serving the guest and then Stinging Nettle.

Fox Tail took a gulp of the tea and singed his lips.

"Careful, hot," said Stinging Nettle. "We are all adults here. What is it you wish, Fox Tail?"

"Since the *mistshimus* that serves you is a woman now, I would lay claim to her this month."

Stinging Nettle took a deep draught of the tea and savored it. "Ah, so you wish to lay claim upon *mistshimus* Nika. What do you offer in return?"

He gestured to Fire Stick, who handed him the rabbit pelts. "I have brought these five rabbit pelts, the best I have, tanned and soft."

"Hmmm. They are tanned well and very soft."

She glanced up and saw Standing Bear running for her hut. "There is another who has thought to lay claim on *mistshimus* Nika. And here he is."

"Stinging Nettle, Fire Stick, Fox Tail."

"Standing Bear," she said. "Would you like tea?"

"I would state my business, Stinging Nettle."

"A warrior who gets right to the point. Go ahead, then."

"I would lay claim to your *mistshimus* who has just come to womanhood this very day. I offer two blankets in exchange."

"To the point, I like that in a man." She took the blankets. "They are not new, but they are soft and quite welcome this cold winter." She looked to Fox Tail.

"No, the five pelts are all I can offer. She is yours, Standing Bear. Thank you for the tea, Stinging Nettle."

"There is no dishonor in being beat at a bargain, Fox Tail. Perhaps you would share my bed some evening. I would not charge you."

"Thank you, Stinging Nettle." He rose and walked away with much ribbing from his friend Fire Stick.

"You may have her three times this month as is custom. I can get by without her tonight if you wish? One night in the middle of the month and one night toward end of her moon cycle."

"Tonight, would suffice well enough, Stinging Nettle. Thank you." He rose and with no glance at Girl-With-No-Name left their presence.

Stinging Nettle gathered up the two blankets and motioned Girl-With-No-Name inside. "I would warn you not to arouse any affection from Standing Bear, but one look at that boy's face tells me it is too late for that. It is an honor to be chosen by the *Tyee's* son as his first, but it is a great danger as well. If the *Tyee* thinks there is any bond between a noble born, especially his only son, and a *mistshimus*, there will be payment exacted. He will punish you both, but yours will be the greater. Much greater, I fear."

"I do not know what to do, Stinging Nettle, truly."

"I do not either. We take the path of easy water sometimes, but it may just as easily carry you over Celilo Falls as to a peaceful back eddy. If you see still water, swim for it, is all I can say."

"Yes."

"Now, the worst thing that could happen was if you were to get with child from this exercise. That would shame the *Tyee*. I will give you herbs, and you should be fairly safe tonight, just a day after your moon cycle. Also, if we can push the third meet to close to your moon cycle's beginning that is safe as well, or as safe as could be. For the mid-month, we will have to depend upon just the herbs. Now, little Nika, get some rest. You will get none tonight."

"Thank you, Stinging Nettle. I know I am not supposed to even own the thanks to give you, but I give what I do not have then." She took herself to a corner of the hut and curled up to sleep.

The time came soon enough. Standing Bear was at the doorway and Stinging Nettle pushing her out. "Do not shame me, *mistshimus*."

Standing Bear's eyes brightened upon seeing her, then he caught himself and cast them down. "Come, *mistshimus*. I have prepared a place." He turned about, and Girl-With-No-Name followed. They did not turn toward his family's longhouse as she expected but toward the creek. At the hut where they had first kissed, the same hut she had hidden in during her belated escape attempt, he entered. She followed him in.

There was a small fire there in the newly dug out fire pit and a nest of sleeping rugs toward the back behind the freshly restacked debris.

"It was the best I could do," he said almost apologetically. "At least we will have some privacy here.

"I am *mistshimus*. You could take me in broad daylight at the salmon festival, and I would make no objection. I could not," she said.

"Please do not say that. I like you. I cannot help that."

"I am *mistshimus*. I must say it. I like you too, but I am *mistshimus*. Never forget that."

"Fine. Eat with me, *mistshimus*. I will want you to be strong and compliant all of tonight then."

They sat on their heels and ate of the little feast Standing Bear had brought. He spared no little thought on the details of it, and Girl-With-No-Name had to admit she enjoyed it thoroughly. Every so often she glanced up from her downcast eyes to notice Standing Bear looking at her. He wore no breechclout as men sometimes did in winter and she saw another part of him paying attention as well.

"This *mistshimus* thanks you for the meal, Standing Bear," she said when she could eat no more nor bear the tension between them any longer.

"Come to the sleeping rugs, *mistshimus*."

"Yes, Standing Bear. The *mistshimus* will be as a reed before the storm."

"We shall see how reed-like you are. Remove your cape and moccasins."

That was easily done, and as that was all she wore, she soon stood naked before him, the flickering firelight dancing over her skin.

"Touch me, *mistshimus*, like you did before."

"To hear you, warrior, is to obey you," she said. She touched his chest and felt his chest muscles tighten. "Here?"

"Yes, and lower."

She let her hand drift down to his stomach. She dragged her fingernails across his hard abdomen. "And here?" She saw the head of his sex protruding beyond its hiding place of skin.

"Yes. *Mistshimus,* you know where I want to be touched. Do not tease me, or I shall be displeased with you."

She knelt before him. "Ah, Standing Bear, you mean here." She grasped his quivering organ in her hand and slid the covering skin up and down. She laid her cheek upon it.

"Ah, yes," he said.

"It is the proud spear of the warrior you bear, Standing Bear."

She could feel a strange response echoing his desire coming from her own body. Though she had indeed thought upon this moment a few times since he had kissed her in this hut and felt some shimmering heat in her loins before, she had never explored what that meant. Now, it felt as though some part of herself was readying itself for him. The act of sex itself was not strange or unnatural to her. Neither she nor anyone she had ever known was not aware of it. Not only were her people, the *Nimi'ipuu,* aware of sex from a very early age in dogs, cats, and horses, but her people and indeed these Chinook were not shy about coupling. True, many would seek their sleeping rugs for such an act, but that was only for comfort, not to hide away. They might just as easily find a soft place in the grass near the village. Any who walked by would hardly notice. If they did, it was more in amusement or to make some jocular remark.

Still, she was, in spite of being around sex from an early age, not knowledgeable of how it would affect her personally. She knew that the mare would back up to the stallion when she was ready, but not how she would back up to this.

"*Mistshimus,* lie down on the sleeping rugs."

"Like this," she knelt down, her face to the furs, her hips lifted high like the mare before the stallion.

"No, *mistshimus.* Turn over. I want to see your face when I take you."

Girl-With-No-Name rolled over and parted her knees wide. Something strange indeed was happening down there. She could feel a wetness forming, and she was opening to him.

"This may hurt some. I will go slowly." He knelt between her legs and placed the head of his organ just into her opening.

"Do not fear of pain for me. This *mistshimus* has been beaten to the ground by the mothers in your clan as well as the other *mistshimus*. Take me like the warrior you are."

This angered him, and he plunged suddenly into her. There was a sharp tearing pain that rose from her sex, along nerves she never knew she had, to her breasts and throat. Not a pain like the beating she had taken, more like a worrisome infected tooth being pulled—exquisite pain followed by an outflow of relief.

Her legs wrapped around him as he drove deep inside her again and again. All too soon, he lifted his chest up high and ground into her and cried out. He held this position for a hand of moments as she worked his organ, then collapsed on top of her.

So, was this it? The excitement of anticipation, the wet flow beforehand, then a very short time of fierce pumping and it was over? It seemed he had enjoyed it immensely, and she was not displeased by that. But she had thought there would be more somehow.

He rolled off her, panting. "We have a time for you to rest, *mistshimus*. Afterward I shall want to take you again."

"I shall await that moment with pleasure, warrior." At least there would be more. Mayhap it would last a little longer next time. She felt sticky between her legs. When she drew her hand between them, it came back bloody. "Ah, warrior, I must wash."

She dashed for the exit, fearful that her cycle had begun again, then remembered the tearing pain. It was not her cycle at all. She felt silly running and walked to the stream. Squatting to pee, she let his seed run out of her. She was glad of the herb tea Stinging Nettle had made her drink and hoped that it would work.

White Mouse chittered something in her ear.

You are right, White Mouse. This is nothing worrying will help at all. Thank you, little one, for watching over me.

She splashed water on her face and over her loins. Running her fingers over that place, feeling his seed, and her wetness, she also felt something else extraordinary. White Mouse squeaked some other "mouse" words.

It is true, White Mouse. There is another seed there that I never knew about before. She ran her finger just above where her flower opened. She shivered at the sensation. This is a curious thing, White Mouse.

Now that she was aware of it, it became hard to ignore. As she walked back to the hut, her swollen lips seemed to rub against it. She squeezed her legs together.

No, that doesn't make it go away at all.

When she entered the hut, Standing Bear lay on his side watching her every move. "Come here, *mistshimus*. I have want of you."

She began to lie down as he had requested before, but he interrupted her. "No, *mistshimus*. I will take you as the *hyas talapus*, as the wolf takes his *talapus klootchman*, his bitch."

Girl-With-No-Name got on her hands and knees and lifted to him. He positioned himself behind her and slipped in. So easy it was and so quick. He began a rhythmic motion, and this time it seemed it was going to last more than a short time. She lay her breasts and shoulders down on the furs looking to one side and tried to match his movements. Occasionally, he would slip out and brush against that seed upon reentering. The jolt it sent through her body lasted only a instant or two, but she knew she liked it. She reached a hand beneath her to feel his organ move in and out of her and brushed against the seed accidentally. The seed was swollen up proud and hard. She began touching him but allowing her hand to slide across that spot that was becoming increasingly sensitive.

Someone was moaning. Girl-With-No-Name realized it was her own voice. His stroke was increasing in a kind of violent need, and she found her own need beginning to match his. Her nose was running, and her mouth hung partway open with her tongue out. Now, she was the bitch, and he was the wolf. She needed him and would not let him go, not until he satisfied this urge that was upon her. As she stroked her seed, the root of her need that had spread to her breasts and thence to her whole body, he thrust deeper and harder. He twisted as if trying to climb inside her. She could feel the surge coming and did not know if it was him or her, only that they needed so badly to be joined. She forgot about the force behind her and focused on her own pleasure now, rubbing harder and faster. She did not know that her hips rocked against him, but she felt it coming. The building of it like the breaking of the ice on a winter river. First, a small piece would break off, then a larger one. At last, the whole of the river would surge up and break the dam.

They collapsed together onto the sleeping rugs, her fingers still twitching spasmodically for a moment then clamped down between her legs. It was done, and it was good. Now she knew why some of the women liked this thing.

They lay together for some little time on the sleeping rugs until Girl-With-No-Name finally fell asleep. At some point during that long night, she felt the rousing of Standing Bear's organ pressing against her. Sleepily she rolled onto her back and took him into her. For her, it was not as the second time had been. This was no forest fire or flood, just a quiet acceptance of Standing Bear's need. As such, it was a pleasant enough experience, and Standing Bear seemed to like it, as his groans and final surge proved. In some way, in her way and her tribe's way, it was proof of her womanhood that she could attract and please a warrior. She was not unhappy with that. She had no way of judging it. She was a woman. She was *mistshimus*. He desired her, and she pleased him. As woman and *mistshimus* she could do no better. This was as much as she was allowed to take for herself, so she took it and held it to her breast along with White Mouse.

The sound of Standing Bear packing up the food and his other property roused her. It was just before dawn. She rolled out of the bed they had shared, the first bed she had shared with a man ever in her life and folded the furs. She saw that they were exceptionally fine. Standing Bear had taken care in picking them. She brought the furs to him and stood waiting.

"Yes, *mistshimus*," he said a bit short.

She would risk it just this one time, then she must say no more. "I know I am *mistshimus*, and you are the *Tyee's* son, Standing Bear. You have honored me with your choice." She looked down uncertain how to continue. Finally, she decided to get it out once. "I like you very much. It is forbidden any feeling between us, I know that. I just wanted you to know that you are dear to me. Forgive me for saying too much. I know that I have done so."

She did not know what to expect from him. Anyone could have seen that he had been angry the previous evening.

Now what will he do?

What he did was unexpected. He took her into his arms and just held her. Though he was a warrior, he was also only fourteen summers. "I do not know what to do, *mistshimus* Nika. I do not. You are the only one who I can truly talk to, and we are forbidden to talk together. I can give you commands, and you can accept them, but we cannot speak together. I am forbidden to like you or show any affection, yet that is all I wish to do. It saddens my heart."

She held onto him as if he were a tree in a windstorm, her only anchor. "You are a warrior of the Chinook, Standing Bear. Whatever comes, you will always be my warrior. You must be strong and treat me as the low *mistshimus* I must be." She looked into his eyes and saw tears there. As she had once done with her eleven-year-old brother, she slapped him with all the force she had right across the face.

Anger sparked immediately in his warrior's eyes. "You dare strike a noble born warrior, *mistshimus*?"

"You are my warrior Standing Bear, my first. I am your *mistshimus*. This is how it must be."

Understanding cleared the fury from his countenance. "I understand. You are wise for a *mistshimus*."

She gathered up all his burdens as well as the sleeping rugs. "I will bear these back to your longhouse, warrior Standing Bear."

Standing Bear took one last longing look at her then shook it off and resumed his arrogant bearing, "Follow me, *mistshimus*. Do not drop anything."

He exited first, drawing his cape about him and the fading sting of her slap. She followed demure and subservient. People were about in the village and many made humorous comments. She bore them with inner pride and an outer show of willing compliance. They entered the longhouse, and she deposited the remaining foodstuffs near the cooking fire, then took his sleeping furs to his pallet. Carefully, she arranged them and, when no one was looking, held one to her nose and drew in one last breath fragrant with the smell of him and her together.

"Do not dawdle, *mistshimus*. You may tell Stinging Nettle your performance was satisfactory. You are dismissed to your duties."

Girl-With-No-Name left humbly chastised. She returned slowly to Stinging Nettle's hut. For this short time, at least, she could be herself. No one was watching, and she could feel the brisk breeze blowing downriver, see the sun passing behind a cloud and just as quickly emerging. A thin winter sun shone upon the life of this small village of Chinook, a warrior, and his *mistshimus*.

Stinging Nettle asked nothing, just directed her to her next task. During that day and the next, several of the *mistshimus* made oblique references to her night with Standing Bear, but as it involved a noble born, Girl-With-No-Name chose not to answer. Taking this as proper, they continued chatting about mundane things and the work at hand.

When they met again in the middle of her cycle, after the initial explosion of pent-up passion, Standing Bear lay with her tucked under his enclosing arm. "Have you had any problems, *mistshimus*?"

"The other *mistshimus* are curious but dare only sidelong comments or questions. Those I ignore, and they take this as proper behavior of a *mistshimus*. Stinging Nettle has not spoken of us, though I know she suspects."

"With me, it is much different. Some of the warriors make bawdy jokes, and I have to resist being angry. Fire Start and Fox Tail have been persistent pests. Every day, sometimes several times each day, they have a dirty joke or story to tell me. They ask how you compare to this one or that one."

"What do you tell them, my warrior?"

"I tell them the Nez Perce women are overrated. That as *mistshimus* you will do as I bid but only that, and you lie like a cold salmon beneath me."

She doubled up her fist and hit him on the shoulder. "A cold salmon. I will show you what kind of cold fish I can be." She rolled on top of him and settled down upon his organ rocking forward and backward.

"If I told them about this, they would find a way to outbid me next month."

She stopped her movement of a sudden. "Perhaps you should. Let Fox Tail or one of the others have me for a month. I could play the cold salmon. The interest would die off."

The sting of the slap on her buttocks brought her thoughts back to the moment at hand. "Do not talk of Fox Tail, *mistshimus*. I am your warrior. I want you."

She resumed her motion. "As you wish, Standing Bear." However, the thought would not leave her mind entirely.

If I am such a cold salmon, why would Standing Bear want to continue with me? If he does continue then why would he lie? She could see the fish trap down the river even if he could not, and the river currents bore her inexorably toward it.

They finished their night together, and Girl-With-No-Name could tell that Standing Bear was not happy. She tried and failed to bring him back by teasing or even in anger. Standing Bear left their conjugal hut with a frown, and she followed.

Their third meeting ten days later was even more stormy. It was not just heavy clouds on the horizon this time. The clouds built and enveloped them. While that brought a new urgency and fire to their lovemaking, it also troubled their talk.

"You must let another have me after my next moon cycle, Standing Bear. I know you see it. If I can be the willing but cold salmon with Fox Tail or some other, then we may continue." There was pleading in her voice.

"I know what you want. Now you have had Standing Bear you want to try another. You want to go with Fox Tail." His arrogance as a noble born and the hurt of the fourteen-year-old warrior both fought for control.

"No, my Standing Bear. I do not. I... I like you. Truly, I do. With all my heart and what spirit a *mistshimus* may have, that is all I want. I am afraid of where this path leads, my Standing Bear. I am deadly afraid. I beg of you. Let someone else have me. I will not care because I will be doing it for us."

Her pleading was not winning out. He could not see it.

"I cannot," he said.

She lay back down, her head on his deep breathing chest. She could feel his heart beating, quick tempoed with anger. "We must go over the falls together and see if we still live."

OVER THE FALLS

CHAPTER 9
JANUARY, 1854

A S GIRL-WITH-NO-NAME prepared to go to the moon cycle hut the next time, she asked, "Stinging Nettle, I know a *mistshimus* may not ask her mistress for a favor, but I truly do not know what to do."

"Does this regard the warrior, Standing Bear, who is apparently taken by you?"

"Yes, it does," she said and began to cry. "I have told him he must allow someone else to have me, Fox Tail, if he is still willing, or anyone else. He will not hear it."

"I will speak as friend to you. A man's pride is a thin thing. It may make him a fierce protector and a fury in battle. This I have seen. But it may make him stupid as well when a woman can see the clear water in the current ahead."

"He insists on taking us over the falls when there is a portage," Girl-With-No-Name said. "I do like him. I had to tell him that much, and that I fear—"

"Was a mistake, *mistshimus* Nika."

"Yes, it was. And I knew it was when I told him."

"That opportunity to stop this foolishness has passed you by. I will try to think of what I can do, but I warn you it may lead to worse consequences. If I arrange for Fox Tail to have you, Standing Bear and his pride may wish to fight him. A fight over a *mistshimus* girl is almost unheard of. It will bring the *Tyee's* attention directly upon you. You will pay the higher price. He may not kill you, but he will exact a price. This I know."

"I am saddened that I have brought this upon you, Stinging Nettle. I know, even now, you miss your *mistshimus* Nika. I shall never be able to take her place. I should have done what you said, and I knew it. I just could not."

"You have made your own place here," said Stinging Nettle. "I could wish it were different or that you were different, but truly I do not. The flood of the *Wimahl* brings what it brings. Coyote has said this, and this I truly believe."

"This the *Nimi'ipuu* believe as well. Thank you, Stinging Nettle."

"Be a proper *mistshimus* and get on to the moon cycle hut. Take these herbs for Bears-Many-Children and tell her this is not a favor. I am healer to this, the Bent Creek Clan."

She hoped this was going to work out well, but she had no illusions as she walked to the moon cycle hut. When she got there, Bears-Many-Children lay curled on her sleeping pallet, and the same *mistshimus* attended her.

Their cycles must be almost identical. She made up the tea and gave it to the *mistshimus* to give to Bears-Many-Children. Girl-With-No-Name entered the sweat lodge to begin her own cleansing ritual.

Four and a half days later, she emerged to a light snow, splashed herself off one last time in the creek and made her way to Stinging Nettle's hut. She wondered what this day would bring and worried that, whatever way the day went, it would not turn out well in the end.

The *Nch'i-wána* bears the clever upon its back and drowns the stupid who stand in the flood. And sometimes it drowns the clever as well.

When she entered Stinging Nettle's hut, Stinging Nettle beckoned her to the back. "I have arranged, as is my right as noble born, to have you go with Fox Tail this very night. Standing Bear does not know it yet, but if I know Fox Tail, he will soon. You are to go to the longhouse to Fox Tail's bed at full dark. Be a good *mistshimus*. Be attentive. Be pliable. But you don't have to be enthusiastic or energetic."

"That role I know how to play. Thank you, Stinging Nettle."

"I fear, with Fox Tail's good-natured joking, Standing Bear may take offense, but it was the best I could do. Rest now, and we shall see, Nika."

A couple hours later as Girl-With-No-Name rested in the back of the hut, Standing Bear entered.

"Standing Bear, sit and be welcome," Stinging Nettle said.

"I come to make claim on your *mistshimus*, and I hear from Fox Tail that her services are already given," Standing Bear said, "to *him*."

He almost spat the words out.

"Calm yourself, Standing Bear. It is my right to do so."

"I was not even allowed to make a competitive bid."

"She is a *mistshimus* in my service. As such, she is my property. Mine to dispose of as I see fit."

"I am the *Tyee's* son. I will see what he thinks about this." Standing Bear made to rise.

Girl-With-No-Name, from her position in the back of the hut, cried to see him in such pain over her, a *mistshimus*. It hurt her to the bone, but it must be done.

"Sit down, Standing Bear," Stinging Nettle said.

He hesitated half standing.

"Sit down—*now*."

He sat.

"You may indeed be the *Tyee's* son, but even as such, I sit at a higher place on his mat than you do. I am elder, and you will listen to me. If you do this thing you are contemplating, you will likely get my *mistshimus* Nika killed or at the very least punished in such a way as you will never forget. And mark my words, boy, for compared to me you are a boy only newly arrived to manhood, I will never forget it, either. Do you understand?"

"I understand, Stinging Nettle, that you have the right to dispose of your *mistshimus* as you see fit."

"And?"

"I will not object to you exercising that right."

"Good. Be calm, and be restful. This may work out right in the end."

Standing Bear rose and left.

When night came, Girl-With-No-Name made her passage toward the *Tyee's* longhouse. Entering, she took a deep breath. The odors of sixty or more Chinook boiled over her. The smells of salmon, smoke, and human—and all that comprised—swirled about her. Food, and the blood and fat on the skins stacked along the rafters, and sleeping furs spiced with the taint of sex were this people's life and her life, as well.

She spied Fox Tail sitting at the central fire with Fire Stick and some others. Fire Stick saw her and gave Fox Tail a poke. Fox Tail attempted to ignore his friend, but as usual Fire Stick's exuberant approach to life could not be hidden beneath a basket. She also saw Standing Bear sitting near the array of foods gnawing on a strip of venison. He lifted his blank gaze and stared in her direction though their eyes did not meet.

Girl-With-No-Name squared her shoulders to her task and approached Fox Tail.

"Fox Tail, Stinging Nettle has sent me to serve you," she said in her most demure and servile *mistshimus* voice.

Fox Tail spared her a glance. Though he did not mean it so, it was an appreciative look at her nubile form. "Ah, *mistshimus*, go to my sleeping furs and await me there."

"I shall await you like the bending willow awaits the wind, Fox Tail." She turned and walked head down to Fox Tail's pallet.

"She does have a well-formed ass, I will give you that, Fox Tail," Fire Stick said. "Like two ripe apples rubbing when she walks." He mimicked the action with his fists.

Girl-With-No-Name removed her cloak and moccasins and crawled onto Fox Tail's bed furs. She lay down and waited. If these furs were examples of Fox Tail's skills at tanning, he did have a gift for it. Though tanning was generally left to the women, some warriors tanned special skins. These were extremely supple and the fur upon them almost like it was still upon the live animal. She drifted a bit and woke only when she found Fox Tail standing above her.

"So, little *mistshimus*, are you pleased to see me," Fox Tail said. "You know I was one of the warriors who carried you off from your home." He knelt on the furs.

"I do remember. It was difficult for me at first, but I will do my best to serve you now. How would you like me?"

"Lie back and spread your knees."

She lay back and parted her legs a little. "Like this? Please pardon this *mistshimus* for her inexperience."

He slapped at her knees. "Farther apart."

She widened the gap. Something funny was happening down there. She could feel the moisture beginning to flow. That wasn't supposed to happen. She didn't even want Fox Tail. "Is this better, Fox Tail?"

She looked at him. She hadn't meant to, but this was the man who was about to enter her, even if it was a sham. He was well formed, with a lean body and hard muscles. She glanced at his organ. It stood proud, and the glistening head peeked out from its fold of covering skin.

He is well formed. Stop that. Think of Standing Bear. Fox Tail's spear was a little stouter than that of Standing Bear.

He nosed his organ into the mouth of her sex and then plunged without warning all the way in. A gasp and a cry escaped Girl-With-No-Name's lips.

Why was he able to slide into me so freely? Do I want him? He has just bought me for this night from Stinging Nettle. I cannot want this. I must be still for Standing Bear.

She looked up at Fox Tail. He was smiling either at his own pleasure or the effect he had on her. After that first writhing cry, she was still as he indulged his need. Yes, she felt some inner desire for this man or any man. Perhaps it was just a pent-up demand from her body for any kind of comfort, but she remembered her goal. She couldn't do anything about her increasing wetness in that place, but she could control her muscles, and she refused their push to reciprocate his movements. And in a hand of moments, she could feel the intensity of his strokes ramping up to his peak. She closed her eyes, lay perfectly still or as still as she could be considering the force that was building within him. He finally spent his seed with a loud groan and collapsed over her.

In a few minutes, he rolled off her onto his back and just lay there breathing heavily. She closed her legs and lay as servile as a reed, waiting, just waiting.

A half hour later he was ready to begin again. This time she was ready, and no cry of surprise or pleasure escaped her lips. She was like a wet piece of soft leather being tanned, neither resisting nor encouraging the tool. Accommodating would be the word to describe her actions. She accepted his organ within her but bent no energy toward his or her own pleasure. To some degree, it hurt to deceive Fox Tail, but he also had earned it in his own fashion, being one of the primary writers of her current existence as *mistshimus*. For that alone, he deserved a cold, dead salmon.

After fifteen minutes of exertion, he was done. This time when he rolled off her, he said, "That is all I require of you, *mistshimus*. You may go back to your own sleeping rug."

"Thank you, warrior. I hope I may be able to serve you again in this or any other capacity."

"Yes, yes, just go on, *mistshimus*. Go away, and let me sleep."

As she gathered up her moccasins and cape, she heard him mutter under his breath, "Three pelts for that. I did not bargain well."

Girl-With-No-Name made her way to the stream. The snowfall was wet and wind-driven, but she did not feel it as snow. She felt it as a cleansing power of the cold which hit her then immediately melted to carry away the scent of sex that covered her. She splashed off in the stream and let the seed of Fox Tail fall out of her. She knew it would do no good to wash it out and hoped she did not catch a child from this experience, but she would have to trust the herbs and the timing of nature for that. It just felt good to have him washed from her both without and within.

Now, it was getting cold, and she ran back to Stinging Nettle's hut. She hung her worn cape of tired rabbit pelts on a peg, curled up under her sleeping furs and went to sleep.

I have played my part. Now if only Standing Bear will play his.

Girl-With-No-Name awoke just after dawn. Stinging Nettle was not in the hut. That meant she was probably in the longhouse, and she hurried to put her moccasins on and throw her cape over her shoulders. Outside, the sun might have risen, but the snow was falling thickly, and the wind still blew hard downriver. She could see the white caps on the edge of the *Nch'i-wána*. The water would be like the gray steel of the soldiers at the fort at the trading place, The Dalles, and as harsh to the unwary.

She hurried to reach Stinging Nettle and hoped that Standing Bear would be still a little longer. Entering through the opening in the totem that fronted the *Tyee's* residence and home to most of the clan, she pulled the flap shut and shook off her cloak of snow. The warmth of the longhouse hit her after the chill of the cold winter day without.

During the warm summer months, the Bent Creek Clan spread out, and many slept outdoors. Even during the chill fall, they might do so. In winter they congregated here in the longhouse to work, eat, and tell stories. The few children played quietly in the corner. The *mistshimus* worked at various tasks or served their nobles. Though technically the *mistshimus* belonged to the tribe and clan as a whole, in practice, they were assigned to various title born. As the *mistshimus* she had seen in the moon cycle hut with Bears-Many-Children was assigned to her, so was Girl-With-No-Name assigned to Stinging Nettle. She may as well be owned by Stinging Nettle for most purposes. However, the *Tyee* could punish any *mistshimus.*

Some of the older boys and younger warriors, including Fire Stick and Fox Tail, sat near the fire telling jokes and stories. Standing Bear sat a bit apart. At present, he was no fan of Fox Tail. She saw Stinging Nettle sitting in her accustomed place among the women. She had her mortar and pestle and was grinding some herbs.

"Sit, *mistshimus* Nika. Take some food and break your fast, then assist me. My wrists grow tired of this interminable grinding." She had a large basket of acorns by her side. Girl-With-No-Name sat and took the mortar and pestle from Stinging Nettle. Grinding was a rhythmic activity that took no thought, and Girl-With-No-Name let her attention wander the room. Her attention was drawn to the humorous conversation between Fire Stick and Fox Tail. More truthfully it could be called jesting by Fire Stick and defensive avoidance by the other.

"Fox Tail, tell us. How was your little adventure with the *mistshimus?* The one that cost us two hours of morning sleep and you three fine rabbit pelts."

Fox Tail looked up from where he had been morosely poking the fire. "It was the worst *mamook* I ever did. Are you satisfied?"

Fire Stick could not be stopped so easily. "So, was it the first, worst *mamook* you ever did? Or the worst, first *mamook* you ever did?" A couple of the younger boys laughed.

"What are you going on about, Fire Stick?"

"Was it your first, worst *mamook* or your worst, first *mamook*? That's what we want to know."

"And what would you know about it?"

"Well, I have lain with three in this tribe, including the memorable Pollen Flower yonder. And none were a first, worst or a worst, first *mamook*. All were quite nice."

"If you really need to know, the *mistshimus* that I *mamooked* because of your infernal needling lay like a dead fish. And because of you, it cost me three rabbit pelts." Fox Tail's voice had risen.

Girl-With-No-Name saw that Standing Bear had arisen and was gravitating toward the fire. Instinctively she began to rise herself, but Stinging Nettle laid a hand on her arm, and she sat back down.

"I seem to recall that it was you, my friend, Burr-Up-My-Ass, who was set on outbidding Standing Bear for the *mistshimus'* services. You, who were certain that Standing Bear lied about yon apple bottomed *mistshimus* when he said she was not that memorable. You, who got us up at the twinges of dawn just a week ago to beat him to the bid. So, you got your first, worst first *mamook* ever. Snap out of it." Fire Stick gave him a friendly push on the shoulder.

Standing Bear was almost upon them.

"You are right, Fire Stick. Still, it cost me three pelts, and I don't even want to *mamook* the *mistshimus* again. She is a lousy *mamook*."

Standing Bear was over his back and on top of him in seconds. Fox Tail was larger, but surprise had taken him, and Standing Bear was on his chest and hit him across the mouth. "Take that back. The *mistshimus* is not a lousy *mamook*."

"I'll take nothing back, Standing Bear. Everyone knows you are stuck on a *mistshimus*. The salmon that floats belly-up downriver after she has expended her eggs, that is your *mistshimus*. I wish I had never met her, and I had my pelts back. She is not even worth one pelt."

Standing Bear hit him again before Fire Stick could pull him off. He was trembling in his fury. Tears ran down Girl-With-No-Name's face as she watched her warrior, Standing Bear, her first love she realized, reduced to such a state.

"What is going on in my longhouse that two warriors fight?" *Tyee* Running Blade's low voice rang out.

"It is nothing, *Tyee*," Fire Stick hurried to quiet the situation. "Just a scuffle. That's all."

"I think not. Do you seek to fool your *Tyee*, Fire Stick?"

"No, *Tyee*. My ill-placed humor caused this. I sought only to bandage the situation."

"Come before me, Standing Bear and Fox Tail. Fire Stick, when a warrior strikes another warrior over a *mistshimus*, it is too late for bandages. I heard your humor, and while it was ill-placed, jokes about the *mistshimus* are not forbidden. They are property after all. Your responsibility is dismissed."

Fox Tail and Standing Bear now stood before the *Tyee*, Standing Bear still shaking with rage and something else.

He is just now realizing what he has done to us. She hated what was to come, but she could not help feeling proud of her warrior.

"So, you fight over a *mistshimus*, Standing Bear?"

"Fox Tail never hit me. He is only guilty of bad talk. I hit him. Twice."

"I am sorry I said what I said, Standing Bear," Fox Tail said. "I wish only that I had never made such a bargain."

"Did you say anything about Standing Bear, Fox Tail?" the *Tyee* asked.

"I said Standing Bear lied when he said the *mistshimus* was a bad *mamook*."

"Let us not be so vulgar. Was she bad to *moosum*?"

"To me, *Tyee*, yes, she was. And I said that Standing Bear was stuck on a *mistshimus*. That was my greatest offense toward Standing Bear, to say he held affection for property."

"That is an offense to a warrior's honor, especially a title born. You should know that."

"I do know that, and I knew it at the time, *Tyee*. I stand ready to accept my punishment."

"Hold out your left arm palm down."

Fox Tail did so, steady now and calm.

With one quick move, the *Tyee* sliced the forearm of Fox Tail, not deeply but enough that blood welled from elbow to wrist. "Bind that up, and this event is forgotten."

"Standing Bear, you stand accused of forming a bond with property, with a *mistshimus*. This goes against all our laws and traditions for a thousand summers."

"I am guilty, *Tyee*. I have come to realize that the *mistshimus* are not just property. They are people too and deserve some respect."

Girl-With-No-Name had stood, and she did not know when. She knew, with tears streaming, that Standing Bear was burying them deeper with every word, but for that moment she did not care.

The *Tyee* Running Blade's anger was rapidly building to fury, and it was evident upon his taut facial muscles.

"The *cultus* whiteman has slaves, and even among them, their slaves have names. We despise the *cultus* whiteman yet they overrun us. I think this way of thinking is wrong. I know you do not, father, *Tyee*. I stand ready to accept your punishment."

"Bring the *mistshimus* bitch forward."

Girl-With-No-Name stepped to a place beside Standing Bear.

"Did you attempt to bring this infatuation upon Standing Bear?"

"I did not attempt it, but I am responsible for it, *Tyee*."

"I respect that answer. I have never said that the *Nimi'ipuu* were not brave and honorable both as allies and sometimes as enemies. Always it has been so."

"Among the *Nimi'ipuu*," Girl-With-No-Name said, "we have slaves. We treat them differently and frequently adopt them into our families. Here, I am not a *mistshimus* among the *Nimi'ipuu*, I am *mistshimus* to the Chinook. And so, I respect and honor your traditions as best I am able. If a wrong was committed, it was solely by myself, and I did know it at the time. I tried to resist, truly, but I failed. I stand ready to accept my punishment, *Tyee*, whatever it may be."

"Heat my blade," the *Tyee* said. The steel knife was placed in the coals. "Your response was honest and honorable, *mistshimus*. It has saved your life." When the blade was the color of the coals themselves, he commanded, "Hold out your left arm palm down."

Girl-With-No-Name held her arm out and looked at the *Tyee* through honest eyes.

"Don't move," he said in a whisper. He cut her from shoulder to wrist, not a deep cut but enough to make his point. He made the cut slowly and carefully. The knife cut cauterized as it cut, and the smell of burnt flesh invaded her nostrils. Her face was pale when he finished, but she did not cry out. "Stinging Nettle, you will rub ashes into the wound so that this scar will always be visible."

His knife blade was placed back onto the coals, and they were blown up to red heat.

"Hold your left arm out palm down, Standing Bear." The boy did so. He was trembling but held steady. Leaning in close so only Standing Bear and those closest could hear he said, "Let the example of this *mistshimus* teach you what true honor and bravery are. I have eyes. She has been trying to save you both from this." With that admonition, he held out his hand for his knife, and it was slapped into his palm. Again, he made the cut from shoulder to wrist.

"Stinging Nettle, you will rub the ashes of this fire into Standing Bear's arm and bind it."

"I will, *Tyee*."

"And you, my son, will sit with the children. For now, you will be Little Bear until I decide differently.

Stinging Nettle led Girl-With-No-Name to the fire pit. She took a piece of charcoal from the edge of the pit and rubbed it the length of the wound. As the wound was already cauterized, there was little blood, but with a quickness that surprised her, there was suddenly a lot of pain. She did the same for Little Bear, who walked suddenly numb as if his whole world was turned upside down.

As they walked back to her hut Stinging Nettle said, "I was sure he was going to kill you, Nika. You do have bravery and honor. For that, I respect you, not as *mistshimus*, but as a person."

THE BARGAIN

CHAPTER 10
MARCH, 1854

A T THE ENTRANCE to Stinging Nettle's hut, Girl-With-No-Name peered upriver toward the creek and the end of the village. Absently she rubbed her left arm and the scar along it. The cut had healed with no infection, but it was still reddened, and the scar was shiny and pinkish. Girl-With-No-Name carried the scar in her own mind as a badge of honor. She had acted with honor and paid for it with this scar. She had not had a chance to talk to Standing Bear since the judgment by the *Tyee*, only seen him look sadly at her when they crossed paths on her visits to the longhouse. Stinging Nettle was keeping those to a minimum. There had been no more bids for her services since then, and she was not unhappy with that outcome.

Stinging Nettle joined her. Through the early spring light on this morning they could see a large raft filled with goods, as well as a smaller canoe pulled up to the bank near the abandoned longhouse past the midden pile. A strange whiteman's boat was huffing backward puffing out black smoke. It was not a large boat, not nearly as long as one of the Chinook's bigger canoes, perhaps ten running paces. Its deck was stacked high with cargo, and a half dozen whitemans lined the rails or sat upon the load. With a piercing whistle, it set off upstream belching black smoke and steam from its single stack. A whiteman with long reddish-blond hair and a scruffy beard was there on the beach. He was perhaps twenty or twenty-two years old. It was always difficult to tell with whitemans. They all looked the same to Girl-With-No-Name.

"Stinging Nettle, who is that whiteman? Why is he here?" Girl-With-No-Name asked.

"Who he is, I do not know. He was here last month during your moon cycle. He looks to make some kind of trade with *Tyee* Running Blade. I do know they made some sort of bargain last month. Beyond that, I do not know. Get back in the hut, nosy *mistshimus*."

As Girl-With-No-Name eased back into the hut and the man approached the *Tyee's* longhouse, she had an ominous sense of things changing, like one has sometimes when a storm approaches. Something was upon the wind today.

———

MARSHALL JOHNSTON APPROACHED the *Tyee's* longhouse.

What was his name? Should've paid better attention last time I was here.

At that time, his plan seemed more a fanciful dream than a possible reality. He had come out on the Oregon Trail four years before. Like many, he hoped to make his fortune in the Oregon country. Like most others, he discovered, it was much more challenging than he first appreciated back in Missouri. He departed Missouri with a wagon load of goods and supplies and two year's wages. Four years of struggle later, and everything he owned was on that raft pulled up to the gravelly bank, and two hundred dollars in his pouch.

It was Chief Running Blade, that was it.

Tyee Running Blade eyed Marshall Johnston as he walked up. By his judgment, a scrawny man and a needful one. This should not prove so difficult as he once had imagined, though the very thought of it made him shudder. He drew himself up taller and adopted a sterner look. The morning light glinted off his silvered hair and the several chains of whiteman beads and shells he wore about his neck. A clasp of steel graced one bicep and a wrap of tusk shells the other. Over his shoulders, he wore the cream elkskin cape he always wore to the yearly trade meet at The Dalles.

"Chief Running Blade, I return as promised," Marshall said.

"No chief. Chinook have no chief. *Tyee* Running Blade."

"*Tyee* Running Blade then, but you still speak for the tribe? For the Bent Creek Clan?"

"I do. You still want wife and place with tribe as you said before?"

"Yes. You can see, I've brought all my worldly goods with me there on that raft. I hope the arrangement we struck last time still holds."

That was a mistake. Never admit you don't got nowhere else to go.

"If it don't," he said quickly, "there are other clans on both sides of the river I can deal with."

"Let us go to sweat lodge first to cleanse ourselves, then we bargain."

As far as Marshall could tell the sweat lodge was a small, smelly structure covered with clay and reed mats and more clay. The opening was just large enough to crawl into and made him feel closed in before he even got in there.

"Leave clothes out here on rocks," the *Tyee* said removing his cape.

Marshall began undressing as a group of Chinook gathered to watch. Several old women in their mid-thirties were at the forefront. Marshall stripped off his shirt and boots and then began to shuck his pants. Whatever words they said he did not know, but they seemed to be comments about him.

"Why whiteman wear so many clothes?" asked the *Tyee*.

"For warmth, protection," Marshall said.

"Warmth in this fine weather? Protection from what?"

"Some wear clothes to show off their status."

"Ah. Clothes are property. You wear your wealth to show all. That makes sense. You even have clothes under your clothes. Very rich man you are."

Marshall looked down at his undershirt and shorts. At least he had worn the good ones today. He stripped those off and carefully folded them on the stack of his other clothes.

They entered, and the *Tyee* indicated a seating place. "Position of honor, my friend."

The sweat lodge was not as small as it had appeared from the outside. It could hold six people. The ceiling was low, and smoke coated from many years of use. It smelled in here, too, of bodies, smoke, and the ever-present

salmon that pervaded all of these villages. Marshall needed for this to work.
He had visited or tried to visit several villages before this one. Some had
received him and laughed at his offer. Some had not even allowed him to
land. They had all wanted trade, but he wanted more than trade.

A little light leaked in through the flap door and the vent in the ceiling.
The heat and the oppressive closeness, as well as the unusual odors, made
Marshall squirm.

"Damn, it's dark in here," Marshall said, "and smoky, too."

"*Cultus* whiteman. Be patient."

Not only could Marshall not see very well in the sweat lodge, but he
felt damned uncomfortable as well. He scratched his pale white belly and
shifted his position.

"You sit on ant hill?" asked the chief. "You want wife? Don't think on ant
hill." His flattened forehead glistened in the dim light.

Marshall schooled himself to be still. The sweat was beginning to stream
from every pore.

This is a test of sorts. A test to put me off balance and increase his
bargaining power.

Marshall tried to still himself again and succeeded for a few minutes.

Damned Chinook, who's he think he is anyways? What if I am sitting on
an ant hill? He did not see any ants, but then he could not really see anything.
And he felt itchy all over.

When they emerged finally into the bright reflections off the Columbia
River, Marshall could not see anything, but he did hear the giggles. His
flesh was beginning to get gooseskin from the chill breeze coming upriver.
He squinted his eyes to see a gaggle of four or five slack tittied old women
chuckling at him. One in particular, lifted her sloped forehead high and
rotated her hips. The others laughed. The chief flicked his hand, and they
dispersed still giggling.

"Those you not have. Not slaves. High caste," the chief said. "Sit here,"
indicating a spot on the mat.

Marshall sat. The chief sat. "So, you want Chinook wife?"

"Yes, if the price is good," Marshall said.

Now we begin the haggling. Good. Damn! The chief had sat him so the sun was in his eyes.

"You not have Chinook wife. No Chinook wife for *cultus* whiteman."

Damn. Was this all for nothing then, the wait, the sweat lodge, the embarrassment.

"But you said—"

The chief cut him off with a hand wave. "I say, no Chinook wife. But I have Nez Perce slave for you." He turned and signaled.

A girl-woman of about fourteen stepped forward and knelt next to the chief. Through the glare, Marshall tried to examine her. She wore no clothing at all and was about five foot, lithe of build, small hipped and small tittied. Her face, bronzed of skin, had a proud look even though she covered that with a demure slave countenance. She had thick, straight black hair cut short and a red cut running down her left arm that she self-consciously rubbed with her right hand.

Marshall sensed a bargaining opportunity. "What's wrong with her arm?"

This aggravated the chief. He looked at the girl, who immediately lowered her right hand. "She is round-head *mistshimus*. She sleep with high caste and attract his affection." The chief coughed. "With my son. Both have been appropriately punished." He beckoned, and a boy, a young man in Chinook terms, stepped forward. "Show the *cultus* whiteman your arm."

The boy-man stood firm before the *Tyee's* gaze and held out his left arm. The cut ran down the biceps to his wrist and had ash or charcoal rubbed into it. "Sit back with the *tenass tilikums,* the children, now, Little Bear.

"She is not cut in a way that hurt her work. Only marked to remember. They mate like dogs in the brush, but she is not with child."

"A little bit on the skinny side. You sure she'll be able to hold up?"

"Nez Perce always that way. They start scrawny, but you give her a child or two, then she get meat on her bones."

The evening breeze chilled Marshall, and he wanted to speed things up. "So, the bride price was—"

"Two ax heads, two adzes, three new blankets, and three knives."

"Three knives? You said two before."

"Third knife for ant hill in sweat lodge."

Marshall decided he'd better get on with it. "Fine, three knives then. The ax heads and adzes." He gestured, and the boy brought them forward.

The *Tyee* looked them over. "We have examined. They are accepted."

"The blankets." Marshall spread five blankets of various quality out on the ground between them. The bold green, red, yellow, and indigo stripes stood out sharply against the white backgrounds on two. On the others the colors were muted.

The *Tyee* sorted through them. "These two good. Rest are *cultus*. Let's see others."

Dammit. "Fine. Take a look at these." He spread out five more, tucking the best under.

The *Tyee* flipped them all over. Examined the bottommost blanket, the best Marshall had. "This good blanket. Knives?"

Marshall laid two on the mat. The *Tyee* tested them. "These are average quality but will do for skinning." He raised an eyebrow, "And the third?"

"Are you serious? For an anthill?"

The *Tyee* just stared. He could wait forever. For this, Marshall did not have a backup. He slipped his own knife from its sheath at his waist.

"Ha ha. Good knife. One last thing for friendship. I need cup, metal cup."

"I can do you a cup, *Tyee*."

"We have deal then." He beckoned the girl forward, and she knelt on the mat behind Marshall. "You understand terms. This bride price, not buy slave. She still belong to clan. But I give special deal. She give you child, it yours."

Marshall was afraid this bargaining session was going to last all night. "Yes. I understand."

"Good. Good. You take house at end of village. You work, hunt, give share to clan. All good. All happy. Ha. Ha. *Mistshimus* wife of *cultus* whiteman, warm him with blanket."

Marshall noticed he was actually shivering as "his *mistshimus* wife" drew a blanket across his shoulders.

"Now we smoke on deal. Then eat and drink. All good. All happy."

Marshall glanced downriver. The big impressive houses were up here, and they got progressively smaller. His "cabin" was just within sight, just past the midden pile. He wished he were there now.

Maybe I will take a little of this anger out on my wife when I get to my shack. That thought made him feel somewhat better.

"*Cultus.* One more thing. She is *mistshimus,* but she still live by Chinook rule. I sell you wife. I not sell you slave. You may beat her if she disobey. No leave marks that last. Not like arm. That kind of punishment is for me. You make her too unhappy, she leave you. Maybe I beat her for leaving you. Maybe I cut her if I displeased. Maybe I sell her to someone else. But that her choice and my choice. It is our way."

This was not looking like such a good bargain to Marshall.

Well, they would see. They would see.

Marshall got up to offer the *Tyee* his hand, but the *Tyee* had already risen and turned his back to give commands for the feast.

These red men don't know the first thing about common courtesy.

"My husband," Girl-With-No-Name said.

He turned and saw that his *mistshimus* wife was standing offering him his undershirt. He put it on. She picked up his shorts, knelt before him, and he stepped into them. She smoothed them out.

"Such soft material," she said and opened his trousers for him to step into. She buttoned them up showing some amazement at the buttons. His stockings she slid onto his feet and then his boots. Finally, she picked up his shirt, and he pulled it on over his head.

"You look the fine warrior, my husband."

"The name's Marshall."

"My husband, Marshall," she said trying it out.

Maybe this isn't going to be so bad after all, Marshall smiled.

"And what your name, wife?"

"I am *mistshimus.*"

"*Mistshimus,* eh?"

"*Mistshimus* mean slave in Chinook Jargon. A *mistshimus* not have name. Name is property. *Mistshimus* is property and cannot own property."

"Well, you are my damned wife. I can name you."

"Please pardon me for saying this. You are Chinook now. I not argue with you, just tell you."

"Christ, what a shit fuck."

"Please pardon again, husband Marshall. Not place of *mistshimus* to speak unless asked. I only say I can help, if you want."

"Hell, yes. Speak."

"I speak true. You pay too much for me, warrior husband Marshall."

"You saying I don't know how to bargain?" Marshall said getting angry.

"No, not saying that. For trading with Chinook, you did good. But you could have done better if you knew Chinook way. You were guest of *Tyee*. As guest he should have put you in best spot, not with sun in eyes. Chinook rules require it if you are guest. If you are trader, then he put you where he want."

"So, you are saying I could have been a guest?"

"Yes, if you turn this into *potlatch*."

"A *potlatch?*"

"Everything is property to Chinook, names, favors, even a cup of tea. If you give it, then other person is required to try to better the gift."

"That's crazy."

"You want to own name for me? I show you how. I right, I pick name. I wrong you whip me."

"All right, deal. Lead the way."

"Let us go to your raft, warrior husband Marshall, see what you have."

An hour later Marshall approached the feast, his "gifts" under his arm. He was wearing his best frock coat, a hat with a ribbon tied about and a long feather tucked in it, and had magenta ribbons tied on his biceps. About his neck, he wore a watch chain, a necklace, and a silver plate chain that once, a half hour before, closed an old box of tobacco. He had white handkerchiefs folded neatly and tucked visibly into each pocket. He felt ridiculous. His *mistshimus* said he looked a rich man.

If she was right, he would get the name. If she was wrong, then the whole experiment had only cost about twenty-five cents, and he was almost looking forward to whipping that little pair of buttocks just to see what it was like.

She paced behind him four steps, looking both proud of her new husband and her status as a married *mistshimus* and demure as well.

"Ho. It is our trader friend, Marshall. Welcome," *Tyee* Running Blade said. He stood. "Come. Sit in the place of honor."

Marshall swept off his hat and bowed deeply. "I could not. Please seat yourself. I am honored enough just to be chosen as a Chinook and to be in your company, *Tyee* Running Blade."

"As you wish then, friend Marshall."

"I remembered that you said I might bring you a tin cup, and I do have one, but it is worn. I thought that perhaps this would do instead."

Tyee Running Blade looked prepared to be disappointed then leaned forward. Marshall handed him the small box they had prepared. In truth, it was an old box that had once held a jar of pickles, but it was of a wood not seen here, and they had lined it with a piece of shiny red fabric. Within was one old china teacup. Its primary value was that it wasn't cracked or chipped, but Marshall had lost the other three cups that made up the set. It did have a fanciful floral design, and Girl-With-No-Name was fairly sure such had not been seen here before.

The *Tyee* took it from the box with great care examining it from every angle. Bears-Many-Children, for whom Girl-With-No-Name knew it was intended, viewed it with delicious desire. The *Tyee* handed it to her, and she held it gently, almost like a baby, with gratitude suffusing her face.

"That is too great a gift, friend Marshall."

"It is really a slight thing, *Tyee* Running Blade. You have given me the gift and this excellent wife as well."

"As you wish then."

"As some small recompense for this feast and my wife as well, I brought you this little thing."

A flicker of a frown passed over *Tyee* Running Blade's face. He knew this game, but for the moment he could not escape it.

Marshall produced the second object, a second wooden box with a hinged top that once had held tobacco. In fact, the odor of tobacco still emanated from it. They had tied it with two cents worth of ribbon in an elaborate bow.

Girl-With-No-Name saw Swimming Salmon's eyes widen at the ribbon. The *Tyee* pulled the ribbon, and the bow slipped away. He opened the box. Two old brass chains stopped the lid at right angles. Within, padded by two handkerchiefs, glistened a tin of strong stale tea from China. The label was printed in Chinese characters in red on a green background, and the logo was a Chinese Dragon.

"It is something I have been carrying with me for a while now, and I never had a real use for until today. The tea is from China, far across the sea. I thought it could represent the friendship of two very different people, of the Chinook and me. I hope you will accept it as my humble gift."

"It is a great thing you have given, friend Marshall, truly." For a moment the *Tyee* forgot the *potlatch* and just sat in wonder. "Hot water."

He filled the china cup with steaming hot water then put just a pinch of the tea in it. All watched, for what Girl-With-No-Name couldn't imagine, but slowly the odor of the strange tea suffused the air. It was Lapsang Souchong and had a tarry, smoky aroma. Marshall had tried it once and hated it, but it seemed perfect for this situation.

When it had brewed for a few minutes, the *Tyee* held the bone china cup up and took a tiny sip. A strange and wondrous look suffused his face. He passed the cup to Swimming Salmon, and thence it went to Bears-Many-Children and the other high nobles. This was the make or break point. Either they would think it strange and delicious because it was unknown, or they would think he was trying to poison them. When the cup came to him, he breathed in deep of the aroma and took a fair draught letting it lie on his tongue as if savoring it in wonder. He choked it down, but he did not allow that to show.

"Friend Marshall, you have done us great honor."

"Among my people, it is the custom always to bring at least some small gift to such a celebration, *Tyee* Running Blade."

They were on easy terms now, and trenchers of food circulated. Dried salmon and camas bulb, and a haunch of elk had roasted over the fire.

"At least, you must allow me to do you some small favor friend Marshall. Perhaps I could—"

"No, *Tyee.* There is something I would ask of you, if it is not too delicate a matter to discuss here."

The *Tyee* was somewhat displeased to be interrupted but decided to play along, "What then, friend Marshall."

Marshall leaned forward. "Among my people, it is customary for a man to have a name to call his wife. I understand, among yours, a name is property. I wonder, might I ask for a name to be given to me to call her?"

The *Tyee* relaxed. A name would cost him nothing. "What name would you wish for? It cannot be a noble name."

"I hope then it is not. I was thinking, Two Blankets."

Tyee Running Blade remembered the two blankets his son had traded for the Nez Perce *mistshimus* services. It irritated him slightly, but the irony was not lost on him either.

"I grant you the name, Two Blankets, to use for your wife," he said.

This *mistshimus* played the game as well as any the *Tyee* had encountered, with honor and vigor. He felt a little sorry for this *cultus* whiteman Marshall Johnston. He knew not what he had, and likely was too stupid ever to know. At least the *mistshimus,* Two Blankets, he corrected himself, would be pecking away like a woodpecker at the whiteman's head now instead of his own.

TWO BLANKETS

CHAPTER 11
MARCH, 1854

I AM TWO BLANKETS now, a married woman. No longer Girl-With-No-Name. I bury her with the name.

She sat back on her heels behind and to one side of her husband, Marshall. When the food began to be served by the other *mistshimus*, she made up a plate for him. There were venison and the resurrected elk haunch, salmon, roasted camas bulb, and camas cakes as well. She put a small amount of each into the shallow cedar bowl that served as a plate among the Chinook. As she served him, she warned against eating too much of the camas bulb. Excessive flatulence would not do in this feast.

Near the end of the eating she leaned forward and spoke into his ear, "Husband, I would be bold enough to warn you of what is to come."

"Two Blankets, what a fine-looking wife you are," he smiled as he drew her into his lap and nuzzled her hair, laughing. "What is it, Two Blankets?"

"Please forgive me for saying this. At a gathering like this, for husband and wife, they will give gifts. Each gift you get you will be expected to match later. Small gifts like food or a rabbit pelt you can do. The elder Chinook here are wealthy, and some will try to give what you cannot repay. Is better to beg poverty and refuse gift than be broken by gift. Once, I saw a visiting elder broken when the *Tyee* gave him seven slaves. Later he had to match or better the gift, and now he has nothing. I ask again, please forgive if you knew this. I did not want my warrior husband broken his first day among the Chinook."

"Ah, you are a sweet lass, you are," Marshall said. "Thank you for that."

"Husband," she said loud and clear. "I should like to go and prepare our bedding and make ready our hut for you. Do you have sleeping furs and personal belongings?"

"Yes, in the canoe and on the raft. Go along. The boy will show you. I shall be along in a couple of hours, I suspect."

Two Blankets eased off his lap and strode with some pride, as much as she thought a *mistshimus* would be allowed, toward the doorway. She passed Stinging Nettle, who grasped her hand for a moment.

"The blessings of the salmon be upon you, Two Blankets," she said. And quieter, "To me, you shall always be Nika."

Two Blankets squatted down and hugged Stinging Nettle impulsively. "You have become my dearest friend, Stinging Nettle, if it is allowed for a *mistshimus* to say that to a title born."

"It is allowed if I say it is allowed. Go and prepare your hut. I shall need you tomorrow though, Nika. So, do not exert yourself too much tonight."

Rising, she saw Standing Bear looking forlorn and lost. She could not help him now.

At the landing, she found Marshall's raft and canoe, as well as the boy he had brought upriver and paid to watch it. He was about twelve, and his eyes bulged out a bit at the sight of Two Blankets dressed only in a cape and moccasins. Two Blankets guessed he had not had dealings with the Chinook before. One glance by Two Blankets to the crotch of his trousers brought him back to his modesty.

"I am Two Blankets. Marshall say he has gear here? For house?" she asked in Chinook Jargon. It was the trade language, but she had no idea if he understood.

"You name Two Blankets?"

"Yes. Need sleeping furs." The look of confusion on the boy's face told her all she needed to know. She tried what she knew of English. "I Two Blankets. Marshall wife. Got sleeping furs?" She mimed a person going to sleep.

The boy jumped up and onto the raft and handed down a bundle.

"Marshall pack. Him stuff," she said.

He fetched two large securely tied bundles from the canoe.

"Good. Follow." She marched him up to the hut, the hut she had once hidden in, desperate to escape back to her own village so long ago. She laid the furs back in the sleeping area she had shared with Standing Bear just a couple of months past.

The boy set the pack down in a corner. "You want other stuff, Miss Two Blankets, clothes, cook gear, all his household gear?"

All she could think of to say was, "Yes." She had only understood the words "You," her name, and "clothes." The boy took off at a run. The small longhouse was still dilapidated, but Two Blankets decided it was not too far gone. She stepped out and found a piece of stiff brush and pulled it up. This would do to sweep the floor.

She began with the fire pit. The center of any longhouse is the fire.

When the boy came back in with his first load, he saw her at the fire pit. "What you need is a shovel." He hurried out and a minute later was back with a small spade. He handed it to Two Blankets. "Shovel," he said.

Two Blankets looked at it blankly for a moment, then said, "Sho—vel." Immediately, she saw its use. The boy nodded, his hair flopping, to her comment as she used it to clean out the ashes.

"I'll get a bucket," he said and dashed off.

He returned and held the bucket for her as she shoveled the ashes from her visits here with Standing Bear into it. Next followed the ashes from years back, perhaps before the great disease had swept through the village. Such was the nature of life and death here, each accreting a new layer, sometimes to be stripped away to the bone later.

She took the bucket out, at first thinking to dump the ashes on the midden pile but turned toward the edge of the forest and spread them there. She could not consign her memories of three nights spent here with Standing Bear to mix in with the fish bones. She knew it was fatuous. Memories were like fish bones. They were yesterday's meal, but she could not mix her clear memory of the passion they had so briefly felt with the bones of a meal already forgotten.

She returned with an armload of branches. Sweeping the fire pit completely clean, she laid a small fire. She had neither coal to start it with nor any way to make fire. The boy entered with another bundle of "gear." He immediately saw the problem.

"You need a flint and steel." He dug into a pack that rattled like a night demon and produced a small box. Two Blankets watched as he quickly gathered up bits of dried brush and small sticks. He took a small piece of char cloth from the tin box then struck the flint against the steel. The spark carried onto to the char cloth and immediately began to glow. He blew it up into a tiny flame, and then added the dried brush and small sticks. Soon he had a small fire going.

He smiled up at Two Blankets.

"Good?" he said as he put the flint, steel, and char cloth back into the tin.

"Yes, good," she said and smiled back. These whitemans had a tool for everything. At least it had saved a trip to the *Tyee's* longhouse for a coal.

The longhouse was some fifteen feet wide by forty long and dug three feet into the soil. At one time it must have been noteworthy, but that was a long time ago. Now it had almost been allowed to go to ruin. The cedar walls were still good though and the posts that supported the roof. Though part of the roof was gone near the front of the house, the rear seemed still watertight.

Two Blankets sang a *Nimi'ipuu* song as she swept. She wasn't quite sure what her position was in the tribe now. There was really no precedent for a *mistshimus* wife of a whiteman. She knew her situation had improved. Yes, she was still *mistshimus*. She still could be beaten, even killed, but she was also a wife. She had a hut as big as Stinging Nettle. Her warrior husband might be a whiteman and frowned upon by most Chinook, but he had a significant amount of property. No matter what came, today she was better off than yesterday. That was enough.

The boy had finished bringing in Marshall's personal "gear."

"Now what?" he asked.

Two Blankets looked around then fixed on the pile of debris. She pointed and said, "Take. Out."

The boy eyed the pile thoughtfully. It was a big pile. He looked at Two Blankets. She was awful pretty, and he was getting bored waiting at the raft.

"Sure, Miss Two Blankets. I can take that stuff out for you. I'll just stack it beside the building."

Two Blankets finished her general sweeping and moved to the sleeping area. She swept it out and knocked down all the spider webs she could reach. She unrolled the furs and placed them carefully. They were furs of decent quality but not particularly well tanned. She knew she could do better. In another half an hour with the two of them working on the debris pile, and a quick sweep she was done. She surveyed her work.

It is a good beginning, and this could be a fine longhouse. I am satisfied.

She went to the creek, took off her cape and moccasins, and stepped in. Covered in dust and cobwebs, but that was only dirt. That would wash off. She was a married woman now. It still felt strange. And she had a name. She submerged herself in the stream and raked the cobwebs from her hair. With sand, she scrubbed her body all over until it was almost raw and she was certain she was clean. Walking back up to the longhouse she saw the boy watching her. She shook her finger at him, and he blushed and looked away.

She laughed. Why should he not want to look? He is a boy, almost a man, and I am a woman. She glanced his way again. He was still peeking at her but now pretending not to. She gave him her warmest smile and entered the hut.

About an hour later, Marshall came up to the hut. He almost fell the three feet from the doorway to the floor of the longhouse. Two Blankets stood from her place by the fire pit, expectant but not knowing what to expect. If he were *Nimi'ipuu* she would know, even if he were Chinook. She had been with them long enough to predict most of their behavior, when they would react from pride or anger, or sometimes even affection. Marshall Johnston was whiteman. She had no idea.

He stood, looking around at the longhouse that was theirs now, as much as any common property in the village could be said to belong to any one person.

"Warrior husband, Marshall, I have prepared our place of rest as best I could in the short time available," she said, hoping that was an appropriate way to speak.

"What a shithole."

He took his hat off and threw it down. She picked it up and moved to help him with his jacket.

"This god damn circus outfit is Christ almighty uncomfortable. It was hotter than hell in there, and it stank."

She pulled the ribbons off his sleeves and took his jacket. "I can say they were impressed by the wealth of your clothing."

"I looked ridiculous. I'm just glad no civilized person was there to see me."

"If I may ask, husband, how did the gift giving go?" she asked as he began hopping on one foot trying to remove a boot. "Husband, please come here to the sleeping platform, and I will remove your clothing."

Marshall hobbled stepping half on the side of the partially removed boot over to the furs which were arranged on a raised section at the rear of the hut. He flopped down.

"Well, I do have to say you were right about the gifts. Most of the gifts from the, what do you call the common people?"

"*Cultus tilikum*, round-heads is what the Chinook say."

"The gifts from the common people, the round-heads, were normal everyday things as you said."

"They do not have much, but those gifts you can match."

"Right, they seemed friendly given, sincere even. It was the gifts from the …." Marshall struggled to find the right word.

"Nobles or title born?"

"Yes, the gifts from the title born started small, but higher than anything the round-heads gave, and then got bigger as each person seemed to try to top the last one."

Two Blankets worried, "How did you meet this challenge, my warrior?" She had the second boot off and was busy stripping off his "dress" trousers.

Marshall looked at his wife with half-slit eyes. "I have been trading this river for a while now. I was a good trader and met each one with pleas of poverty and thanks."

Two Blankets muttered a small inward *Nimi'ipuu* prayer of thanks.

"What's that?"

Two Blankets thought quickly. "I say you are clever like Coyote with Great Bison."

"Go on," he said his trader instinct sensing a lie.

"This is story of Clever Coyote and Great Bison. They met at *potlatch*, a gift giving ceremony. Now, Great Bison was not ordinary buffalo. He was as tall as the shoulder as two men, one atop the other, and a nearly twice that in length. His horns spanned a man's height, at least. Great Bison was angry at Coyote for fooling him the last time they had met. So, he dropped a giant pile of shit as a present. It was truly a huge pile, as tall as a man and a perfect, how do you say it, cone from bottom to top." She hoped that sounded believable.

"Really. And what did Coyote say to Bison when offered this great pile of shit?"

"He circled the pile and said, 'This is a wondrous pile, steaming, rich in color as spring grass and the golden sun, and truly a mountain in size. Great Bison, I am stunned at this gift of shit, but my den is but a hole under the bank by the stream. It is such a humble abode and so small I could not properly care for or display such a godly pile of shit in the manner it deserved.' Great Bison tossed his head rooting up great clods of earth and grass and strode away quite proud and clever. Clever Coyote retired to his den, glad he had been clever and escaped."

"Ha, ha. Well, that was about it. They tried me and found I would not be fooled by such childish games. So, at last, they gave up and let me go."

Two Blankets only hoped that they had escaped the worst of it. She drew off Marshall's shirt and stood before him. "What would my husband like now? Would you like some tea?"

"Bring me that bottle of whiskey there in the near pack."

Two Blankets hastened to obey. She had heard of this whiteman's drink, though none in *Tyee* Running Blade's clan drank it. Some at the stockade at The Dalles did. She brought over the bottle. Marshall uncorked the bottle and tipped it up, letting it drain into him. At last, he dropped his hand, droplets of the amber fluid running down his thin beard.

"God damn, today of all days, I needed that." He tipped the bottle up again and took a smaller swig and then wiped his mouth with the hand holding the bottle. "I been meaning to ask, what does this word *'cultus'* mean? I heard the *Tyee* say *'cultus* whiteman' a couple times and you just said *'cultus tilikum'* a while back."

This was dangerous ground. "It means 'nothing,'" she said.

"Now I know it means something. Don't be lying to me."

"I am not. *Cultus* means nothing or worthless sometimes. *Cultus tilikum* means 'the worthless people' or the small people, the round-heads. Not always a bad word but can be used as bad word."

"Like when *Tyee* called me a *cultus* whiteman." He took another drink feeling evil and angry inside.

"Yes."

He had finished off the pint and tossed the bottle over near the fire pit. It shattered on one of the stones and the residual alcohol flamed up and as quickly died down.

"Come over here then, Two Blankets. Let's just see what my *cultus* wife has to offer her warrior husband." He looped one arm about her narrow waist and slung her across onto the sleeping furs face down.

"And how may I serve my—"

"You can serve me by shutting the fuck up, and taking what your husband has to offer, *cultus* bitch." He slapped her across the thighs. "Spread them legs, squaw bitch. I am not a Great Bison to be fooled by your Clever Coyote stories."

He pushed into her with his organ and began to fuck her.

He is certainly no Great Bison. It feels more like he is prodding me with his little finger than a man's organ, *cultus wootlat.*

FOUNDATION FOR BROKEN DREAMS

CHAPTER 12
MARCH TO APRIL, 1854

MARSHALL TOOK HER sexually a second time that night, though Two Blankets hardly thought of it as sex. He prodded her with his *cultus wootlat* for a few minutes and then rolled off into a drunken sleep. She slipped out of the furs and went to the creek to bathe his sweat off her body and his seed from within her body.

In the morning, she roused at her usual time of pre-dawn. She swept up the bottle fragments, sad it was broken. A container like this would be a nice thing to have. She built up the fire, gathered more wood and stacked it beside the fire pit.

"I must go to Stinging Nettle to work for her, husband," she said softly in his ear. He opened his eyes and waved her off. "After the morning's work, I return."

She had not thought that the morning after her wedding night she would feel less hampered returning to her life as Stinging Nettle's *mistshimus*, but she had the wisdom to see that she did. While her life with Marshall would offer her more freedom and potentially a stronger foundation for her future, she knew already that it would not be a life shared with a partner.

Stinging Nettle was outside her hut, taking in the morning sun and grinding as she often did, when Two Blankets arrived.

"Sit, Nika. We will talk a moment as two old friends, not as title born and *mistshimus*."

"Thank you, Stinging Nettle. You are kind."

"So, how do you find the marriage bed?" Stinging Nettle was not one to waste words.

"Let us just say he is small in construction."

Stinging Nettle lifted an eyebrow in question.

"His *wootlat* is like this," Two Blankets said lifting her little finger on her right hand.

"Ah, that is unusual. But sometimes small men can still be satisfying. Does he know how to uses this little *wootlat*?"

"He knows where to sheath it, but that is all."

"That is sad. A small *wootlat* used poorly is worse than no *wootlat* at all," she chuckled.

"It is not so much that. Perhaps I could teach him eventually what pleases me even with a small *wootlat*. It is that the river runs shallow within him as the *Nch'i-wána*—pardon, the *Wimahl*—over a sandbar. I can live with him, for it does better my position within the Chinook."

"It does. You have your own longhouse, and he does have much property. Even as *mistshimus* your position is much improved. Also, it removes you from the *Tyee's* eye, and Standing Bear's as well."

"Yes. Those are good things. But I cannot bear the thought of catching a baby from that man. Most men I could accept, but I cannot let his seed take root in me. Does that make me wrong to your eyes?"

"It is a hard question, Nika. But no, it does not, not with the Chinook. And he is truly *cultus*. I will tell you this, but it must remain forever locked within you. It is not ever to be spoken. Do you understand."

"I do. And you know I will die before breaking my vow."

"If I did not know that, I would not even think of saying this. Even so, it is forbidden to reveal this to *mistshimus*. You can continue taking the herbs I have given you. You are relatively safe just before your moon cycle begins and just after it ends. Two or three days on either side. In the middle of the moon's pass you may catch a child, but there is less chance. This is women's medicine. Men do not know we can do this. There is another type of medicine, though. Let us just call it hard medicine. I can give you a seed that will make your husband's seed not take root. He will not be able to father a child upon any woman, and there is the possibility it may be permanent, though usually, it is not. It is a bitter seed, and you must take great care and mix it with his food, so he does not taste it. Understand, I take great risk myself giving it to you. But for you Nika, I will do so."

"I will carry this secret clasped to my heart."

"Do so." Stinging Nettle got up and went into her hut for a minute returning with a small leather pouch. "Mix three of these seeds with a meal each day. It is not certain, but almost so."

"Thank you, Stinging Nettle. I do not know how to repay you."

"One day, Nika, I may ask something of you. I do not know now what it might be."

"I agree to your terms, Stinging Nettle."

The rest of the morning passed in pleasant work. She returned to Marshall's longhouse, to her longhouse, for the afternoon.

"Where the fuck have you been, Two Blankets?"

"I have been working with Stinging Nettle, husband Marshall."

"What? You have to go there every day?"

"It was agreed upon, husband. We must give share to the tribe."

"I agreed to that?"

"When you took me to wife, and the *Tyee* said, 'you work, hunt, give share to tribe,' those were his conditions on the bargain."

"Jaysus."

"Yes, if Jaysus is like Coyote. Every word a Chinook says in a bargain is calculated. I must continue to work with Stinging Nettle as my part of bargain. You will be expected to work, and hunt with clan, and give a share of everything you get to clan."

"Christ, that could be a lot of work."

"It can be. Is Chinook way. But you also have right to eat at the longhouse, and they will share with you. If you get sick, Stinging Nettle will heal. There is no cost or bargain for this. If we need help raising this longhouse, they will help. You do not pay them. You are Chinook. They just help."

Marshall's face got a squint-eyed look that Two Blankets would later recognize as his "seeking an advantage" look. This was the first time she had seen it and was surprised when he finally shook his head and began planning. "Fine, Two Blankets, I can work with that. Meantime, I need your help outside."

They spent the rest of the afternoon dragging a large tarpaulin over the front of the longhouse and bringing the rest of the supplies inside. Several of the tribe stopped by to look, and a couple of round-heads even assisted in the happy way they had of working. After three handspans of time they left with the comment to Marshall, "*cultus potlatch.*"

Marshall looked angry at first and then looked to Two Blankets for a translation. "This time mean free gift. Not bad thing. Just help."

Marshall was industrious. Two Blankets had to admit that. As soon as they had the longhouse secure, he began working on the long-abandoned longhouse neighboring theirs. To her, it appeared a total loss. Only one cedar wall still stood, though many of the posts were still there. The roof had long since fallen in. Yet, Marshall saw something in it, or mayhap he was just foolish, Two Blankets did not know. She went within to prepare a supper for them both.

When Marshall came in at dark, she had the salmon roasting over the little fire pit and camas cakes toasting. During the afternoon, several boys had arrived carrying their wedding gifts. Most were small things, but Two Blankets shuddered to think of the cost of some of the fancier gifts. One was an armband of dentalium shells. These had to be traded for with tribes from the coast. The work that went into it represented a couple of weeks of time just to repay that.

At least no one had gifted him with a canoe. I hoped he would have the sense not to accept something that grand.

Among the gifts, she found two shallow dishes made from cedar and some smoked venison. The venison she put on stones by the fire to reheat. If Marshall did not like salmon, they had meat.

He threw his hat onto the neatly stacked supplies. He spied his chair turned leg-side-up and set it down beside the fire. Rummaging about, he pulled another pint bottle from a crate, uncorked it, and took a deep draught.

"Ah, that is much better. So, we've got salmon and camas cake."

"And venison, husband."

"Ah, let me have the venison and a camas cake then. I don't know how you eat salmon every day, noon, and night."

She dished the venison and a couple of cakes on his platter and handed it to him. Looking about for anything else to please him, she said, "We also have some acorn cakes." She put a few of these delicacies on his plate.

He took a bite of the acorn and spit it out. "Jaysus, Two Blankets, how do you eat this shit? Bitter as all get out."

Two Blankets bit into one. True there was a slight bitter taste, but these were roasted as well as any she had ever eaten. Whoever had prepared them had leached the acorns properly, which took days.

"I am sorry, husband, that our foods do not please you."

"Don't matter, the venison is tasty. Don't you have no clothes to wear? I can't have my wife running around naked all the time."

"I have no other, husband. A *mistshimus* is only allowed a covering when it is cold, like this cape and moccasins."

"Well, dammit." He thought for a moment and then got up and fished in one of the packs. He pulled out a red and white checkered tablecloth. He cut a hole in the center and pulled it over Two Blanket's head and tied it at the waist with a rawhide thong. "Now you got a dress."

Two Blankets was stunned by the gift. "Thank you, husband Marshall. And if I need to go into the village to work, I can just remove the thong and turn it, and it is just a cape. So smart of you."

"Just be sure you wear it here. I like your titties and cunt just fine, but I don't want them hanging over me all the time."

After they had eaten, he took another drink, then got up and fetched in a long cedar plank from outside. He lifted it up and began the process of building it into a series of shelves near the entrance. Two Blankets was amazed at the number of tools this whiteman owned—two different saws, an auger for boring holes, a hammer and others she did not know the purpose for. He also had a whole cask of metal nails. Truly he must be a rich man.

This evening, when he went to toss the empty pint bottle, Two Blankets took it from his hand. If he were going to throw it away, she knew of several people she could trade it to. She found the cork and hid it away. She thought then he would *mamook* her like yesterday, but instead, he fell across their sleeping furs and went to sleep. Two Blankets removed his boots and covered him, then curled up and slept herself.

The next morning, she woke and Marshall had already left the longhouse to work. She threw her cape on, tied up her moccasins and threw some sticks on the fire for light as much as anything. Several bent nails were scattered on the floor, and she gathered these up for trade. Drifting outside she saw Marshall up along the creek chopping down a small fir tree.

She tried to estimate its size in U. S. Government feet. It is about ten running paces tall so that would be about thirty feet. And half a foot across.

It fell, and he bucked off the branches, then began hauling it back to the abandoned hut.

Who knew what a whiteman was going to do. She walked up to Stinging Nettle with her salvaged bottle.

"Greeting, Stinging Nettle," she said upon approach.

"Greeting, Nika," Stinging Nettle said.

"I brought you this in exchange for your bedding gift. I don't even know which gift was yours. Husband Marshall did not keep track." She handed over the bottle. "If it is not enough, I will find you something else to add."

"No, no, this is a wonderous gift." Stinging Nettle held the bottle to the light. "You are very thoughtful."

"I am glad. Perhaps you can help me by remembering who gave what gift? I do not want to start a *potlatch* fight, and I do not want to insult anyone."

Later in the day, she saw the whiteman's steamer coming downstream trailing a drift of smoke. It blew its whistle and nosed into the raft. The boy was up and aboard quickly, and Marshall was there handing him a piece of paper and a small pouch. The boy nodded and the steamer puffed off.

Knowing her husband's tastes a little better now, she thought to enter the *Tyee's* longhouse to see if any meats were still roasting. It was still within, but she did find a small amount of venison as well as a large piece of elk meat. She thought Marshall would be happy with this.

And so, her days went. Marshall worked on the "barn," he called it, building up the missing walls with logs. He spent his evenings working on the "shelves." He finally tore down the other cedar plank wall and built more shelves, and then stacked his "goods" on them.

When the *Petonia* returned upriver in two weeks, they unloaded another raft load of cargo. The boy came up with them as well and began immediately to remove it to the log barn. Two Blankets remembered to turn her dress about and found that Marshall had managed to convince the captain of the *Petonia* to wait a hand span of the sun while he invited the half dozen whitemans into his longhouse. He had finished building his shelves as well as a long bench along one wall. The men took whiskey, and there was an exchange of coin. They examined some of the other goods he had on the shelves, and Marshall pulled down some fur pelts as well for them to look at. More coins were dug out of pouches, and one man went back to the *Petonia* to show Marshall some trade goods he had. Marshall chose two knives and a set of six metal arm bands. When the men left, four of the glass bottles of whiskey left with them. Marshall seemed happy with the exchange, and she was happy for him.

That night he fucked her three times, and she hoped the three seeds she had put into his whiskey bottle would work. She knew this was the dangerous time for catching a baby. On the third fuck, he pulled her head down into his lap. At first, she did not know what her husband wanted, but he lifted his little cock to her lips, and she understood. She took the soft organ entirely into her mouth and stroked it with her tongue. It began to grow harder, yet she could still take the entire organ in her mouth. His hips moved against her.

He really likes to *mamook* me this way. If I could get him to want to *mamook* me this way, I would run no risk of catching a baby.

It was a strange thought, but people were strange in their own ways and preferences. She began actively to try to please him with her mouth and hands. Experimenting with different sucks and licks and observing his reactions. She grasped his testicles accidentally, and he groaned.

Interesting. She massaged them and stroked his shaft. His hips jerked to her rhythm.

She took his entire hard *cultus wootlat* and his testicles into her mouth and stroked the whole of him with her tongue working him with her mouth and cheeks. His reacted immediately, and his back stiffened. He seemed not to be able to even breathe. She felt the surge coming from him and managed to catch most of his seed on her breasts rather than in her mouth. He fell straight back, a vacant stare to his eyes.

Two Blankets said, "Are you pleased, my husband?"

To her statement, he only looked at her like he did not even know where he was.

"I am happy then. I hope we may do this again soon, my warrior husband, Marshall." Two Blankets slid off the sleeping furs and outside to the creek to bathe his *cultus* seed from her breasts.

TALES OF HUNTING, SEX, AND COMMERCE

CHAPTER 13

APRIL, 1854 TO JULY, 1854

WHEN NEXT THE *Petonia* docked at Johnston's Landing, as Marshall had begun calling it, it unloaded the usual cargo for him, and the men came into the longhouse to drink and trade. Marshall offered all a drink, and congenial bargaining commenced. The men seemed to like trading with Marshall, especially the odd and various metal objects for native furs and pelts. Here, although his selection was small, they could get a slightly better price and still do their major trading at The Dalles above the Cascades. Always they seemed to leave with a few bottles of Marshall's whiskey.

After he had the load on the barge transferred to his storage shed, which now had log walls all around but still lacked a roof, and the specific goods stored within the longhouse, he called Two Blankets to attend him.

"Two Blankets, I have something for you."

"Yes, my husband." She approached wearing her tablecloth dress and stood before him as she had learned was appropriate in these circumstances.

He handed her a package wrapped in paper and tied with string. She unwrapped it with care, smoothing the paper flat and coiling the string.

"Enough with fooling with the paper and string." Marshall moved to throw them into the fire.

"No, please do not throw away," she said. "I value gift I receive from you, husband."

It was a small lie. She could already think of two persons she could trade them with.

"Fine, then." He held up the contents of the package. "It is a dress, a proper dress for the wife of Marshall Johnston of Johnston's Landing."

In truth, it was a simple shift, something even the poorest woman in Portland could afford, but to Two Blankets it was something miraculous.

"Well, put it on," Marshall said.

She shucked her cape and folded it and put the dress on over her head, having some trouble getting her arms into the long sleeves. Marshall had to assist her with the buttons up the bodice. Two Blankets had never felt so rich before. She swirled about testing it. She stooped forward, tried squatting on her heels. The dress covered her from ankles and wrists to her throat. So, she was encumbered. The dress pulled at her in odd ways when she made common movements.

How whiteman's women wear these every day, I have no idea. And yet, this dress is property, given to me by my husband. He will want some trade in return.

"It is, how you say it, *cultus potlatch,*" Marshall said. "I need you to wear it especially when other whitemans are here, understand?"

"I understand my husband. Maybe I give you something in return," she said. There was no question of what she meant.

"Later, perhaps. Now I need to restock the trading post."

"I will go to the *Tyee* to see where I can wear this. If I could wear it outside it would help, yes?"

"Yes, good idea," he said, but she could tell his head was already spinning plans and arranging his goods.

Two Blankets unhooked the button loops one by one and folded up the dress. She donned her old pelt cape and left for the *Tyee's* longhouse. As she passed the tanning area, she saw Fox Tail there. He had a string of women's beads about his neck and a skirt of cedar bark. Sitting back on his heels he scraped the hide before him with newly acquired skill and conversed happily with the other women. Apparently, she had missed much with her separation from the main flow of events within the tribe living with Marshall.

The morning was still somewhat cold, and *Tyee* Running Blade sat within his longhouse in his customary place. She approached with caution, never knowing what his reaction might be, although lately it had been mostly resigned acceptance.

"*Tyee* Running Blade," she said by way of greeting.

"*Mistshimus*, wife of Marshall." He would still not say the name she had adopted, and Marshall had placed upon her, Two Blankets.

"If I may disturb you and speak openly?"

"You may. Hope you do not disturb me too greatly." A look of apprehension had creased his face.

"I seek your counsel and judgment, *Tyee*. My husband Marshall has given me this whiteman's dress and instructed me to wear it when whitemans are present in his longhouse. He apparently would prefer me to cover myself at all times. No *mistshimus* may wear clothes except moccasins and a cape. I do not want to anger my husband in his whiteman's ways or distress the Chinook by violating the clothing taboo."

The *Tyee* relaxed somewhat. "It is good you brought this to me, *mistshimus*. Within his longhouse, you must do as he requires. It is outside that is the question." He thought a minute in clear silence. "Let us say, if you are on the other side of the midden pile you may wear what he wishes. On this side, you must follow Chinook custom."

"Thank you for your wisdom, *Tyee*." She exited his longhouse.

On her way back to Marshall's longhouse she decided to stop at Stinging Nettle's. She had been involved in other tasks for the tribe these past two weeks and hadn't been able to see her. As Two Blankets approached, she was pleased and surprised to see Stinging Nettle surrounded by a certain glow. White Mouse chittered in her ear, a voice she had almost forgotten these last few months.

"Stinging Nettle, this *mistshimus* is pleased to see you."

"Ah, Nika, sit a moment in the fine sun."

Two Blankets sat down on her heels. "I think I am pleased to see both of you, Stinging Nettle."

Stinging Nettle stroked her slightly protruding abdomen with pleasure.

"You are observant, Nika. Yes, I am with child and am to marry Drifting Smoke. He is eleven years my junior, but he is a fine man."

"I remember him. He was one of the three who took me," Two Blankets said. "But he is an honorable man. His first encounter with me does not diminish that. I apologize for that comment."

"I am happy. He is a strong warrior, and he is noble and true."

"I remember that he admitted his mistake to the *Tyee* immediately and took all responsibility. Even then, I could tell he was one with the river."

"Have you heard the news? Fire Stick is to be newly married."

"I feel as if in a fog. Where have I been? Who can he be marrying?" Two Blankets ran the possible title born prospects through her mind. She could think of none.

"Well, the *Tyee* has had to adjust his strict policy somewhat, the tribe has shrunk so much. Although he doesn't like the non-traditional clans, he is forced to be a little non-traditional himself." Stinging Nettle was stretching this gossip like a hide on a frame, thong by thong.

"A round-head?"

"Yes. He is to marry Sweet-Pollen-Flower. She will still be round-head of course, nothing can change that. But their children will be title born."

"That is—simply amazing. I have always liked Sweet-Pollen-Flower."

"Yes, it is amazing. Though that is not the most amazing thing."

"No?"

"No, he will also marry Fox Tail, who is a woman now."

"I saw Fox Tail with the women, stretching hides in a skirt with women's beads across his—well, er, across *her*—chest. She seemed happy and relaxed."

"Yes, she is. Fox Tail and Fire Stick have been close friends since childhood, and Sweet-Pollen-Flower likes her, too. I do not know if Fox Tail, who of course cannot *moosum* with Fire Stick like a woman, or Sweet-Pollen-Flower, who is not title born, will be first wife to Fire Stick. But I think they will be happy together."

Two Blankets missed the next small event later in the month because she was in the moon cycle hut. She definitely heard about it from the laughter and jokes coming from outside the hut to many retellings of the story.

Several of the warriors were planning an elk hunt, and they invited Marshall to come with them, partially to test his skill and partly in good-natured humor. He took down the possession in which he took the most pride, his M1841Mississippi Rifle. He joined his Chinook compatriots, who jogged up the creek. When they reached the point where Two Blankets had turned to the south in her escape attempt, they continued on, reaching another small tributary heading west, and turned up that. Up on the plateau, they headed for the distant tree line. They could see a herd browsing near the treeline.

The Chinook began circling the herd, hoping to get within arrow range. Marshall judged the distance to be some two hundred yards. He lay down in the new grass and adjusted his sights. One of the Chinook looked back and saw him. He signaled for the others to stop. What was this whiteman doing? At two hundred yards, one could hardly see the elk, let alone bring one down.

Marshall sighted down on a prime specimen, not the largest of the elk, but plenty big enough. When he felt the certainty of the shot, he squeezed it off. A huge "Kaboom" echoed across the plain, scattering the herd. His target took one faltering step and fell. Marshall reloaded the muzzle loader and walked toward his kill, the Chinook following. It was a perfect heart shot, he was sure of it. Pride in his marksmanship suffused him. He was tired of being called a *cultus* whiteman as if he had no value at all.

When they reached the elk, Marshall saw that he was right.

"Shot penetrated both lungs and the heart if I'm not mistaken."

"It is good shot, Marshall Johnston. We take back to camp." They cut down a sapling and tied the elk's legs over it. Two of the more brawny hunters shouldered it, and they headed back.

When they reached camp, they marched the elk up to the *Tyee's* hut. The *Tyee* looked the elk over. "Kill shot good. I thought you go for three or four. Why you only get one?"

"Marshall took first shot at least four bow lengths out. He make kill good but rifle scare away rest of herd. He is a good shot. I say that," Drifting Smoke said.

"From now on, Marshall take last shot, after bows. If bows miss, we still get one. Bows hit we get three or four."

The others nodded to the wisdom of this.

"Hang him, bleed him, and butcher. Save brain for tanning. Skin go to Marshall and his choice of meat. Rest to tribe."

In commerce, Marshall's business improved with each visit of the little steam scow, *Petonia*. Fox Tail paid the trading post a visit in late spring. Two Blankets was there to meet her. Marshall looked with disgust at the skirt-wearing Fox Tail, but Two Blankets carried no such prejudice. She looked to her husband, and he spat tobacco juice and waved her to deal with the oddity.

"Greetings, Fox Tail. I am pleased to see you."

"I do not know how exactly to greet you, *mistshimus*. It is strange. But if I tell the truth, I am happy to see you, as well."

"Let us go with that. I know I will always be *mistshimus*, but we have known each other since the beginning. There are stronger bonds than those of *mistshimus* and title born."

"It is generous of you to say so, *mistshimus*, since I was one of the Chinook responsible for your slavery."

"I am Chinook now. I am *mistshimus*, Marshall wife, and I am your friend, too, I hope. I do like your Two Spirits necklace. The beads are so pretty."

"Thank you, is it Two Blankets? I would like to trade these pelts." Here she placed two brace of beaver pelts on the counter Marshall had made in his latest improvement project.

Two Blankets examined them, probed and stroked the fur. She turned them over and noted how consistently the skin had been scraped, and how evenly the hide had been tanned. "Fox Tail, these are as fine as I have ever seen. Of course, we would want them. Your tanning skills have certainly improved since you bought me for a night."

Fox Tail's face reddened slightly. "I remember that day. In some ways, I have you, a *mistshimus*, to thank for awakening the woman spirit within me."

"Oh, Jaysus," Marshall said, and stalked out.

"Do not worry, whitemans do not understand Two Spirits persons. What would you like to trade for?"

"I want a present for Fire Stick, to show my friendship, love, and value of him as my warrior."

"Ah," Two Blankets contemplated. "I think I know. What do you think of these?" She fished down two of the remaining armbands. She polished them up on her dress and set them before him. "They are steel, I believe."

Fox Tail looked into her own reflection in one. "They are very beautiful."

"Steel is strong like your warrior, long-lasting as your love, and true as your friendship. If you give him two, it can also say that there are two who love him, both you and Sweet-Pollen-Flower."

"Are my four beaver skins enough for this gift?"

"Two skins are enough. I will wrap them for you." She got out her paper from her dress and tore off a piece to wrap the armbands tying the package with a bit of string.

"Thank you, Two Blankets." There was a softness in her eyes that Two Blankets hadn't seen before.

After she left, Marshall asked, "Why did you only take two beaver for the armbands? Clearly, he had no idea of what they were worth." His tone was accusatory.

"Forgive me, husband, I know the metal armbands are discards from some other process. They are worth little to you, as I have seen you trade them for less than the two beaver I received."

"That was to men who knew their value." He was still angry, but he had to admit she was right. They had only cost him about thirty cents.

"By making a fair trade with Fox Tail, or what he thinks is fair trade, more Chinook will begin to trade with you. Please excuse my ignorance if I was wrong."

That was a turning point for the trade at Johnston's Landing among the Chinook of the tribe. Before Fox Tail, the Chinook had treated the trading post with suspicious acceptance. After his visit, they came in ones and twos once every week or two. They traded what they had locally for what they could only get at The Dalles once a year. They knew that they could get a slightly better bargain waiting for the yearly trade at The Dalles, but this was easier. Marshall suspected, and Two Blankets knew, that most still held out their best goods for The Dalles, but what was the cost of trading a less than perfectly tanned elk hide, or beadwork they knew could be more perfectly done, for something they wanted or could use now.

At the same time, the bi-weekly and later the weekly, visits from the *Petonia* developed into a regular stop. Two traders began to trade at the post exclusively, at least when the goods were available. That saved them the cost of the portage above the Cascades. If they completed their trade at Johnston's, they would camp at the Cascades and wait for the downriver trip. Whiskey was always a popular trading item to the men on the scow, though no Chinook ever asked for any. If they did drink it, then it was from the summer trading event at The Dalles.

The months rolled on into summer, past the wedding of Drifting Smoke and Stinging Nettle and the wedding of Fire Stick to his two wives Fox Tail and Sweet-Pollen-Flower. It turned out that Fox Tail was to be designated first wife as she was entitled and Sweet-Pollen-Flower second as a commoner, but to see them, Two Blankets thought there would be no formal first and second wife in that marriage.

THE GREAT HUNT

CHAPTER 14
JULY, 1854

IN THE SUMMER of 1854, between the summer and fall salmon migrations as the grasses on the plateau above began to dry, came the great hunt. Though it was not something the Bent Creek Clan did every year, the *Tyee* decided their food stores for winter needed to be supplemented. The store of brains for tanning was low as well, and the clan could always use more skins. All in the Bent Creek Clan would be involved except the smallest children.

Early in the morning, after three days and nights of dancing, appeals to the spirits for a good hunt, and apologies sent up on the drifting smoke of the central bonfire to the animals that would be taken, the clan began moving up the creek. They took the same path as the elk hunters had taken with Marshall. The *Tyee* led the group and was followed by the title born in order of precedence, then the round-heads and finally the *mistshimus*. Two Blankets and Marshall closed the group.

When he had first heard of the hunt, he began to get down his M1841 Mississippi Rifle, but Two Blankets halted him. "Pardon, warrior husband Marshall, but it is not that kind of a hunt. You will see."

When they reached the plateau, the clan spread out from the edge of the steep ravine which dropped to the creek, to the forest two miles away. The wind blew away from the river, which was a good sign. Every two hundred feet or so stood a person. In the early gray light just before dawn, Two

Blankets saw a flame flare up near the forest edge. Another was started near the edge of the ravine. The fastest runners in the clan raced with torches toward the center. As they ran the mile toward the center, they lit the torches carried by each of the long line of Chinook. In the mists of the morning, it was a slow-moving line of fire. Another fire sprang up at the cliffside and ran toward them. Backfires were started along the ravine and the forest two miles away. Marshall had a torch as well, and he saw what was happening. The cries of the hunt sounded out along the line, and Two Blankets and Marshall joined in.

Timing was everything in a hunt such as this. They had no desire to trap the animals and cook them in a wildfire. The object was to drive the animals, elk, deer, rabbit, and snake closer and closer to the bluff overlooking a shallow beach alongside the *Nch'i-wána*. A great bull elk charged up to the edge of the fire, the herd bull Marshall had seen before. Fear was in his eyes, but also rage. A small gap existed between Marshall and his neighboring hunter where the fire had not taken well. Grass smoldered and sparked. The bull elk eyed it. Marshall moved to fill the gap, but Two Blankets stayed him.

"Some must always escape for the future, and see how noble he is."

Marshall nodded. "That is the very reason I did not shoot him on our last meeting."

The bull elk roared, then bugled. He charged the gap and trampled a path that was followed by two cows. They were singed, but they made it through before the fire closed off the escape route.

The hunters followed the fire inwards a short way behind to allow the burnt grass a chance to cool. Occasionally one would dash forward through the smoke and sparks and relight a portion. For the most part, they just followed it in. Two Blankets saw the creek and forest were out of danger having been backfired.

As the half-circle closed and the animals were crowded closer to the edge of the bluff, Two Blankets and Marshall and other Chinook encountered creatures that had been overcome by smoke. The first was halfway down the line. They heard the *"Ayiee"* of the hunter as he cut the animal's throat. A fox had collapsed from the smoke before Two Blankets. *"Ayiee,"* she called and dispatched it. A short prayer for the animal's spirit followed and thanks to it for giving up its life so others could live.

The circle was tighter now, and Chinook began leaving it to trek back down the creek and gather on the beach. Soon it was Marshall's and her turn to join them. They picked up the fox, a snake, and four rabbits on the way back. Nothing was wasted in this life. Even a snake had its use and was appreciated.

It was a long trek down the creek. By the time they reached the village most of the animals had either succumbed to the smoke or taken a plunge off the bluff at the west side of the village.

Two Blankets stripped off her cape and moccasins. She turned to Marshall. "If it pleases my husband, I suggest removing all clothes you do not want to be ruined." Marshall nodded and began shucking his clothes. He stopped short of his drawers, and he left his boots on. They piled their clothes in separate stacks next to the *Tyee's* longhouse and advanced toward the bluff. Marshall and Two Blankets dropped the sooty creatures they had collected, and Two Blankets picked up a flint knife from the skinning station. Here, Two Blankets could see eight or nine skinning racks set up, consisting of crossed logs with a log running across the top.

A hundred yards past the village they rounded the edge of the bluff. Marshall just stopped and stared. "Jaysus. Jaysus H. Christ," was all he said.

The gore was overwhelming at first. The smell of blood and feces was thick, and the bellowing and crying of critters that had not died in the fall penetrated to someplace deep in the brain beyond tribe and civilization.

"Any that have not been killed from the fall, we kill," Two Blankets said. "Offer a prayer of thanks for the food and sacrifice of the animal, be it elk, snake, or mouse."

They began, and Two Blankets slit the throat of each animal she came across. She offered a prayer to each. The children of the village were slitting the throats of the smaller creatures and hauling them back to the skinning station. Two Blankets saw a three-year-old carrying a mouse with reverence. Older children carried a fox, or sometimes two would carry a fawn of the deer or calf of the elk. Marshall moved to a large elk and picked up one end of the pole between her legs. Drifting Smoke held the other end.

She shouldered the pole on the front half of a deer. *"Ayiee,"* she said, and the woman on the other end echoed the cry. They carried it back to the village. Two Blankets saw this area, though slippery with blood, hair, and offal of the dying animals was already cleared of the carcasses. The whole village moved as one organism when a task such as this was involved, and there was little wasted motion.

At the skinning station, they laid their deer down and removed the pole. She stood a minute beside Marshall watching. The creatures were arranged by size, with the mouse and snake and fox going to the short rack, the deer and small elk going to the mid-sized racks, and the great elk awaiting the largest.

Already the *mistshimus* were cracking the heads of the animals and removing the brains to be used for tanning. The brains were collected in a large waterproof basket. The Chinook had a saying, "The brain of every animal is large enough to tan his hide."

"Why do they take the brains?" Marshall asked.

"You do not do brain tanning of leather and pelts?"

"No, I haven't done that."

"That is the secret you are missing to your pelts, then. Your tanning skills are good, but the brains provide the ingredient to make the softest leather. You could ask Fox Tail to show you. She has become one of the best tanners in the tribe."

"You want me to ask a sodomite?" He turned to her in disgust.

"She is Two Spirits and honored in the Bent Creek Clan. Forgive me, husband, but you are Chinook now. It would not do you or your trade well to go against it."

"There are a lot of things I can do to please your Chinook. Associating myself with a freak of nature ain't one of them."

Four warriors worked the frame nearest them, which stood the height of two men. First, they hoisted the largest elk, which could be just somewhat shy of the height of the frame and weigh a considerable amount, and slit him open from anus to the chest cavity along the soft tissue. The entrails were stripped out first into a large basket for later washing. The guts of the animal, stomach, bladder and intestines, were valuable once they were washed in the river and dried. The internal meat organs were pulled next into a separate waterproof basket. Finally, the heart was taken and placed carefully in a separate basket. They turned the animal, so it hung head down and drained the blood into another waterproof basket. Nothing was wasted.

The same process applied to the smaller frames where deer and elk calves hung. The smaller creatures, the several foxes, coyotes and one wolf who had been trapped by the fire were treated likewise. At the smallest frame, the children worked practicing their craft on snakes, gophers, and even a few mice. Although Two Blankets doubted much of what they did would make it to the pot, they were observing and participating in the process.

Two Blankets picked up an end of the pole and headed back for another carcass. This would be the work of many trips and would be a long day. She could see it would be a rich day as well, one that secured the clan for the winter, a day to be celebrated.

As the sun began to sink in the west, Two Blankets looked along the bluff. Marshall and three others struggled with the massive carcass of an old bull elk. He was of great size and must have once been the herd leader. Now he had finally met his end. Hoping his spirit was not too displeased with the Chinook for taking him in this way, she offered a soft song of a prayer to his great spirit that had lived so long, and now his meat body would help them through the winter. All she could hope for was that it would be accepted. She followed them up to the butchering. After the brain had been taken, Marshall helped hoist the great elk upon the frame. He slit him open with his steel knife and reached in and dragged the entrails out, then the meat organs and the heart. Two Blankets was glad he had observed. They flipped him around. He was so long his antlers dragged the ground. The blood drained into the basket. The other Chinook on his team looked at each other, the white and the brown. All were covered from head to toe in blood, hair, and offal.

One of the Chinook began to laugh, and the others followed.

"He sure was one big old bastard. As big as I've ever seen," Marshall said.

"Yes, a big bastard for sure," the Chinook said.

"One big old bastard," echoed the others. There was laughter all around.

They all headed for the river to wash off. It was one thing to be covered in blood when the work needed to be done. When the work was complete, and the blood began to dry on her skin and hair, and the flies were buzzing, it was time to get clean. Two Blankets submerged in the *Nch'i-wána* and let the current wash away the filth. She scrubbed with beach sand over her entire body. The sand hurt her tender parts but ridding herself of the day's gore was worth it. Once she had washed her hair twice and scrubbed her body down again, she emerged from the water enlivened. Marshall emerged as well, shivering but with an overtone of pink to his pale flesh.

"Your drawers are ruined, I think, my husband. Mayhap you may save the boots," she said as they walked back up to where their clothes lay.

"You can burn the drawers for all I care. Still, it was a good day's work. Now I just want to go home and lie down."

"I think we must attend the feast tonight, worthy husband. It would be a great insult to the *Tyee* if we did not. There will be plenty of meat roasted tonight to eat and no salmon."

"The Chinook rules would put any fancy noble Englishman with his Rules of Etiquette manual under his arm to shame. All right, let us make our proper appearance. But I do want to get a pint first."

"I will get it for you husband, if I may. And you can get dressed." Two Blankets was already dressed in moccasins and cape.

"Aye. Come back with that pint. We'll eat and make festive and then go home to a proper bedding."

Two Blankets was off before he had finished. She fetched him a pint of whiskey and put on her tablecloth as a cape. The opportunity to attend a feast of this magnitude excited her, and she realized that she missed the community of the *Tyee's* hall.

They entered the *Tyee's* longhouse, and she sat on her heels with the *mistshimus.* Accorded the status of highest of *mistshimus,* but that did not allow for seating with the common born. Marshall sat halfway up in that grouping. That was far above where he would have been seated just a few months ago. His position was being elevated, and hers as well. Among the Chinook, such things were noted.

Several of the *mistshimus* fingered her red and white checkered "cloak" and made kindly remarks.

The *Tyee* Running Blade stood, and all in the longhouse quietened. "We have had a good hunt. All among the Bent Creek Clan of Chinook have participated to make this possible. From the highest of the title born"—he gestured to those seated at the high mat—"to the common people"—his gesture expanded to include the round-heads—"and among the common people, even our friend Marshall, to the lowest *mistshimus*"—his arms spread to include the whole clan—"every one of you has made this possible. Because of your efforts on this day, we have food for the winter and beyond."

He paused and let that feeling of community sink in. "Tonight, we eat of the many animals who died today to give us life and renewal. We eat of the hearts of our prey, and we give thanks to them for sacrificing their lives so that the Chinook and our way of life may continue. Before me, you see the heart of the elk, the heart of the deer, and the hearts of one of each creature that died today in service to us." He indicated the shallow cedar bowls before him, each containing a heart. "Of these creatures, none was higher than any other. For each, the sacrifice was the same. And so, shall we be on this one night of the Great Hunt this year. Pass down the hearts. Each of you take a piece, chew on it, and give thanks."

The *Tyee* lifted the bowl containing the raw heart of the mighty elk and tore off a piece. He chewed and said a half-silent prayer of thanks. The bowls were passed with no attention to rank or privilege. Two Blankets saw Marshall bite off a piece of what looked to be deer heart and saw his lips move. When the bowl came to her, she took a bite from what she thought was the heart of the red fox, or it could have been coyote, and she said her fervid and heartfelt prayer to the animal's spirit.

The *Tyee* gestured, and large cedar platters of roasted strips of meat of every kind were brought forward to each eating group. Bowls of camas root that had been buried in the dirt beneath the hot coals and roasted for hours were brought forth, as well as toasted camas cakes. When all was set forth, the *Tyee* Running Blade stood a second time.

"On this night of the Great Hunt we Chinook of the Bent Creek Clan observe a tradition that only occurs once every several years. On this night, we celebrate the contribution of every member of this tribe as equals. Some of you may have experienced this many times in the past. For some, it will be new. It is not something we ever talk about on other days. For this one night, we stand as one tribe, one people with no rank or privilege between us, as once our ancestors did when they came to this land. For The People were formed by The Old Woman who threw down the eggs of the Thunderbird. The old giantess did not throw down title born and round-head and *mistshimus* eggs that became Chinook. All the eggs she threw down became the Chinook who lived along the great river, the *Wimahl*.

"And so, I instruct you remove all your clothes. Remove all your jewelry and any signs of office." He began removing his cape and jewelry and placing his property with solemn grace where he sat. "This night, it will be as it once was, when The People were first created. This night, there is no rank. This night, there is no title born or *mistshimus*."

Those who had been through this celebration before—it had not occurred in Two Blankets tenure here—removed all traces of clothing, jewelry, and rank. Those who had not, looked about and followed suit. The *mistshimus*, who had nothing other than a cape or moccasins on, rapidly removed everything and stacked it neatly next to them.

Tyee Standing Blade stood proud and naked before them all. The other title born stood as well, followed by the rest of the tribe. "Now we stand before these creatures we have killed to continue ourselves, and before our spirits and kin as nature first made us. My last command as *Tyee* before I relinquish it for this night is this, move about, eat, *moosum* with any you wish, be happy, my people." He stepped down and came to the *mistshimus* area, sat back on his heels, and began eating. Some round-heads moved to the area reserved for title born, looked about guiltily then began to eat. For the *mistshimus* who were used to being told what to do it was most difficult.

The *Tyee* looked up, "Go, go on."

He might be naked and eating where the *mistshimus* regularly ate, but to them, he was still the *Tyee*. And he had said, "Go." So although they were uncomfortable doing so, they did as they were bidden.

Running Blade caught a young *mistshimus* girl by the wrist as she was passing by and pulled her into his lap. She smiled up at him, uncertain. He kissed her full on the lips, savoring the taste of her. She settled herself on his stout organ, her legs about his waist, and he fed her roasted meat from the platter.

Two Blankets was drifting now amidst a sea of organized confusion. She saw Marshall, who had not changed position, being stripped of the last of his clothes by both Swimming Salmon and Bears-Many-Children. Both were laughing and clearly enjoying themselves. Bears-Many-Children put the long end of a strip of roasted elk between her teeth and dangled the other end into Marshall's mouth. Marshall began to nibble on the end, and Bears-Many-Children smiled. Swimming Salmon ducked in and nipped off the bite Marshall had been chewing and swallowed it down. Marshall took a deep draught from his pint, and another, and Bears-Many-Children pushed him back to the floor of the longhouse. She placed the next strip of meat partway up into her furrow and knelt over his face, dangling it just beyond his bite. Swimming Salmon stroked his now erect *wootlat,* and though it was indeed small, it stood as proud as it could. She sank down upon it and slowly rocked, nibbling on a camas cake.

Two Blankets spied Standing Bear standing alone. He was like a sun to her planet. She could not help being pulled by him. He moved toward her, slow and resolute. She glanced back over her shoulder at the *Tyee.*

Surely, if he notices he will be angry. If not today, then tomorrow the punishment will come.

His head lifted from the *mistshimus* girl, and she saw him take in the scene before him. She knew he saw Standing Bear and herself moving obliquely toward each other, the slow dance of circles as each rotated in the other's orbit. She saw the recognition on his face of their attraction each to the other. And then she saw—she could not really believe it—she saw him really see them both and nod. He knew, and he accepted—at least for this night—the love that his son and Two Blankets felt for each other. A slight smile spread across his normally taciturn face, and he resumed his rocking pleasure with the *mistshimus* girl.

She and Standing Bear passed nearer to each other, each testing the bounds of this pull. At last, he grasped her and drew them both to his sleeping area, which was partially screened off from the commons.

"We may have only this one night together, Two Blankets, but I would seize it and hold it dear."

She held him close to her as they lay back down on his sleeping furs. Her skin trembled to his light touch. "I would too, my love." She realized what she had not before, that she truly loved Standing Bear. The pain and drawn sweetness of it were so bittersweet, she teared up.

"Let us not waste a moment, Two Blankets, on what we do not have. We know we cannot be together. Perhaps we will not get this chance ever again. But if we should not, I would rejoice in it to my dying day."

"Oh, sweet warrior, you were always my warrior, Standing Bear, please hold me and fill me up so that I may remember only this, my sweet."

Slow and gentle he slipped into her, hard and proud and seeking. She was wet, and she bit upon his shoulder as he filled her. Her legs lifted over his hips and she tried to pull him into her deeper, though he was already as deep as he could go. Yet still, there was that feeling that there was another half or quarter of an inch of him that he had not given her yet, and her legs crossed behind his back. Her hips lifted to each thrust and twisted against him. Her moon circled his earth. His earth circled her sun. She knew she was crying, felt the tears upon her cheeks. They were the tears of joy. They were also the tears of sadness and desperation. Sadness because this might be their only such time together, and that did make her immeasurably sad. And desperation as she clung to this tiny scrap of driftwood in the torrent of the *Nch'i-wána* spring flood. She was small, a tiny thing, but she was *Nimi'ipuu* and so proud of this warrior man, Standing Bear, who possessed her. He was the boy she once knew as Little Bear no longer. This was a man who took her, and this was the man she wanted to take her. Only the man within him could ever truly match her. Only the Chinook warrior who surged within her like the *Nch'i-wána* could truly take and master the *Nimi'ipuu* woman who lay entirely open and vulnerable to him.

"You are my Chinook warrior, Standing Bear, and you shall always be mine," Two Blankets said. Her tongue half lolled in her mouth and her nails dug into his back.

"My *Nimi'ipuu* woman, Two Blankets, as the fire today you have burned me to the bone. I will ever be changed for loving you."

She reached between them partly to feel him moving with her and partly to open herself and her seed of pleasure to him. She pressed it against his cock as it thrust within her and let it drag along him as he pulled out. She could feel the surge coming from him in his frenzied movements, and she matched it. She needed this, needed this completion, and she rode it now for everything she could get. It was coming. She could feel it now, beginning at her nipples and drawing tighter. She was so close, so close. Two Blankets knew she was there, and he was, as well. He heaved twice more, then his whole body went rigid, and she ground out the last bit of her own pleasure against this oak of a man until he fell upon her, gasping.

All around them Chinook were engaged in various sexual activities now, resultant from the bloodlust that had overcome the whole tribe. It was perhaps the tribe's way of praying, this frantic sexual activity. After the day of bloody killing, they felt a primal release, knowing food would be abundant this winter. The release of anxiety over food, though the tribe had little enough to feel anxious about during most years, was an outpouring of life force.

Two Blankets knew, however, that the experience that she and Standing Bear had just had, while undoubtedly influenced by the general mood, was much more than simple copulation and the enjoyment of bodies. The craving she had within her to be joined with Standing Bear was only physical in the smallest sense. She could not have him. She knew that. Yet she must have him. And this night at least, as she clung to him, he was hers entirely. This was her sadness and her victory.

Tonight, you are mine. Tonight, you are solely and utterly my own, and I will cling to this memory.

CHANGES

CHAPTER 15
AUGUST, 1854 TO JANUARY, 1855

OVER THE NEXT several moons, Two Blankets experienced a series of interruptions to a routine, rather than any one sequence that built up to a dramatic consequence. For example, Stinging Nettle had her baby, which she named informally Wind-from-East after the gorge winds that arrived in the winter down the *Wimahl* Gorge. More often she just called him Squall.

Sweet-Pollen-Flower caught a baby, and no one knew whether the father was Fire Stick or Fox Tail as both acted as proud parents. Several other pregnancies occurred, some of which seemed to date from the Blood Feast. Among these was Swimming Salmon. The Chinook viewed children differently than the typical whiteman, and they frequently allowed their wives and women to have relations with outsiders. It was believed that the child belonged to the woman and that outside blood, even white blood only strengthened the tribe.

Thus, Marshall's fear that he might have fathered a child upon the *Tyee's* second wife was unfounded, but no explanation by Two Blankets could convince him. Finally, she just said, "Swimming Salmon lay with two other Chinook men that night. Any of you three could be the father." She was fairly sure it wasn't Marshall, since she was still giving him the seeds with his whiskey. At the same time, she hoped to catch a child from Standing Bear, though deemed that unlikely as well, due to the tea Stinging Nettle gave her.

Another thing that happened during this period of time, was that first one, and then two steamboats began running the river up to the Cascades. They were the side-wheelers *Belle of Oregon City* and *Multnomah*. Though they did not make regular stops at Johnston's Landing, Marshall developed a strategy to get them to bring cargo to him and, in this way, get them accustomed to making the stop. Always he had whiskey ready, complimentary to the captain, and gradually the stops became more regular.

One day in November, Marshall made the announcement that he would be going by steamboat to Portland the following week, returning about a week later. Two Blankets accepted this news with equanimity, especially since she was due to begin her moon cycle during that period. She made sure that Marshall had some good sex to remember her by and waved goodbye as the *Belle* departed with a shrieking whistle and the churning of her sidewheels. Marshall, once he boarded, never looked back at her.

It felt strange to be alone in the longhouse, and she soon fell back into her old *mistshimus* ways. It wasn't so much that she liked being a slave to the Chinook, as it was that the role was comfortable. The Chinook accepted her as one of them now and among *mistshimus*, round-head and even title born, she was accorded a certain respect. Possibly it was because of her unique status of being *mistshimus* and a whiteman's wife that placed her in this position. Whatever it was, she was determined to enjoy it.

She visited her old friend Stinging Nettle, who made no distinction any longer of Two Blankets being *mistshimus*. To Stinging Nettle, she was just Nika, and Two Blankets had developed a similar affection for Stinging Nettle. They ground herbs together and laughed at Squall's tremendous voice.

Later that evening she took a meal at the *Tyee's* longhouse. Marshall had lately been trying to teach her to fry bacon and make proper raised biscuits, cornmeal mush, and cowboy fried potatoes. All these foods, save the bacon, held no flavor to Two Blankets, but Marshall liked them well enough, so she tried. This meal was the typical salmon and camas cake and a coming home for Two Blankets. Some of the women were playing a game with beaver's teeth marked on the various sides. They threw these "dice" down then counted the score.

As she exited from the longhouse, she was caught by Standing Bear in the dark. He drew her into the shadows alongside the longhouse and held her tightly. She did not know if she should dare it, but it was a battle she was doomed to lose.

"Come to me at Marshall's longhouse, and we will steal such time as we can," she said.

He nodded and slipped off into the shadows. The night was moonless and black with overcast as she made her way back. Once to the doorway, she looked about for Standing Bear. It was so dark that he was almost upon her before she saw him and drew him within.

Once they were inside, they took no time for talk. This was time stolen from the moon, and someday perhaps there would be an accounting for it. They fell into the sleeping furs and made love with a furious intensity that belied the word. This was not the vulgar *mamook,* nor simple *mosuum.* It was love, but it was a love stolen. They did not speak one word during this time. The silence was by some unspoken agreement between them and the forces of the night that surrounded them. There were primal cries that penetrated the air but no words. Words somehow would break this spell they lived within, timeless for a time, a space beyond space where two could become one, where all that was known became unknown.

Standing Bear shuddered his climax and lay first on top of her and then rolled his hard weight to the side. Two Blankets curled beneath his arm and clung to him as a sailor fallen overboard will cling to any piece of flotsam, watching the stern lights of his ship diminish over the horizon.

After a time, his *wootlat* hardened under her resting hand, and she slid her head downward to take it into her mouth. She certainly could not take in all of him as she had Marshall, though she did not think of this. She thought only of the pleasure of being with her warrior. She laid fierce claim to him and, like a mother badger, would have torn any competitor for her mate to pieces in that moment. When she could begin to feel the surge building within him, he pulled her back away, so her seat of pleasure was within his mouths range. He quivered but his seed did not erupt, and she sat back and ground herself against his hungry mouth and tongue. This was not something she was used to, a man sacrificing his own immediate needs for hers, but she took it like a feast and gorged herself upon it. When at last she felt the imminent burst possess her she fell once more upon his still hard *wootlat* and brought the surge that was just sleeping to the surface. Now his seed erupted into her mouth, and she allowed it. His seed was of him, and her passion was for him. It was thick and warm and slightly bitter. It was certainly sticky. But it was of him, and he was hers, his body and his seed. She collapsed along his side, her head on his thigh, her hand clasped tightly still about his sex.

Their night passed like that, somewhat short periods of intense mating followed by increasingly longer periods of rest. In the early gray hours, he slipped silently from the sleeping furs and left, her hand trailing from his body. In the deep coal lit shadows, she watched him leave, and then turned onto her side curled into a fetal position and slept.

Two nights passed like this before Two Blankets felt the onset of her courses and entered the moon cycle hut. This was a familiar routine of cleansing, fasting, and rest for her. She was alone for two days, then joined there by Bears-Many-Children and the round-head, Wind-on-Water.

Bears-Many-Children saw her, nodded and said, "Two Blankets."

The round-head with more friendliness said, "Hello, Two Blankets."

She had never been anything but *mistshimus* to Bears-Many-Children before this, and her mouth must have fallen open, for Bears-Many-Children poked Wind-on-Water, and they both laughed.

"Your husband, Marshall, may have a *cultus wootlat,* but he is like the whiteman's gun, the revolver. He can shoot it many times," Bears-Many-Children said.

"I fear, Bears-Many-Children, that he will never understand the way of The People, either the Chinook or the *Nimi'ipuu.* He is not bad to me, but the whitemans only strive to compete, to beat one another. And always they are alone."

"These are true words, *mistshimus* Two Blankets, and The People will suffer for it, this I believe."

Wind-on-Water did not say anything. Certainly, she had never heard a title born speak to a *mistshimus* thus before.

Two days later, Marshall arrived on the steamboat *Belle*. After getting his cargo ashore—which included among the normal trade supplies a cow, two pigs, and a crate of chickens—and having his drink and a little trading with the captain, he went looking for Two Blankets. He went first to Stinging Nettle.

"I am looking for Two Blankets," Marshall said irritably. "She wastes a lot of her time here with gossiping and such women talk. Do you know where she is?"

"Friend Marshall, would you care to sit down, and I can tell you?"

"No, I do not care to sit down. Where the hell is she?"

"She is in the moon cycle hut, but you cannot go—"

Marshall stalked off before she could finish her sentence. He stormed up to the moon cycle hut. Even his anger wouldn't prompt him to go in, but he pounded on the frame of the doorway and said, "Two Blankets, come out here."

The blush of shame suffused Two Blankets's throat and face. She looked to the other women. There was no precedent for such an action by a man. She moved to the doorway. Perhaps he would just go away.

"Two Blankets. Come out here *now*, bitch."

Some underlying force of a thousand years of culture and mores filled her with a power, the shaman woman's power when her courses are upon her, and she swept the door flap open.

"It is about time you came out. I—"

"Husband Marshall, I will say this only once. What you have done violates the greatest taboo of the Chinook, the *Nimi'ipuu*, maybe every other tribe of The People. No one, not even the *Tyee* himself, would dare such a thing. If you do not go immediately without another word from this moon cycle hut, I will leave you. Without me, you will likely be expelled from the Chinook and sent as a pauper from this place."

She turned and closed the door on his bewildered face.

Marshall, for his part, walked away, looking fearful at how close he had come to losing all his dreams.

"I am deeply apologetic, Bears-Many-Children and Wind-on-Water. I do not know what to say about this *cultus* whiteman." It was the first time she realized that some part of her hated Marshall Johnston. "I would beg you not to hold it against me."

"I have met many whitemans, and there are some that understand the ways of The People. What they do not understand, they attempt to. That *cultus* man does not, and I say truly that I believe he will not."

"I am ashamed, Bears-Many-Children. As his wife, I feel I bear some responsibility. I have tried to teach him, as much as a *mistshimus* wife can instruct any person."

Bears-Many-Children moved to Two Blankets side. "This is a women's council affair, and no man can decide this. As wife of the *Tyee* and second only to Swimming Salmon among women I decree that you, *mistshimus* Two Blankets, are absolved in this matter. The shame does not lie with you, Two Blankets, but upon the man Marshall Johnston. I, Bears-Many-Children, witnessed this act and am adamant. We will speak of this no longer."

Two Blankets looked up at Bears-Many-Children. "Thank you, Bears-Many-Children," she said.

Bears-Many-Children looked upon Two Blankets and said, bemused, pulling out her pouch of beaver teeth, "Shall we play Roll the Dice?"

In another day, Two Blankets was ready to leave the moon cycle hut. Before she left, Bears-Many-Children embraced her, which made Two Blankets feel odd. Never, with the exception of Stinging Nettle and of course Standing Bear, had she felt any real closeness to any of the title born.

"We women must bear many things from the men we are bound to, Two Blankets, but there are limits. Perhaps you have met yours. I certainly would consider walking away from this *cultus* whiteman, Marshall Johnston. You may not be Chinook by birth, but I have watched you, and you are Chinook now."

"I thank you, Bears-Many-Children. I fear that the *Tyee* Running Blade will have heard of this event."

"I am certain he has. The whole camp may have heard of it by now."

"Then perhaps I should go to him first."

"A wise choice, Two Blankets. Only you can make that choice, but that would be my advice if I were asked."

"I will do that, then," said Two Blankets, and she left the moon cycle hut.

It was with apprehension that she approached the *Tyee's* longhouse. The *Tyee* was not sitting outside as he so often did, so Two Blankets gathered her courage and went within.

He was sitting in his usual place and beckoned her forward. "I have heard of a bit of noise coming from the vicinity of the moon cycle hut."

"Yes. To my great humiliation, there was. Marshall came to the hut and pounded on the door frame. I did not know what to do, so I went out to him and explained he had violated a great taboo by interrupting the women there. He seemed not to understand, or perhaps he just did not want to understand."

"I suspect it is both. The *cultus* whiteman does not, nor does he want to. He feels he is superior to the laws of the people."

"I am saddened by this, *Tyee* Running Blade. I feel as *mistshimus* and his wife that I have failed in my duty to explain it to him."

"You were not born to us, little *mistshimus*, but you have learned our ways. The Nez Perce believe much the same in this matter as I understand?" He left this last as a question.

"They do."

"So, you are not to blame, and if you decided to leave him, there would be no punishment on you. You would go back to being a common *mistshimus*, of course."

"I understand, *Tyee*. I will think on this."

"Know also that I am somewhat aware of the goings on between my son, Standing Bear, and you."

"I am shamed by this, but I do not deny it."

"Wise that you do not. If you should decide to leave Marshall Johnston, know that your relationship with Standing Bear would have to cease. I could no longer ignore it. As the wife of that *cultus* whiteman, I can ignore it and take some pleasure in doing so."

"You are generous, *Tyee*, to a *mistshimus*."

"I am not generous to you, *mistshimus*. It pleases me to allow it to continue because it is a secret aggravation to the whiteman. But know this, *mistshimus*, if the *cultus* Marshall should become aware of it because you were angry and let it slip, or merely careless, I will have to kill you and punish Standing Bear as well. As much as it would grieve me to do so, my honor and the bargain I have made with Marshall Johnston would require it. We shall talk no more of this."

"I understand and respect that honor would require that. Thank you, *Tyee* Running Blade. I shall think on this dilemma."

She left the *Tyee's* longhouse with a true dilemma on her mind. She could leave her husband and go back to her previous role of *mistshimus*. If she did, there was no doubt in her mind that she would have to give up Standing Bear completely. The *Tyee* had made that clear.

As she approached the longhouse of Marshall Johnston, which she could no longer think of as hers, she saw in the makeshift corral that Marshall had built alongside the shed several animals—a cow, two pigs, and in a separate wire enclosed area, a dozen chickens. It seemed odd to her to keep meat animals when the surrounding area provided so much, and they did not have to be fed and cared for.

She entered the longhouse to find Marshall at work stocking supplies.

"Your wife has returned, husband Marshall."

"About time, too. What was that business you gave me at the women's hut? About taboos?" His anger was starting to build.

"The *Tyee* summoned me to him. I had to explain that you did not know of the taboo, although I do not think he believed me. All the people I know of have such a taboo. He said, and forgive me for saying this, I only report to my husband what he said, he said I could leave you if I wanted and rejoin the tribe as a common *mistshimus*."

"Hah. You cannot do that." He fished in his pack and produced a piece of paper and slapped it down on the counter between them. "See that? That's a proper marriage license, stamped by the county clerk and registered. See these words here? It says Marshall Johnston, husband, and Two Blankets Johnston, wife. We are man and wife, recognized by the courts of the U. S. of A. What do you think of that?"

Two Blankets picked up the piece of paper. She could not read it, but she saw under his finger was his name a signature, and under her name an *"X."*

"What is this 'X' here?"

Marshall flustered a little. "Well, since you weren't there I put down your 'X' as your agreement."

"So, as I understand what you are saying, I have to make my mark on this paper to make it real?"

"Well, yes, technically speaking, you do."

"And did I make my mark?"

"Not actually, no."

"Is there a penalty among the whitemans for making such a mark for another person?"

"I see where you are going with this. No court is going to take an Indian's word, or a woman's, over a whiteman's."

"Here among the Chinook, none will take the word of a *cultus* whiteman over even a lowly *mistshimus* who is a member of the tribe. The *Tyee* said I could come back after your actions at the moon cycle hut. Please forgive this *mistshimus* when she says he seemed almost to look forward to the day. That would be when you would be required to leave and trade no more among the Chinook. And believe me when I say this, word would be passed along to other Chinook clans. It might be that few or none would trade with you."

"Dammit, you are *my* wife. You can't do this."

"I can do it," Two Blankets said, her back straight. "I am willing to remain your wife, husband Marshall, and cook your meals, clean for you, and warm your sleeping furs, but you must promise me one thing on whatever honor you hold dear."

"And what would that be?"

"You must honor your vows to be a Chinook. You must pay the respect due from you, give your share to the tribe, and respect the taboos. If you accept that, then I will stay with you. If you cannot, then you must bear your shame alone. I will no longer continue to be humiliated by a man who does not respect our traditions."

"So," Marshall said, as cunning lit his eyes, "if I agree to respect the tribe, generally speaking, you will be my wife? And you will accept this mark as your own?" He pointed to the paper.

Two Blankets took a deep breath. This man was a devil, and she knew she was making a deal with one, but she could not give up what she had with Standing Bear to return to *mistshimus* life. That would truly break her.

"On my honor as a *Nimi'ipuu* and as a Chinook, I will."

"Good. We are in agreement then. I'll drink to that. And then you can warm my furs because I have missed that mouth of yours and your little cunny as well." He grasped her between the legs and leered into her eyes.

SCHEMES, TIME, AND THE TREATY OF TEARS

CHAPTER 16
JANUARY, 1855 TO JULY, 1855

FOR SOME ODD reason, Marshall was extremely happy and industrious over the next several months. He made no more attempts on the moon cycle hut and seemed to take his vow to honor the Chinook way seriously. Trade with the band had dropped almost to nothing for the month or two following his almost fatal error in judgment, but it gradually built back up with his apparent efforts. The two steamboats making the run to the Cascades stopped more frequently and not always because Marshall had cargo delivered. The men who came were like the men who had stopped on the *Petonia*, but frequently of a slightly richer class of trader. They stopped for the whiskey and companionship, and usually left with trade goods.

Two Blankets learned how to milk the cow and feed the pigs and chickens. Marshall was happy to have milk, which seemed disgusting to Two Blankets, and chicken eggs, which she was surprised that she was beginning to look forward to. Perhaps, whiteman's strange habits were not all bad after all.

In the meantime, over the months that preceded the summer of 1855, the mood of *Tyee* Running Blade and some of the other elders became increasingly more somber. The whispered talk was always out of earshot of Two Blankets, and even in the moon cycle hut, either the women she met did not know, or they refused to talk about it.

Marshall had asked for, and received, the *Tyee's* disgruntled permission to take the little-used longhouse just on the other side of the midden pile. This was a big trade apparently, because Marshall's stock of metal goods, beads, and tools diminished sharply upon the conclusion of their agreement. It was a strange trade, because a small group of eight or ten individuals had to make their accommodation now in the *Tyee's* longhouse. Not that his longhouse wasn't large enough. At one time, it might have held a hundred and fifty Chinook easily. But why make such a trade? And for the benefit of just one man and his wife? It just didn't make sense, at least not to begin with.

Marshall immediately set to work modifying the longhouse to his purposes, raising shelves for trading stock and shifting some of his bulkier stock into this longhouse. All of his untanned hides went there as well, which uncluttered the Johnston's Landing longhouse to a considerable degree. Johnston's Landing became more "genteel" without all the raw hides and Marshall's tools stacked about.

Marshall still demanded Two Blankets warm his furs and his other parts. He liked what she had learned to do for him, but was increasingly frustrated that she did not give him a child. Of course, she could not admit she was still taking the herbs or that she made sure he took his without his knowledge. She would not stop those. He might become increasingly frustrated, but she lived a life of fear that she would catch a child from him.

She and Standing Bear had the opportunity to meet twice just for a quick and fevered union of bodies in the woods behind the village. The time stolen may have only been an hour or two for each meeting, but for that hour they were alone in a world of their own making, a world constrained only by their passion.

They also had one short time together when Marshall made another trip to Portland. It was toward June of 1855, and he was gone for four days. He was excited to be going and mentioned meeting two whitemans named Joel Palmer and Mr. Metcalfe, an Indian Agent. At the time, it didn't make much sense to Two Blankets. It only began to make sense a couple months later.

For four days and four nights Marshall was gone, Standing Bear and Two Blankets met in an almost continual passionate embrace. This time they were together long enough to talk a bit.

"I do not know why, but Marshall is excited about meeting Joel Palmer and Mr. Metcalfe in Portland. It must have to do with his trade business, but Marshall has never been this way before," Two Blankets said during one interval as he held her close, lying tucked in the crook of his arm.

"The elders do not speak with me, but there is much negotiation with the whitemans going on at The Dalles," Standing Bear said. "Each time they go to negotiate, my father returns more disgruntled. He is truly saddened."

"Mayhap it will not affect us," she said.

"I think that will prove not to be true, Two Blankets."

"I agree. It is like seeing a massive winter storm brewing over the *Nch'i-wána*, and the wind is blowing downriver. You can hope it doesn't catch you crossing the river in your canoe, but you had better paddle fast."

"I am afraid we will not be able to paddle fast enough to avoid this storm, Two Blankets. Not nearly fast enough."

"Hold me fast then, dear Standing Bear, and make me forget that a storm is coming."

He bent to kiss her and soon they were moving together in that dance of bodies older than words. To Two Blankets it was very sad and very sweet, and she relished both feelings, for both made her feel quite alive. They only had four nights together, and she meant to feel quite alive as much as possible.

As she walked the camp during the day, she was certain that virtually everyone knew of how she and Standing Bear spent their nights. No one would tell, of that she was equally certain. Although she was *mistshimus*, she seemed to enjoy some strangely elevated status. This status was directly related to the love she and Standing Bear shared and the fact that they were doing it under the cultus whiteman Marshall Johnston's nose.

In April of 1855, there were four births celebrated, all within days. To anyone counting, they all led back to one date, the Great Hunt and Blood Feast of the previous year. Within the tribe, no one seemed to care who the fathers were. The births of four new members in a group of eighty-seven was a huge cause for celebration. Among those four births was the child of Swimming Salmon. Though she had gone through childbirth before, and following children were supposed to be easier. Swimming Salmon was old as such things were counted, in the gray of her hair and the wrinkles of experience she wore on her face. It was a hard labor, and the whole tribe held its breath.

One of the reasons that breath was momentarily suppressed was the curiosity of whether the baby might be of Marshall's siring. He was nervous about that possibility, though Two Blankets did not understand why. The baby would belong to the mother. That made sense to anyone with any sense at all. The father only provided the seed, and any seed would do to start a plant growing. It was the watering and feeding of the child within the mother's belly that determined the outcome of the child. It was the mother's spirit that guided the new life into the world and her breast upon which the child would suckle.

Her labor was hard and long. A patient woman, in her way, was Swimming Salmon, but her patience was wearing thin. Finally, in the early hours just before dawn, the contractions began to come in earnest. The child was positioned correctly as determined by Stinging Nettle. There should be no problems. Swimming Salmon bore onward now with the determination of a spring flood. The child emerged, and she collapsed from her squatting position onto the floor.

As the cord pulsed its final life into the child, Stinging Nettle held her up for all to see. A beautiful baby girl, as beautiful as babies covered in birth-blood can be. She had a voice to her as well, which she used to let everyone witnessing know how displeased she was to be passed into this cold world after spending nine months in the warm vitreous fluid within Swimming Salmon's body.

"A fine voice she has," said Swimming Salmon and no one present could disagree.

When the cord went slack, Swimming Salmon bit it off and tied it. The afterbirth followed shortly and was gathered up for her later. She held the new child to her breast and began to lick her clean just as a cat would. The baby pursed her lips and began to suckle on Swimming Salmon's nipple. Her breasts, a year ago slack and sagging, were now full of milk. Swimming Salmon smiled, exhausted.

"I did not think to feel this again. It has been years since the birth of my son who died. I am pleased and satisfied," she said.

All who looked upon the baby also noted, perhaps to their relief though none would admit to such belief, that there was no *cultus* whiteman in this child. Nothing was certain, of course, but all there felt it.

When Two Blankets carried the news to Marshall, he seemed relieved on the surface. He knew he didn't want a baby in this way, one who belonged to the woman who bore the child. Most certainly, he did not want to be responsible for Swimming Salmon's child, the wife of the *Tyee*. He had not tried very hard to understand the Chinook's apparent lack of concern over paternity.

"It's just downright strange, close to damn obscene, that you people don't care who the father is. It's unnatural," Marshall said.

"Ah, husband, The People, and I mean the Chinook, the Wasco, the Cayuse, the Nez Perce, all The People I can think of, think this whiteman's obsession over who the father may be to be both a fruitless question and a demented one. It is obvious to us it is the woman's child. You will never know for certain whose child your wife carries when she gives you one."

"I would know. I still say it's damn unnatural." Under the surface of his relief was a strange undercurrent of unhappiness.

Did he want the child to be his in some odd way? Would that have proved something for him? That he was a man and could father a child?

———————

AS THE EARLY summer progressed, there were increasing visits to The Dalles by *Tyee* Running Blade. Though it was not uncommon for him to go to The Dalles to inspect and participate in the tribe's fishing, these trips seemed different. Each time he returned, he met with the elders who had remained in the village. Two Blankets was not privy to these conversations, of course, but even she could sense the seriousness. The large influx of whitemans along the river and through the Cascades over the past year, and the building of four new steamboats to serve between the Cascades and the forty or so miles upstream to The Dalles, were proof enough of the diminishment of importance of the Chinook, the Wasco, and Wishram along this stretch of the river.

Two Blankets heard talk of similar displacements of natives downriver, along the Willamette upstream from Portland and all the way to the mouth of the great *Nch'i-wána* where it flowed its life into the ocean. Though such stories were rarer, they did filter into campfire talk in the evenings of even the fierce Makah tribe being forced to treat with the United States Government. Everywhere, it seemed to be happening at an increasing pace. The People, weakened by whiteman's disease, were giving way to the increasing flood of whitemans.

In the meantime, Marshall seemed to be growing larger, to be taking up more space. He contained his exuberance when the *Tyee* or other tribal members were present, and merely looked sympathetic to their questions and talk, but with Two Blankets he was not so self-contained. In fact, if anything, he was more confident and even gloated upon occasion.

"I have been telling you, Two Blankets, of the power of the white man against your pitiful people. You do not use the land to great purpose, only to make a few individuals, like the title born, rich. Our way is going to prove itself superior, you mark my words."

He took a drink. He was drinking a fancier whiskey now. Two Blankets couldn't tell one whiskey from another by look or taste, but she could see that these bottles were more finely made.

These whitemans are like grasshoppers. They consume everything in their path, and only the seagulls can stop them.

No gulls came to eat these grasshoppers, only more and more whitemans.

"I tell you, Two Blankets, I will be proved the better trader. The *Tyee* has made of me a fool, and I have had to grovel for what I have earned, but in the end, I shall have it all." He took another long drink and another.

Two Blankets worked silently. She had learned that quiet was the best approach when Marshall was drinking. A few times she had ventured a different opinion and received a bruise as payment. She knew if she just quietly went about her business, he would soon drink himself into a stupor.

She would have peace for a time. This was a more difficult payment to make for her occasional meetings with Standing Bear than was the mating with this man.

It is odd that I feel this way. Truly, the mating is not pleasant or fine as it is with Standing Bear, but it is no more difficult for me than gutting and cleaning salmon. What is hard is listening to his talk. The mating I can forget almost immediately. The talk haunts me.

On July 25, 1855, many elders of the tribe gathered together on the beach. They all wore their finest beads and cloaks. Their hair shone, newly woven with beads and shells. Armbands of both shell and metal bedecked both man and woman. It was a solemn and sad procession to the *Tyee's* canoe, a procession of fourteen elders and twenty of the best round-head paddlers in the tribe. *Tyee* Running Blade stood and addressed the Bent Creek Clan of Chinook.

Two Blankets, being *mistshimus,* stood near the back. Even Marshall took time off from his busy "trading work" to listen to the *Tyee* speak. For him, it seemed merely curiosity at how the *Tyee* would handle this situation, or perhaps it was his secret gloating that drove his motivation. In either case, he was there.

"My people, my Bent Creek Clan of the great Chinook, today I go with the elders of the tribe on a sad mission. For tens of years, we have suffered under the onslaught of the whitemans. First, it was his disease that weakened us and took four of every five of us away from this world along the *Wimahl,* the Great River. Many of you do not remember those dark days, but many still live with the memory of those days and with the spirits of those taken. Once we were a mighty People, and this village alone supported two hundreds of The People. Another village, only slightly smaller upriver had one hundred and fifty. Downriver, a third village held a hundred. After the *cultus* disease had spent itself, there were only eighty some people left, and they all came to live with us. We welcomed them, and we survived.

"There were few whitemans upon the *Wimahl* at that time. Now we are diminished, and they are like the swarms of the locust and cannot be stopped. We go now to sign a treaty with them to preserve what we can. It is all we can do now. We will speak more on this and explain this agreement upon our return." He signaled his paddlers, and they began stroking the waters of the *Wimahl* in cadence. With *Tyee* Running Blade standing proud and straight in the bow of his brightly-painted canoe, they moved off into the distance upriver. Only those who were near him could see the tears running from his eyes.

Two Blankets returned to the longhouse she shared with Marshall with not just her personal tears, but also the tears of a people and a culture displaced streaming her face.

"I told you it was coming," Marshall said. "I told you."

"Forgive me, husband, but shut your fucking mouth."

Marshall's backhand caught her across the cheek and knocked her down.

Two Blankets got herself up and took a moment to regain her balance. She picked up a hunting knife off the table that she had been using to cut up vegetables for the evening's meal.

"If you strike me again like that," she said, "hope that you kill me. For if you do not, I shall cut off those useless testicles and that *cultus wootlat* of yours and make you eat them for your supper. To take joy in the slaughter of an enemy, when you have done nothing, is not honorable for a warrior. But I have married no warrior, only a *cultus* whiteman."

Marshall looked at her aghast. This was not a Two Blankets he was used to or knew how to handle.

"I am going to the *Tyee's* longhouse to await his return. I do not think this would be a good time for you to be anywhere near there." She swept out the door.

A handful of days later, the *Tyee* returned. All greeted him on the bank, but he signaled silence and proceeded to his longhouse. The rest of the Bent Creek Clan followed in subdued silence.

Two Blankets entered the longhouse, a part of this saddened gathering, near the end of those crowding in. Marshall was there as well, but when he made to enter his way was barred by two warriors.

"Why can't I enter? This meeting of your people affects me, too."

"You are no Chinook. You are not even of The People. You wait outside."

Two Blankets turned back and saw the argument and turned away.

Marshall did not belong here. Her admittance to the gathering was not disputed. To them, she was Chinook.

When the last had entered, the door flap was closed, and the two warriors stood one to each side of the doorway.

I do not think Marshall will attempt entry, not into the mood of this gathering. He will be angry later, and I will pay for it. Even this knowledge was not enough to make her question her decision to stay and listen to the *Tyee*. This was her place, and in her place she would remain.

The *Tyee* strode to his usual spot and turned to face his people. "My people, we have returned with this document that we have put our marks to. This document, the whitemans call a treaty. In truth, there was not much to treat about. The whitemans stated their terms, and all we could do was agree and dispute the small points. We have tried, along with the other tribes on the treaty, to protect as much of our life as we could. Now, we are so weakened and small, and the whitemans are strong and many, I fear we have given away the blood of our clan and received only water in return."

The subdued clan looked to each other for comfort or understanding, but finding none, returned their attention to the *Tyee*.

"I was not alone in voicing my disappointment with this 'treaty' document, this Treaty with the Tribes of Middle Oregon 1855, as the whitemans name it. It is an agreement, a barter if you will, between the tribes and the United States of America, which they say will last for eternity. In this, I would believe brother Coyote the Trickster before I would believe these *cultus* whitemans.

"There are many provisions within this 'treaty' with the whitemans, and I will tell you of these," *Tyee* Running Blade's voice faltered. "Please, excuse me," he said in uncharacteristic earnestness, "I will speak as a friend to a friend, a father to a son, not as *Tyee*. I cannot speak of this as *Tyee*. This *cultus* whiteman's paper demands that we give up our life on the Great River *Wimahl* where we have lived for tens of tens of summers and move to a reservation along the Deschutes River. We are giving up fifteen thousand square miles of their measurement for one thousand square miles.

"I know these are whiteman's measurements, but even if you do not know what a square mile is, or cannot imagine a thousand, every trader knows what an exchange of fifteen for one is."

"A bad trade," came the voice of a young warrior.

"In that, young Fire Stick, I would agree with you. A very bad trade."

"We should fight," said Fire Stick.

Several of the other young warriors agreed.

"I do not disagree with the warrior's way. I would not forbid it or punish any who chose that path. Just know this. If you fight, you will die. We have all seen the guns and cannons of the whiteman's military and seen their numbers. If you go to fight them, we will honor your deaths at the campfires at Warm Springs. Your bodies shall be placed in canoes of great size and raised above the ground upon posts. You may be sure that your wives will be cared for and married to your brothers if they exist. If they do not, still, they will be cared for as if you were still alive. Your children will know that you died to protect our way of life."

"Thank you, *Tyee*," Fire Stick said. Others chimed in with agreement.

"Where shall we live at Warm Springs? There are few forests thereabouts. What shall we do for a longhouse? Or food for our children? Where will we fish?" There were many such questions. The very idea of moving from the Great River some distance up the Deschutes River was hard for anyone there to imagine.

The *Tyee* appeared wearied, but he still stood erect. "This paper says we will have the rights to travel from Warm Springs to the *Wimahl* and Celilo Falls to fish as we have always done. This was something we fought to get included." This statement provoked some encouragement among those gathered.

"As to how we shall house The People, the whitemans seem to know little of the way we live. They propose to build houses for us at Warm Springs, one house for each family. This is the whitemans way of living—a separate house for each family group."

"Maybe after they build all these houses we could tear them down and build a longhouse, a proper place to live," one man said. This was met with laughter as they imagined the look on the *cultus* whiteman's faces as the newly-built houses were torn down by their prospective tenants.

"Perhaps we may do that," Running Blade said a slight smile on his face. "I should like to see Joel Palmer or Mister Metcalfe as we did that. They propose to build for us a grist mill, a blacksmith shop, a wagon, and plowshares shop, a school, and a hospital, and to staff them for a time. All to the effect of teaching us to be whitemans."

"They would have us be farmers?" an unbelieving voice asked.

"This they will do, they say as well, they will pay us certain monies and grant land based upon each family's size to farm. Please excuse me, my people." The *Tyee* Running Blade sat, his face drained of its natural vigor. He continued, his low voice trembling with the effort. "I know I have failed the Bent Creek Clan, my people, the Chinook. I did the best I could to bargain with what I had. We all did." Here he gestured to the other elders present. "We fought hard for every point, and yet, we have still made a bad trade. Other tribes have fought and been crushed or forced to relocate a thousand miles away. It is with tears in my eyes and shame in my heart that in a year's time, when we have prepared, I shall go to Warm Springs and struggle to keep alive what we can of the Chinook People. That is all your *Tyee* Running Blade has to say."

THE CANOES
OF DEATH

CHAPTER 17
AUGUST, 1855 TO OCTOBER, 1855

THE NEXT SEVERAL months were a strange time for the Chinook and for Two Blankets. The Chinook must continue their way of life to continue living. There was no escaping that. That meant the remainder of the summer and the fall salmon runs. That meant the drying and pounding of the salmon into *ch-lai*. It meant continued hunting for elk and venison as well as the collecting of the camas root, another staple of the tribe. The list, if such you could call it, was endless, and to omit a part of it would be like omitting a part of life as well as to risk the tribe's existence over the coming winter. They survived by hunting and gathering, and none of that could be skipped just because, within a year, they would all move to a new area and have to start life anew. Certain things they could cut back on, and these they did.

The tanning of hides, for example, could be deferred. The Chinook had an immense supply of partially-tanned hides bundled and hanging from the rafters of the longhouse. They had, as well, a large number of hides from the Great Hunt that were only scraped and were drying in the longhouse. These would keep, and the tribe could resume tanning them after the move. That, in itself, left a hole in their lives. Some, like Fox Tail, were expert at tanning, perhaps not so good at other things. Fox Tail was amenable to doing whatever must be done, but it hurt her and her esteem that she could not do what she was best at.

Stinging Nettle, on the other hand, had to gather additional supplies of herbs, barks, and roots for her craft. She did not know when, or if, she would be able to return to the traditional places where she and her forebears had gathered back through the centuries. So, she kept busy, and she kept Two Blankets busy as well. Almost every day, they were about with digging tool, or bark stripper and collection basket, trying to gather at least a three-year supply in just a season. Fox Tail, the Two Spirits, often went with them on such ventures, both as the protection of a warrior as well as a competent gatherer herself. Two Blankets liked her company and took joy in her ability and soft humor.

"How is your family, Fox Tail? Fire Stick and Sweet-Pollen-Flower and the baby?"

"They are the joy of my life. It is odd how such things work. Fire Stick has been my friend since we were just boys together. We played at being warriors and other games as well. Fire Stick could always beat me at all the warrior games. He is a natural born man and warrior too. I am proud of him. He always used to tease me endlessly about everything. As boys, it was about the games we played. Later it was about the girls."

Two Blankets laughed easy in Fox Tail's company. "I remember some of the comments he made."

"But always, he was kind to me as well," Fox Tail said. "Always there was a bond between us. Now that bond is complete with him and Sweet-Pollen-Flower. It is a bittersweet bond between us though."

Two Blankets didn't mean to pry, but they were talking as two women might. As two women, she was allowed if she were sensitive. "Forgive me if I am intrusive, Fox Tail, but why would it be bittersweet?"

Fox Tail turned eyes toward Two Blankets. Her eyes were large and soft, and Two Blankets could see pain there. "It is his insistence that we fight the whitemans. He obsesses over it, and I know it is the warrior's way for him to do that. Truly I do. Sweet-Pollen-Flower as well. We are both proud of our warrior husband. But it makes us fearful, as well. The chance of him dying in a futile effort to get some kind of justice from the whitemans makes us both cry. We keep it from him, of course. He is our warrior, and we are so proud of him. That does not stop us from being sad at the thought of losing him forever."

Two Blankets turned to Fox Tail and put her arms around her. They stood that way for some time just holding each other. "It is always a woman's burden to bear the weight of her warrior husband's pride. It is how we honor him, but it does not make it any easier to know that."

"No, it doesn't," Fox Tail said. "But having another woman say that does help. For that, I thank you."

One of the great questions raised at the "Treaty" meeting at the longhouse was "What of our dead?" This was a question not so easily answered. For a people who had inhabited an area as the Chinook had for ten thousand years, and certainly as a tribe as currently identified as Chinook for at least a thousand years, ten lifetimes for a very old man of one hundred, or twenty for the *Tyee*, there seemed to be no simple answer. Would the dead, who had been raised into the trees in a nearby forest to rest in ceremonial canoes for an eternity, understand? Did they care, or were they too involved in other things more important to their current state to care about the living left behind? There was no question in any Chinook's mind, or in Two Blanket's, as a Chinook and Nez Perce, that they were there.

To the living, the spirit realm was as real as the one that provided the salmon for their daily life. It flowed like the river over them and their every activity. The prayers offered to the elk or rabbit they killed for food were not just a meaningless ritual to them. They believed that the spirit of the animal would hear such a prayer if earnestly offered, and believed it to their bones. If cast off perfunctorily, then such prayer would fall far short, and only evil could come from the taking of a life without the proper supplication and thanks.

Two Blankets, of course, had knowledge of the burial place, if such it could be called. As *mistshimus*, she had no reason to roam there, but then no round-head or even the title born wandered there without purpose. She did not understand the whiteman's "cemeteries" as Marshall had once described them. A place where people visited whenever they pleased to leave flowers on the grave of the passed. It was the whiteman's way, and she could not conceive how the dead got any rest that way with people frequently coming about and talking with them.

For the Chinook, the passing to the other realm and the care of the dead itself was a much more serious matter. Even those people disregarded or disliked in life, acquired a greater presence when they passed. Of course, this consequence did not apply to the *mistshimus*, who were routinely cast upon the midden pile or left at the edge of the forest for the scavengers. A *mistshimus* who was particularly liked might be cast into the river to be taken by its current. Once, it had been the custom to have a slave die with their master, though this had not been practiced for two or three generations even among the more traditional clans like that of *Tyee* Running Blade.

When Two Blankets had walked past the sacred grove on the few times she had errands or gathering, she had felt the presence of the dead there like the susurrus of a breeze stirring cool on a heated day. There was calm within the grove. Not that it wasn't inhabited by the normal creatures that commonly lived in such places, for it was. Everyone knew that the forest creatures lived already in harmony with the Earth Mother and thus would pay no attention to the spirits of the dead.

Along the edges of the grove, as Two Blankets looked in, she could see the canoes both of the greatest size, those of past *Tyees*, to the smallest, some as small as a child. Many of the nearer ones were painted in bright colors and those deeper within the grove evidenced by the faded colors of age. The canoes were raised up into the trees and rested there in the forks or were supported by four large posts of cedar. All she could see had been raised in an earnest sense of seriousness for death was not a casual thing to the Chinook.

All this had been talked about at the "Treaty" meeting at some length, and apparently much more among the various elders once the decision to accept the whiteman's treaty had been made. She had not been privy to these meetings at all, but the talk after the "Treaty" meeting was more general, and she was a good listener.

"What do we do with our ancestors?" Swimming Salmon had asked. "I do not know, and I do not know how to discover what they would wish, other than that they would prefer not to be disturbed by queries from the world of the *Wimahl*."

"What do the *shamans* say?" asked Stinging Nettle. "Those who walk freely in the sacred grove and sometimes speak with the departed."

Bone Rattler shook her staff of bones. All talk ceased, and a respectful silence fell upon the women. "I have walked among the dead many times these past several weeks with that very question in front of me," she said. "In truth, little beyond this has occupied me lately. I feel we must care for the dead as they wish and each time I go there, I fast and go to the sweat lodge to purify myself of all but this question."

All nodded to the ancient, for Bone Rattler was the oldest of them all, and although she came to them from a clan gathered in after the whiteman's cursed disease had left them reeling and wasted, she had always been true.

"The question I carried was this. 'We must leave this place soon. Would you prefer to stay here where you have been for centuries and grown into the trees, even into the land itself? A place so steeped in the dead it is sacred beyond all others? We cannot come to see you anymore, and no new dead shall come. Or should we try to take you with us to this new place and honor you there in a place of virgin ground?' Mind you, I did not ask the question as I have told it to you. That cannot be done with the spirits. I can only say one must hold the question firmly in mind and listen."

"Did the spirits reply?" asked Bears-Many-Children, the question on all the women's minds.

"Patience, Bears-Many-Children. I have been to the Sacred Grove during each phase of the moon. I have gone five times, five being a sacred number. Each time I have fasted and cleansed myself to the best of my ability. Truth to tell, it may be that this question is one that has no great answer. The spirts seemed confused by the mere asking of it, as if they could not conceive of a situation where we, the living, would have to leave them. I fear I have failed, and yet I have tried with everything I have in me." Bone Rattler slumped from her rigid posture and wept.

This alone was such a strange visage. No one there could ever remember seeing Bone Rattler weep.

But then, no one there had ever been in this position before.

Late in the fall, a Chinook did die, and the question was raised again. This time the death was of a child, not a newborn, as newborn deaths were not any more infrequent among the Chinook than they were among the whitemans. This was a death of a five-summer-old child and a title born as well. Her mother, Bright-Feather-Bird, wailed at the death of her child, only yesterday running and playing with the other children of the clan, now lying in a tiny canoe, as still as a flower. She looked as if she might be sleeping. She had run along the *Wimahl* and slipped and fallen into a deep spot near the bank. The water was calm there. The current had not taken her, but by the time the other children found an adult to save her, it was too late. The body lay in the pool, swirling round and round with the edge of the current, unmoving and never to move again.

"What shall I do with my little heart's blood, my Falling Flower, now? Do we take her to the Sacred Grove and let her rest among her ancestors? Or take her later to the Warm Springs place where there will be no spirits to comfort her? What do I do?" In truth, this question bothered her more than the loss of the child, which distressed her to the bone.

"For now," Bone Rattler said, "she must be set to rest here in the place her ancestors rest in and where her spirit may take comfort in their company. Next year you may decide to take her body with us on our sad journey away from our home." Bone Rattler leaned forward from the heel sitting posture and hugged Bright-Feather-Bird. "We are all at a loss here. We know not where we are going."

After the requisite days of cleansing passed, they walked as a clan toward the Sacred Grove. Two Blankets followed, as did the other *mistshimus*. They followed somewhat reluctantly at first, in quiet sadness, for in truth none had ever been allowed to venture in before. Now, it seemed, things were somewhat different. The Bent Creek Clan's imminent departure, only a few months away, made the unthinkable, thinkable. Somehow, because the clan was so threatened and so close to being torn asunder, every member of the Bent Creek Clan, even the *mistshimus*, were allowed to participate. It was as if a mother bear had been wounded and driven back into her den, her cubs behind her. She needed every ounce of her strength to fend off the attackers.

This became a matter of dispute when Two Blankets tried to explain to Marshall that she was going to be unavailable to him, both sexually and as a general cook and partner in life, for the next several days.

"Tell me again why I gotta do without my wife for five days just because some kid fell into the river," Marshall asked.

"Forgive me, husband, I will try to explain the Chinook way. A child has died. All the clan is in mourning. For three days, a sacred number of days among the Chinook, all of the clan will fast and cleanse in the sweat lodges several times. During this time, it is like the moon cycle. There is no mating. Then comes the internment in the Sacred Grove. The child will be placed in a canoe, and all in the Bent Creek Clan will shear a lock of hair. Some may cut all their hair and place it with the child's body. She will be carried into the Sacred Grove. I do not know if the *mistshimus* will be allowed to enter. Usually, we are not, but times seem different with the coming of the whitemans and the need for the Chinook to vacate the land we have held for ten hundred summers. I will return to my duties in five days."

"I still don't understand," Marshall said. His voice took on an almost childlike whine that Two Blankets had heard much of lately, often when things just didn't go the way that Marshall wanted them to. "I understand how it can be for the child's family, how sad they must be. You act like the clan is more important than your own family, than your own husband."

"Again, forgive me, I know you do not want to hear it, but the Bent Creek Clan and the Chinook tribe are more important to me than my own family. That doesn't mean I don't care. It is just a fact among the Chinook, and among the *Nimi'ipuu*, my tribe before. There is the small family, and there is tribe, the large family. We might survive the loss of the small family, but we cannot live without the larger family."

"Well, it still ain't right," Marshall said. "You people just got a backward way of looking at things. Just get on out of here then."

"Thank you, my husband."

So, the fasting and cleansing began. Bright-Feather-Bird wept and sometimes wailed at the edge of the forest, as was proper and civil. She sheared off all her hair, as did her warrior husband, and laid it into the tiny canoe. Others sheared off a forelock and placed it there, although Bright-Feather-Bird's *mistshimus* wept and shaved her hair off to the scalp and placed it there. She had been close to the child and had served Bright-Feather-Bird for many years.

The child was gowned in an almost white elk hide cape, and many dentalium shells were placed around her. Her moccasins were made with care of the same white elk hide and decorated with dentalium and finely beaded. Other gifts as well had been placed into the boat, from the simple flowers of the *mistshimus* to carved bone. There was a small carved stone statue set up in the prow. Everyone had contributed.

The clan seemed to need every member, no matter how low the status, to fend off the press of events as they swirled about the tiny boat that was born by four warriors. The procession was solemn, as if a chief were being taken up into the trees. This was not common. In the past, a child might indeed get a "burial" such as this, and still not be treated with such respect springing from the need of the Bent Creek Clan to respect its traditions.

When they got into the Sacred Grove, the brightly painted canoe was hoisted up into the fork of an old man oak tree and wedged in securely. All gave a prayer to the child's spirit. All there gave prayers to the surrounding spirits, who were so evidently there, they could almost be seen. In fact, some did claim in quiet moments to be able to see them swirling about in a many-colored haze.

At last, they were done and proceeded out of the Grove, Bright-Feather-Bird, the last in a long line of some eighty or so Chinook. When they were on the outskirts of the forest, she dropped to her knees in supplication and began her intermittent wailing. All knew this was proper, and soberly passed into the village for their own two days of recognition of a life lost.

BITTER WINTER

CHAPTER 18
OCTOBER, 1855 TO FEBRUARY, 1856

THAT WINTER, THE winter of 1855-1856, was a bitter winter, or so it seemed to Two Blankets. Perhaps it was just the looming deadline approaching ever closer at its leisurely pace that made it seem so. She did wonder why this winter seemed so harsh among all those she had spent here as *mistshimus* to the Chinook, and those she had spent in her now increasingly distant childhood as a *Nimi'ipuu*. When she compared it to previous winters, she could not pinpoint any factor that would have made it so.

Yes, it was cold, and the ground covered in ice often in the mornings, or sometimes with snow that lasted for several days. These she had experienced before. True, the *Wimahl* iced up from bank to bank during January of 1856. A few traders even walked upon the iced-up river near its entire length. The small creek that ran through their camp was frequently iced over. When the river finally cleared, and the *Fashion* and the *Belle* steamed up, they told stories of the Columbia frozen up clear to its mouth at Astoria. Again, these things had happened before. It was only a matter of extremes. The Chinook worked continually at their various communal tasks to ensure provision to the clan. Two Blankets worked along with them.

One thing that did stand out was that, although most all the tasks pursued had not changed because of their imminent departure, they were pursued with no joy. Always before, even the most onerous tasks were pursued with some kind of joy of the work. Even when the task itself, be it the endless drying and then grinding of *ch-lai* into dried salmon strips that would keep for years, or the tedious scraping of hides for tanning, brought with it a communal sense of contribution at least. Now, they were just tasks to perform, and the same tasks would await them in the morning.

Thus, a sort of depression settled over the whole tribe. They still performed each job to the best of their ability. To do otherwise was an unthinkable slap to the face of the whole clan. None would shirk their duty in this dark time. Neither did they take pleasure from it. This was a big change, for Two Blankets had seen previously the lowest *mistshimus* take inordinate pleasure in a job well performed, even though it made no difference to her station in life. A *mistshimus* was a *mistshimus*. It had always been so among the Chinook. As far as anyone knew a *mistshimus* would always remain *mistshimus* until the day she died. Her children would be *mistshimus* as well. So, it wasn't as if they were working for an improvement in their life's standing, for they were not, nor for a future that was substantially different.

But they had been working toward a definable future. True, it would be much the same as the current one. Did the *Nch'i-wána* complain because it must always rush past the same rocks along its long path to the sea? No, any could see that it did not, and so it was with the Chinook of whatever station. They took the path of Easy Water and floated upon its downstream rush along with all life.

Now their path lay to the Warm Springs Reservation. It was along a river they knew, the Deschutes River. She knew it would be drier, more of a windswept prairie than this moist river land. The forests there were different, too. First, the trees would be sparse, and second, of different varieties. It wasn't that they couldn't exist there. The Cayuse and *Nimi'ipuu* existed quite comfortably in such territory. And it wasn't unknown territory. She had passed within a day's pony ride of Warm Springs in her failed escape attempt. Even the plateau just above this village, not more than a mile away, was very similar.

But we do not live there, on the plateau. We, the Chinook, live here on the *Nch'i-wána* and have lived so for as long as anyone can remember. It is as if the Great River runs through these people's spirits and the thought of leaving makes them wither inside.

While the Chinook withered, Marshall Johnston seemed to thrive. Each day that to the clan was another expended toward their demise, was a day to Marshall closer to some undefinable great pleasure. Two Blankets did not understand.

Will not this event disrupt his life and plans as much as it does the Chinook? Why would any man take such joy at the demise of another's fortunes?

Yet, joy he did take. He met each paddle wheeler, and smaller boats as well, with the jovial tradesman's smile, with whiskey and a great shaking of hands. His trade had not actually increased as far as Two Blankets could tell. Their stock did not significantly change, but his attitude waxed with the waning of the Bent Creek Clan. Each steamship from Portland brought with it a stack of newspapers, *The Oregon Spectator, The Western Star,* and *The Oregonian.* Marshall read them all.

Two Blankets wondered at the stack and once asked Marshall about them. "I understand the idea of reading. But why do you need three newspapers from the same town, Portland? Do they not contain the same information?"

"It is something you probably cannot understand, Two Blankets," he said, for once patient and not angry with her. "Each newspaper has similar news, that much is true. What is different is how it is presented, the slant of the news."

"The slant of the news? But is not news information? And information is either true or not true, just as the *Nch'i-wána* is today frozen along its banks. There would be no point in saying it was not."

"I thought it would be a hard concept for you to grasp, living as a primitive all your life. But here is an example. *The Oregonian* reports that a new steamship is being built and will be ready for service on the Columbia by March of next year. *The Statesman* has the same story but reports that it won't be complete until June next year and that there is speculation on whether it will serve on the Columbia or is destined to go up the Willamette River. You see how the slant makes a difference?"

"As you say, husband, it must be my primitive upbringing. I cannot see how the addition of one more steamship on the Columbia or the Willamette will make a difference."

"Surely, you can see that it might make a difference in my trade here. Another steamboat means more people wanting goods, another boat stopping here at Johnston's Landing. If it goes to the Willamette, then it means more trade for those up that river."

"You are right, husband. It all means the end of The People on this Great River. The end of a great people and their way of life."

They butchered the pigs in late fall, and it seemed odd to Two Blankets that they should feed animals for several months only to butcher them when elk, deer, and other creatures waited in the forest to be taken for meat. The same situation existed with the chickens, which had now become a great flock of more than twenty individuals.

Why would a person want more eggs than he can eat? It is ever thus with the whitemans. They always want more and seem very good at finding ways to get more.

The steamboats came, and their passengers seemed to really like the eggs and the pork. There actually wasn't that great an oversupply. What they had was gone with the first two steamboats. After that, they only had the extra eggs, a couple dozen a week, and they were traded out as soon as they were laid. Marshall proceeded to get a shipment of six more pigs and two dozen more chickens, as well as half a dozen sheep.

The other thing that Two Blankets noticed, in a peripheral way, was that Marshall always seemed to have a paper written for the captain of each boat that came in. These papers appeared to be different from his usual orders, which were delivered to the captain in his tradesman manner. For these papers, Marshall always took the captain aside and delivered his reports seriously. The tone of the captain was serious as well.

Thus, it proceeded for most of that winter. Marshall was accepting of Two Blankets's efforts at whiteman's cooking. She felt she had gotten the knack of cooking biscuits, gravy, bacon, and cornmeal. She was better at traditional native cookery, but Marshall was less and less satisfied with that. It came to a point where, except for venison or elk, she cooked no more traditional dishes for him. They had a small garden alongside the longhouse where she grew potatoes, carrots, onions, and other whiteman's vegetables. The same puzzlement passed over her as she hauled water for the potatoes.

Why go to all this trouble growing these potatoes when camas root grows just for the taking? The camas root tastes much better. These potatoes are just white paste.

As winter waned and a hint of spring drifted up the *Nch'i-wána* upon the occasional warm day, the shipments to Johnston's Landing began to alter. It was as if Marshall were preparing for something different. Two Blankets could, of course, see that there would be a change. The Chinook would soon no longer be there, but she could not see what would come after that. Marshall apparently could see it coming.

One day, they received a very large shipment from the steamboat, and the unloading took an hour. Marshall was all over this shipment like a bee upon honey, shouting to be careful of this crate or that one. Finally, a great large crate was lifted, with much steam by the boat's derricks, onto the shore. The boat had to position its bow onto the shore to accomplish this feat. Fortunately, this was a sternwheeler with shallow draft, as Marshall explained once, and it was ultimately achieved to Marshall's satisfaction. The next hour was spent in the usual whiskey-induced trade that had become the hallmark of Johnston's Landing. The florid-faced captain shook Marshall's hand vigorously before leaving. With two piercing whistles, the steamboat reversed its paddlewheels and backed off the bank.

A young whiteman warrior had gotten off the boat. At least that was how Two Blankets classed him. All young men of age sixteen, with the occasional exception of Two Spirits men, were warriors to her. This man was of such an age and dressed rather shabbily in hard-worn work clothes.

"Nice squaw you got there," he eyed Two Blankets.

"She's fine, and she's mine. Keep your eyes on your work," Marshall said. Together they moved what Two Blankets surmised were the usual trade goods either to the shed near the animals, the new storehouse, or to more secure storage in their own longhouse.

Finally, they were left with two large crates and the very large crate. Two

Blankets wondered what could lie within. Marshall and the young man tried moving one of the two smaller crates, but it was too heavy. Marshall looked up to see if any help might be available from the tribe, but all were suddenly occupied elsewhere.

"Damn Chinook. When they want help, you got to help them. Part of the bargain, they say. When a man could use a little assistance himself, they're suddenly nowhere to be found. Nothing to do but unpack it and repack inside. But be careful, Joseph. Them's window glass in both these crates. You break one, it's going to cost you."

"This ain't the first box I ever unpacked in my life," Joseph said. "Just tell me where you want them."

Together they unpacked the window glass. Two Blankets knew of glass, of glass beads and the wondrous glass bottles that Marshall was so quick to throw away, and which she husbanded for her own trade, but this was sheet glass as clear as water, or at least as clear as slightly green water. It wasn't quite the crystal clear that many houses in Portland would demand, and in some, there was a slight sagging near the bottom, but it left Two Blankets with a sense of amazement. What did Marshall plan to do with all this glass? There must be a hundred sheets of it.

When the glass was packed away, Marshall pried the cover off the last huge crate. Two Blankets had not ever seen such a machine before.

"Pretty thing ain't it," Marshall said. He was like a boy with his first bow.

Two Blankets looked within the crate. She truly did not know what to say. Never had she seen such a contraption.

"Of course, it ain't put together yet. There are the bed and the motor. It's powered by steam like the steamboats. So that there is the boiler, and there's where the blade attaches."

"I ain't never seen a portable one before," Joseph said letting out a long whistle. "She'll make short work of the trees hereabouts."

Two Blankets could see all the things Marshall pointed out, but to her mind, they made no sense at all. Small machinery she could grasp with her mind if she forced it, but this was just too big and too complicated. "I see what you say, husband Marshall, but what is it?"

Marshall turned to her with pride in his eyes. "It's a steam-powered portable sawmill, that's what it is."

"It sure is, and she is a beauty," Joseph said.

"Where did you buy such a thing?"

Marshall plucked a sheet of paper from the crate. "This here steam-powered portable sawmill came all the way from Scott and Herndon, Hope Foundry in Fredericksburg, Virginia. I ordered this last August, and it had to come all the way round the Cape Horn to San Francisco by ship, up to Portland by another ship, and finally here to Johnston's Landing by steamboat."

"Pardon my ignorance, but why?" her mind was rapidly computing. So, he ordered it last year, in the dry season.

"Believe me, Two Blankets, this little baby is going to put Johnston's Landing on the map."

"What does it do?"

"It's a lumber mill. One of them cedar planks in our longhouse, it'll cut one of them in just a few minutes. Wait until I get it set up. You'll see."

Two Blankets backed away in fear—not fear of the machine. The Chinook had gotten used to the whiteman's machines. Fear of what this would mean as she imagined the forests this would consume.

Marshall and Joseph began pulling pieces out of the crate and carting them up to the side of the longhouse. Marshall surveyed the buildings that comprised his little settlement and decided that the side of the longhouse away from the view of the rest of the village made the best spot. When finally assembled, it was an impressive sight.

"Let's see what it can do," said Joseph.

"Well, we ought to try one board at least," said Marshall.

They filled the boiler with water and started a fire in the fire box. Once the fire was burning well, they added more fuel, watching the pressure gauge. When it reached the green zone, Joseph fed a log onto the bed. Cogs caught it and fed it toward the blade which Marshall engaged now. Two Blankets, alarmed by the sound, came running out of the longhouse. The machine made a huffing and clanking noise while emitting a cloud of black, sooty smoke. As the log reached the blade, a sharp screeching penetrated her ears, and she put up her hands to shut it out. She pinched her eyes shut. Even so, she still could hear the machine and smell the hot metal and the raw wood as shavings flew everywhere, covering her hair.

Others from the village came running to see what new horror Marshall Johnston had brought to their village. They stood dumbfounded as the first cut was completed. Marshall let up the lever, and the blade whined to a stop, but only for a moment. He and Joseph carried the log, now cut flat on one side, back to start the process again. Marshall adjusted the thickness to two inches and opened the steam valve again. The feed cogs clanked, and the log began its second traverse toward the saw blade. Marshall pulled down on the lever that fed power to the blade, and it whined into action once again. All those in attendance watched—the whitemans with pride in the mechanical advantage, the Chinook in shock at what this represented to their world. In five minutes, Marshall shut down the machine and examined the new plank.

"Sweet work, I'd say," Marshall said.

"I'll say," said Joseph. "How much labor that save you?"

"Well, a plank like this for one man would take at least an hour, maybe two with a long saw. Especially for the first one, it needing two cuts. Two men with a pit saw could do it faster, but this steam powered saw would still beat them six or seven times."

"Should we cut another one?" asked Joseph.

"Well, I don't see any reason why not. We got a nice head of steam going," Marshall indicated the little steam engine and boiler with its brass-trimmed smoke stack, from which a steady stream of smoke emerged to drift downriver toward the rest of the village.

"Marshall, please," Two Blankets said.

"What's that, Two Blankets?"

"Look at the people from the village," she said. She indicated them as surreptitiously as possible.

Marshall turned to look for the first time. The Chinook were squinting against the acrid smoke, but the look on their faces was no longer one of awe. It was rapidly turning to anger. Marshall had seen that look before in Missouri and on the trail west, as well as a few times in Portland. This was a mob building. He quickly moved to shut down the machine, a noisy process in itself since it involved the release of a large amount of steam. Finally, the smoke began to diminish.

Marshall moved before the Chinook. "I am sorry. We didn't mean to disturb the village. Please accept this whiteman's apology."

The crowd began to back away, although Two Blankets could hear the occasional *"cultus* whiteman" and *"cultus wootlat"* comment drift her way. The breeze broke up the smoke, and a confrontation, possibly a violent one, had been avoided.

"Husband Marshall, I do not know what you plan for this machine, but I would suggest waiting until the clan moves before starting it again."

"You may be right on that count," Marshall said, wiping the sweat and shavings from his brow.

"It reminds them so very much of what they are losing and what the whitemans are taking. You do not want them, especially the young warriors, thinking of you that way."

"Let's tarp this mill, Joseph, and tie the tarp down good against the wind," Marshall said. "The more it's hid away from the Chinook, the better."

SUSPICION
OF MARSHALL

CHAPTER 19
FEBRUARY, 1856 TO MARCH, 1856

A FTER THE EVENT with the Hope Foundry Steam Powered Portable Sawmill in February, there was no more trade with the Chinook. Marshall had never been really trusted, but quite a number of the Bent Creek Clan had come to trade with him nonetheless. As was said among the Chinook, "You do not have to trust a man to trade with him. If you do, you are a poor trader."

It was more than lack of trust now. They eyed him with suspicion. Two Blankets noticed that the practice of dumping refuse in the midden pile had changed. She was sure no order had gone out but noticed a new small midden pile growing on the other side of the village. So, they would even prefer dumping the refuse somewhere else rather than cross into "Marshall's territory." This saddened Two Blankets, but there was nothing to be done about it at this late date. All she could do was to attempt to diminish its impact.

"So, I notice that none of your damned Chinook will come here to trade no more," Marshall said one evening, half drunk. "Is what I get. Try to give them good trades, and they spit in a man's face."

Two Blankets did not know if there were any point in trying to mediate the growing crisis, but she had to try. "Husband Marshall, I know I speak from ignorance compared to my warrior husband's knowledge of trade, but—"

"Damn right you do. What do women, especially Indian women," he paused to take a deep swallow of whiskey, "know about trade?"

"You are correct, of course. They do not trade with you because they do not trust you."

"What does trust have to do with it? Trade is about getting the best bargain."

"If you do not trust the man, you will not trust the trade. Your trades with them have been fair. No one contests that. They do not trust you, the man."

"That don't make no sense at all."

"That may be, husband Marshall, but it is truth."

Items began to go missing around Marshall's Landing during the next month. Nothing was stolen that was large enough to be noticed particularly. For example, one morning Two Blankets went out to collect the eggs from the flock of forty-odd chickens. On a normal day, she might expect thirty eggs. On this day, there were only a dozen, on the next, sixteen. She knew that the clan would not be stealing them to eat. They were counting coup in the way they knew how.

When she went into the storehouse puzzling this question over in her mind, she noticed two bundles of hides missing from high in the back of the longhouse.

I wouldn't even have noticed had I not been thinking of the eggs. Of course, it could just be boys challenging each other to see if they could get away with such a thing but stealing from the clan was a serious offense. A dozen eggs were one thing, a dozen hides quite another. It means that they do not think of him as Chinook any longer. If he is only whitemans, he is a target now—not an ally or possible friend.

She hoped it would not affect her relationship with the tribe. Marshall's foolishness was his own, and she would not tell him what she had discovered. She had worked hard, to be honest, and true to these people. Even though they were her captors, she had acted with honor and gradually that honor had returned to her, first from Stinging Nettle, then Standing Bear, even the *Tyee* himself. That respect she would fight for.

"May the river flow through your life," Stinging Nettle greeted Two Blankets when she next arrived to do her share of work. "You appear distressed, Nika."

"I greet you humbly, Stinging Nettle, but with gladness in my heart,"

Two Blankets said. "I am distressed, but this *mistshimus's* problems are not yours to bear."

Stinging Nettle poured some blackberry leaf tea for both of them into carved wooden cups. "I do not offer to bear them, only to listen, Nika."

Two Blankets took the cup and breathed in the fumes. "Breathing in the blackberry reminds me of when we collected these leaves."

Stinging Nettle wafted the fumes into her nostrils. "Yes, I can smell those afternoons as well. There is a happy smell to them. Remember the fox we flushed from the blackberry bush? He surprised me so, I dropped my basket and fell on my rump."

They laughed together. "If Brother Fox held a basket, he would have dropped it, as well," Two Blankets said. "His eyes were as big with surprise as yours were. Blackberry leaf has many medicinal uses. Do you have problems you drink it for?"

"No, Two Blankets, I am fine. Today I drink it just for the taste and the fond memories."

"That simple memory has eased my mind a bit."

"Tell me now, *mistshimus*," Stinging Nettle said in a severe tone, "what bothers you?"

"I shall tell you as *mistshimus*. Thank you. It is my *cultus* whiteman husband. His thoughtless actions are drawing the Chinook to steal from him. Since the day he put fire to the smoke-belching ear-splitting saw, they refuse to trade with him."

"You would not have to be a bird to hear that rumor coming."

"No, of course. I tried to explain why to him, but I think he does not want to understand."

"Or so the bird tells me, he does understand what he does and simply does not care?"

"So, I believe," Two Blankets said, sipping her tea. "He does not care, and so, the people begin to steal from him. Small things mostly, like the eggs from his chickens, but I noticed two bundles of hides missing from his stores, as well."

"That is something the bird did not tell me. But I understand it."

"I, as well. I will say nothing to him of it. Even I have lost all trust in the man, and he is husband to me."

"Ah," Stinging Nettle said. "It is a difficult path you have chosen, Nika. It is your presence alone that is keeping the clan from burning him out."

"Do they blame me, Stinging Nettle?" Two Blankets asked in some fear. "I would not blame them, but truly I do not share his views."

"No. You would hear if they did. We Chinook are nothing if not direct in our complaints."

"Thank you, Stinging Nettle, for that."

It was not long into the month of March before Marshall began noticing little things missing, as well. A spade that he had left out overnight at the animal pen was missing the next morning. A few days later, a chicken was taken. True, it could have been taken by a fox, the pen was not that secure, but his suspicions were aroused.

Over his breakfast of bacon, three eggs cooked over easy, pan cooked biscuits and gravy, he said as if it were no account, "Chicken went missing during the night."

Two Blankets looked up from her toasting of camas cakes, feeling still restricted in her dress. "A chicken missing? Was it a fox?"

"I don't think so. No tracks or digging." He shoveled half an egg into his mouth. "You are getting pretty good at cooking these eggs."

"That is strange, husband Marshall."

"Yes. Only tracks I could see, and that soil by the pen don't take tracks too well, was bare feet and moccasins. Besides my own boot tracks."

Two Blankets could sense Marshall circling. This was his way to distract through casual conversation while he circled his prey, tightening his argument.

"I do not know," she said. This part was true. She did not. She had to be careful because Marshall had almost a sixth sense for lies. He sniffed around them, gnawed them like a bone, and wouldn't give them up. It was part of what made him a good trader, at least by whiteman's standards. "Was the gate open?"

"It weren't latched down proper. But kind of hard to see a chicken pushing out of there. You've been careful closing it, ain't you?"

"Yes, husband Marshall. I admit I have forgotten to latch it a couple of times, but I always close it firmly when I go to collect the eggs."

Marshall mopped up the yolk with a biscuit and popped it into his mouth. "Well, like as not it just got out and now is in the fox's belly," he said chewing and speaking through the biscuit. Though she did not see it, for she was still deliberately occupied with her camas cakes at the fire pit, she felt him turn toward her. She could envision his appraising look. "That's another strange thing." He left the words hanging.

Two Blankets knew he was awaiting a response. She sensed the quiver of the noose of the trap closing. "What is that, husband Marshall?" She looked up at him with no guile showing in her eyes.

Two can play at this trading game. The one advantage I have is that he thinks me stupid and unaware.

Marshall lifted a forkful of biscuit and gravy to his lips and paused with it before continuing, "Have you noticed the egg count's down of late?" The food passed his lips.

"I have seen that, husband Marshall." She got up and fetched a piece of paper from the stack neighboring his record ledger. Handing it to Marshall, she said, "I cannot make numbers like you can, but I have made a count every day and marked it as you taught me, four downward marks crossed by a fifth one for five."

He looked at the sheet and frowned. "This shows lower counts for most days of the last two weeks or so. Why didn't you bring this to my attention?"

Two Blankets eased back to the fire pit to turn her camas cakes. "I am not a sharp trader like you, husband Marshall. Not even like the Chinook. It is not in my blood. I just feed the chickens and collect the eggs. I make the little marks on the paper and put the paper where you said so you could see it."

"This is very suspicious," Marshall said eyeing the paper calculating his loss or the dates it started, Two Blankets could not tell.

"Do chickens have a time when they do not lay much?" she asked, munching down on a camas cake and piece of bacon. "One thing, husband Marshall, I do not like your whiteman's food any more than you like much of the food of The People, but I do like this bacon."

"I don't think so. This all started just a couple days after I got the portable sawmill. We'll see about this," he said. "We'll just see."

Marshall had given up entirely on his contribution to the tribe's welfare and no longer contributed his "share." However, Two Blankets did not see that he could just breach his agreement with the *Tyee*, and so she attempted to pick up some of the burdens Marshall had left unfulfilled. As such, she often worked the mornings with Stinging Nettle, then returned to Marshall to tend to his dinner. After that, she returned to the *Tyee's* longhouse to make herself useful in any way that she could. About four o'clock she would return to the longhouse she shared with her husband to prepare his supper. All of this seemed to her so much more work than when she was merely working for the tribe's welfare.

These whitemans make everything twice as much work because they insist on such a private way of life. She sat pondering one afternoon in the *Tyee's* longhouse.

She was in the midst of cutting up fresh greens they had picked along the creek. They would make an excellent fish soup when the *ch-lai* was added. Looking up from the roots she was scraping, she saw *Tyee* Running Blade watching her. When he saw her eyes lift to his, he beckoned her over. She rose with a grace she had not had two or three years ago, left her cloak in her place, and walked over the short distance.

That is another thing. Why do the whitemans insist on wearing so many clothes? Many times, Marshall had come into their longhouse dripping with sweat. He would remove his shirt, but that was as far as he would go. Our way seems so much better. Why wear clothes when the weather does not ask for clothes?

The *Tyee* Running Blade admired her lithe body and the way she moved. He gestured for her to sit when she approached, and she sat back on her haunches.

"*Mistshimus*, I want true speech from you."

"Always, *Tyee*. I owe you no less."

"Of late, I notice you working here more, and I do not see your husband, Marshall Johnston."

"That is true, *Tyee*. My husband Marshall does not make his share to the tribe. I attempt to do so for him. I am sorry if I have not done enough."

The *Tyee* Running Blade waved off this last apology. "I am not concerned with what you do. You have always contributed your share. Why is it, do you think, that Marshall Johnston does not do his share as we originally agreed upon in the marriage bargain? Does he think I asked too much?"

"I remember that trade. It was fairly done. He may say in the whiteman's tongue that he feels abused by the bargain, but I have seen him make a few poor trades with other whitemans, and he always honors those. I think he knows the tribe is leaving, and he can just wait you out. In the end, he plans on getting it all."

"I feel this, as well. I sense you have more to say?"

Now came the difficult part. "I mean no disrespect to my husband, Marshall, but since the day he received and started up the steam-powered-portable-saw," she said these words as if they were a name, "I noticed first, and now he has noticed, items going missing."

The *Tyee* leaned forward. "And he suspects the Chinook of these thefts?"

"*Tyee*, please forgive this *mistshimus*, but you asked for true speech."

"I did. Please go on."

"In truth, I suspect the clan, as well. They have been small things, eggs from the chickens first. I noticed two bundles of hides missing from his storehouse. A shovel, a chicken. I did not tell him of these things. I knew it was my duty as wife to husband Marshall to say, but I did not." She bowed her head.

"Why did you not tell the whiteman, Marshall Johnston?"

"I felt my duty to the clan was stronger. It is very strange to have these duties fight each other."

"You are not at fault, *mistshimus*. If you were to advise me, what would you say to me?"

"I would not dare to, *Tyee*."

"I command it," he said brooking no obstruction.

"As you wish. I would advise confronting the thieves, who I am sure are children or very young warriors, and command they stop. I would say nothing of this to Marshall Johnston."

"Is that honorable to allow my people to steal from him? Do I not owe him restitution?"

"If he were Chinook or *Nimi'ipuu,* I would say, yes, *Tyee.* But he is not. My husband Marshall does not understand honor. I am greatly shamed to say he has no honor."

"That is a severe thing to say of any man, *mistshimus.*"

"You commanded truth. I speak true. I do not speak of the way I am treated but of the way he sees himself in this world. He does not care at all about the clan. He will avoid the bargain he has made with you any way he can. He means to have it all when you are gone." Two Blankets was nearing tears at this admission but forced herself to look at the *Tyee* so he could see the truth in her moist eyes.

"You know you could be killed for speaking thus about a Chinook?" he said, his anger began to show.

"I know this, *Tyee.* If you had seen the steam-powered-portable-saw, you would understand. It was made in Virginia and brought here by ship on a journey of three seasons. It cost a thousand of the whiteman's dollars in gold just to buy and almost as much to bring it here. The cedar planks this longhouse is built from, it takes a man several days to cut and shape one."

The *Tyee* nodded. He had not been alive when this longhouse was built, but he had seen a smaller one built. "That is true. What has this to do with honor?"

"The steam-powered-portable-saw can cut one in a short hand of time. This I have seen with my own eyes. He has spent the property of a chief to bring this machine here. And ten tens of window panes. When you are gone to Warm Springs, he means to cut down the forests for planks of wood. From one summer to the next, he will have a little whiteman's town here with glass windows in all the buildings."

"I see. Do not trouble yourself by what Marshall Johnston has done. It is not your doing. I shall ponder this. I thank you for your truth."

"Thank you, *Tyee.* Your honor commands the truth, not your voice."

"And you still insist on remaining with this husband when we go to Warm Springs? You know you could come with us."

"You know I could not stay away from Standing Bear if I came with you," she said, the tears finally breaking through. "We would break the taboo against our relationship if I came. I would not be able to help myself. It is to protect the Bent Creek Clan, the Chinook, my people now, that I stay here. I do not do it from any loyalty or bond with my husband, Marshall."

"So, you have said, and I believe you, *mistshimus*. Know that the offer still stands, and I respect your decision."

"Thank you, *Tyee* Running Blade."

CASCADES
ATTACK

CHAPTER 20
MARCH 20 TO MARCH 29, 1856

ON MARCH 20, 1856, four warriors of the Chinook stood before the *Tyee* Running Blade in front of his longhouse where he sat on sunny days. They were Drifting Smoke and Fire Stick of the title born, and two round-head warriors, Bone-in-Nose and Flaming Arrow. They stood proudly before him after having cleansed for three days. Their pores were clean of every bit of salmon grease and wood smoke, and their eyes were clear.

The *Tyee* Running Blade greeted them, "Warriors Drifting Smoke and Fire Stick, Bone-in-Nose and Flaming Arrow. You have come before me seeking my permission, but I suspect you have made up your minds already."

Drifting Smoke, as the oldest title born, spoke for the group. "Long have we withheld our desire to strike back at these whitemans, *Tyee*, in respect of you. We understood the wisdom of your advice and took it to heart. The whitemans do not diminish in number. They are like maggots on a flood-swept carcass rotting on a sand bar."

"True words."

"Now the Yakama, the Klikitat, and the Hood River Wasco mean to strike back at the whiteman's settlements at the Cascades. We wish to join them. Maybe we will not but kill a few maggots, but we will draw enough blood they will remember us."

"I have said before that, though I believe this venture will not end well,

I honor you for your decision. If you die, we will honor and mourn you as warriors for as long as the smokes flow from our longhouses. Go now and fight bravely."

"Thank you for your good words, *Tyee* Running Blade. We go now. We will take a smaller canoe."

As they walked down to the beach, Two Blankets saw the Two Spirits Fox Tail and also Sweet-Pollen-Flower embrace their husband Fire Stick with tears and pride in their eyes. They climbed into the canoe and rapidly began paddling upstream toward the Cascades.

The steamboat *Jennie Clark* came upriver from Portland about midday on March 21, 1856. She was the first sternwheeler built for the Willamette route out of Portland, one hundred fifteen feet long and eighteen feet wide. She always ran the Willamette route, never the Cascades route.

"Husband, what steamboat is that coming upriver?"

Marshall turned from the larger corral he was building to shade his eyes. "It's the *Jennie Clark,* and she ain't stopping here today. She don't run this route normal. I got to get out there." He ran down to his canoe and pushed it out into the river, paddling hard against the current to meet the vessel.

The *Nch'i-wána* was perhaps a half-mile wide here, but the channel swept close to the south side, so it wasn't a great feat for Marshall to meet up with the *Jennie Clark*. Two Blankets watched as he grabbed onto a line thrown from the boat and ran up to the pilothouse. The big sternwheel slowed as she matched the current.

Fifteen minutes later, Marshall was boarding his canoe, and the *Jennie Clark* was once again on its way upriver.

March 27, 1856, the *Belle* passed Johnston's Landing and the Chinook village very early in the morning, her side-wheels churning the water at full speed. Her decks, Two Blankets saw, were filled with twenty to forty cavalry horses and uniformed men. In the afternoon, she steamed past empty of troops bound downriver at full speed.

"Now, we'll see how those savages deal with the U.S. Cavalry." Marshall rubbed his hands on his pants in expectation. "That there is Lieutenant Phil Sheridan and his Dragoons. We'll see the color of their damned backsides now."

March 28, 1856, the *Belle* steamed past bound upriver, followed shortly thereafter by the steamboat *Fashion* with troops from Portland lining her decks.

On March 29, 1856, Two Blankets stood at Stinging Nettle's longhouse shading her eyes against the thin sunlight. Some mist rose from the river, but something was drifting along the bank.

"Stinging Nettle, please look. Is that the canoe that Drifting Smoke and Fire Stick left in just a week ago?"

Stinging Nettle joined Two Blankets then broke into a run. "Come quick, *mistshimus* Nika." As the canoe drifted, bumping along the bank, sometimes swirling backward, Two Blankets saw that it was the same canoe, albeit in much worse condition. When they had left, the painting on the bow had been bright, and the cedar planks shone red in the sunlight. Now it was scraped, and a couple of planks were partially stove in. Within the canoe lay two bodies. River water sloshed six inches deep in the bilges.

Two of the round-heads waded into the *Nch'i-wána* and dragged the canoe back to the bank. They could see now several bullet holes piercing the cedar along the right shoreward side. Drifting Smoke and Fire Stick lay within. Drifting Smoke had a rough blood-stained bandage tied about his left arm. Fire Stick lay cushioned against Drifting Smoke's chest, a bullet wound oozing blood from his right breast.

"Get them into the longhouse," Stinging Nettle said. The several round-heads present rushed forward and took up Fire Stick roughly. "Careful now. If our warriors aren't dead yet, you don't want to be responsible." They finished easing him from the canoe and in slow cadence marched him up to the longhouse. Four more followed with the breathing but only semi-conscious Drifting Smoke.

They lay Fire Stick gently on one of the sleeping shelves along the side of the longhouse and Drifting Smoke on the next one. Fox Tail and Sweet-Pollen-Flower hovered over Fire Stick, worried, yet not knowing what to do.

Drifting Smoke coughed. "Take care of Fire Stick. I'm not that bad. It just feels good to be at home in sleeping furs again." By the time Stinging Nettle had turned to him to answer, he was already asleep. She drew a fur over him and turned her attention to Fire Stick.

"Please, Fox Tail, Sweet-Pollen-Flower, give me a little space." They backed away a few feet, his two wives holding on to each other as two cubs might lie together when their mother was away from the den.

The "armor" that would protect the wearer against an arrow was shattered by the bullet's impact. Stinging Nettle cut the side ties. Caked blood, mud and river water made untying them quite impossible. She lifted it over his head. Beneath it, the right side of his chest was covered in dried blood with fresh blood slowly oozing from a hole in his upper right chest. The minie ball had pierced his shoulder just below the right collarbone.

She bathed the wound first with river water, then with herb-infused water. Two Blankets assisted bathing the rest of his body. For the present, she packed the wound with herbs and wrapped it with a cloth. Stinging Nettle opened his mouth and noted both old and some fresh blood there. She sniffed his breath and didn't like what she smelled. He had the iron smell of blood upon his breath. Finally, she bade everyone be quiet and listened with her ear to his chest.

"We must let him rest a bit to gain strength. The ball is still in his body. I would say that there are bones shattered there. If one has pierced the lung, he will die. If it has not, he may die anyway, or he may heal and be crippled. Both Fire Stick and Drifting Smoke are fevered. Give them both the willow bark tea, and in two handspans of the sun we will see if we can get the ball out. Let us see what we can do for Drifting Smoke."

Aside from various cedar splinters and a minie ball graze across his right ear that had furrowed his hair, he had only the one major wound. Stinging Nettle stripped off his armor and examined the rest of him. Only bruises, and those would heal.

Turning, she saw that both Fox Tail and Sweet-Pollen-Flower still stood in the same position, trembling in each other's arms. "You two, over here."

Unwilling to abandon their position of guarding Fire Stick's body, now resting in labored breathing sleep, but more afraid of the command of a tribal elder, they advanced.

"Make yourselves useful. Cleanse his body as I did with Fire Stick." She appeared serious, and her tone was direct. She awaited an answer.

Fox Tail recovered some of her sensibility first. "Yes, Stinging Nettle. I saw. First the river water, then the herb water."

"Exactly. I want you to pluck out every one of these cedar splinters. Take care with them. Don't break them off. They will fester and delay his recovery. A large splinter wound can even cause death. Remember the *mistshimus* that took the broken piece of cedar in his leg a few years ago? He just ripped it back out and didn't tell anyone. By the time anyone knew, it had festered and was too late. He died."

They were both sober now. "Yes, we understand Stinging Nettle."

While they were about their business, she peeled off the bandage. The bullet had gone clean through his arm, leaving a larger hole to the back. The blood still flowed slowly out, red and clean. She sniffed the wound. She could smell the blood and the raw meat smell, but no bad spirit smells. Cleaning the wound and packing it with herbs took a few minutes. Drifting Smoke moaned in his fitful sleep but didn't wake. She bound a piece of cloth over the injury and examined his head wound. Here the minie ball had just grazed his scalp and taken a piece of the top part of his right ear. A warrior's battle scar, then.

She withdrew a few feet and turned to face the *Tyee*. "Pardon, *Tyee*, I did not see you standing there.

"One can learn much by standing quietly," The *Tyee* said. "What do you think? His lung is pierced?"

"That is what I fear, yes. His mouth has blood in it, both old and fresh, and his breath has the smell of blood. His breathing sounds like he has fluid on his lungs like with the winter chills. He is fevered as well. The ball entered high, but if it broke a bone and that pierced the lung...." She let the sentence hang.

"Then, he will die," *Tyee* Running Blade said.

"Yes. There is nothing I can do. I can attempt to remove the bullet, but I am saddened. It may make no difference in the end."

"It was a foolish venture, but sometimes I think it would be better for all of us to die a warrior's death, like Fox Tail, than live like worms beneath the whiteman's boot." The *Tyee* turned away and walked at a measured pace back to his sitting place.

Stinging Nettle motioned to Two Blankets to attend. Two Blankets got up, careful not to disturb Fire Stick, and approached. "Nika, watch over Fox Tail and Sweet-Pollen-Flower. When they learn that Fire Stick is to die, I fear for them. Do not be obvious, but be there when they learn of it."

"I understand, Stinging Nettle. This *mistshimus* will do as you say."

Drifting Smoke woke from his sleep and sat up late in the evening.

"He wakes. He wakes," Sweet-Pollen-Flower said.

"I see you have seen fit to jab me full of splinters while I slept," Drifting Smoke said. "What of Fire Stick?" He looked over at Fire Stick, who lay upon his pallet breathing weakly.

Stinging Nettle moved to his side. She pressed her hand to his forehead and his throat. "Your fever is subdued. That is good." She leaned in close. "I fear for Fire Stick, Drifting Smoke."

Drifting Smoke looked over at Fox Tail and Sweet-Pollen-Flower, "Ah, I understand."

The *Tyee* stood and stepped to the forefront of the others surrounding Drifting Smoke. "We of the Bent Creek Clan would hear of your adventure if you feel strong enough to tell it."

"*Tyee* Running Blade, if I may piss and have a plate of food, I will gladly tell the story."

The *Tyee* nodded, and Drifting Smoke got up and stood erect for the first time in the last two days. He stretched and hobbled out. In a few minutes, he returned and accepted the plate of food, and sat in the story telling place near the head of the Bent Creek Clan. He took a bite of venison and chewed as if it were his first meal on earth.

Swallowing, he said, "That is the best mouthful of food I have ever eaten. We left the Bent Creek Clan nine days ago and paddled up the *Wimahl* very quickly. All four of us were young, strong, and in high spirits. Fire Stick told his usual bawdy stories, which made all of us laugh, especially Bone-in-Nose and Flaming Arrow, who had not heard them a hundred times. We all laughed. It was a great adventure, and we have not had many of them lately.

"We reached the lower Cascades, and the water was quite deep. We managed to tow the canoe up over them with much slipping and cursing.

It was dangerous, but we were young warriors on our first true war party. All of us were some bruised and scraped when we finally made it above the lower Cascades, but we did not care about the risks we took, and the bruises and scrapes were symbols of that. We camped along the bank that night and lay down filled with excitement. I did not think I would sleep, but the journey up the lower Cascades exhausted us, and all of us fell asleep almost immediately. All but Fire Stick, who let out a huge fart which woke everyone. When we turned to him, he was snoring with a smile on his face. After the stench of it had drifted away on the cool river breeze, we all slept."

Two Blankets could hear the warrior's tale from where she sat by Fire Stick. She dipped another cloth into cold water and bathed his fevered brow, throat, and chest. He slept fitfully and in pain, and his wound still seeped blood. Although Fire Stick had been one of the three who had taken her, she had grown accustomed to his humor and feared greatly that soon it would be gone.

Drifting Smoke stopped his narrative for enough time to gulp down a couple more mouthfuls of food. "The next day, we woke in the gray mists and pushed on. By mid-afternoon, we could see where the creek the whitemans call Mill Creek entered the *Wimahl*. We pulled the canoe up there into the bushes and made it fast on the north side of the river. At that point, we did not know the situation of the place, nor where the Yakama, the Klikitat, and the Hood River Wasco were. We scouted the whiteman's post there. We saw the steamboat *Mary* tied to the bank and several of the whitemans going about their usual business. We knew then that the attack had not started and became more excited. We decided to act casual and just stroll through. It was difficult knowing that soon we would be killing them, but Fire Stick kept his humorous comments in Chinook, and we knew they could only understand the Jargon. I remember, after we had passed, that Fire Stick thought it hilarious that with each whiteman he walked by, he said in Chinook 'You are dead' or 'I will kill you second' and laughed that the whitemans did not know. As we walked through the camp I noticed a thin drift of smoke, just a wisp off to the north, then it was gone. Looking around, I saw no one in sight and motioned our party to follow a game trail in that direction. About a half a mile up, we came across Wasco scouts and made ourselves known to them.

One of them accompanied us into their main camp. Once we had convinced them of our intent, they let us join them.

"We were quite amazed. There were a good two hundred warriors there and most carried some kind of gun. We told them we had known they might be there by the smoke trail, and they immediately doused their fires. For two days, we stayed there as more warriors arrived. We chanted, and we talked of retribution on the whitemans. I did notice that there was not much organization to a plan of attack, just a lot of frustration and hatred. Finally, we were ready to attack.

"We slipped down into the whiteman's village near dawn and stood there in the early morning mists. Many of us lined up along the creek they call Mill Creek, down to the falls, and waited. The whitemans were walking to their work on the bridges for the portage railroad. The first whitemans that saw us stopped and just stared for a moment, their jaws hanging open. Then they ran. A few ran for the blockhouse downriver. Our party fired, some arrows and many rifle shots, and killed one *cultus* whiteman and wounded several others. Most of the tribal warriors followed the whitemans up to the Coe family store. We made an initial attack on the store thinking to take it immediately and were met by such a rain of bullets that I ducked behind a tree. Bark and leaves were flying. I think perhaps some tribal warriors were hit, but I was too busy hiding. I couldn't count how many were in there, but there must have been thirty or forty men, women, and children. One thing you can say for the whitemans is they know how to shoot better than we do."

Drifting Smoke paused to eat a couple more bites. All were silent in the longhouse, imagining the scene that he painted. Drifting Smoke was proving to be a gifted storyteller.

"Thank you. I am so hungry. The wind was blowing hard downriver and some, including the four of us, ran down the creek to where the *Mary* was tied up. We could not see any smoke coming from her smokestacks, and there were only a few men there. Two were on shore untying the lines, and although we tried to kill them, they got away. Another whiteman on the boat was shot through the shoulder. One of our group rushed up the gangplank and was shot dead at the head of it by a man with a pistol. A boy, not more than fourteen or so, climbed up on the upper deck and shot another of our party at close range and killed him. By now we were all firing upon anything that moved on the *Mary*, and we could see that she now had smoke coming from her stacks. We knew that someone had to be in the wheelhouse, that little house they steer the boat from on top, and many fired upon it. Our bows were useless at this point, and the four of us just watched. Splinters were flying from the wood of the pilothouse as the *Mary* began backing up. No matter what we did, we could not kill the boat or the person steering her. Finally, she backed out of range and blew her whistle twice and steamed in the direction of The Dalles.

"Since we couldn't get the boat, the four of us returned to the store. The tribal people surrounded it and were keeping up a constant fire upon it. Some of the tribal party broke off and went to the creek to burn the sawmill there, a couple of houses and a warehouse down by the *Wimahl*. About a hundred or so warriors went downriver toward Fort Rains blockhouse, and some beyond, though I didn't learn about them until later.

"Though the only stairway to the upper floor of the store was outside, soon the whitemans began firing upon us from that vantage as well. They must have cut a hole in the floor of the upper story and then to the little garret above that. This kept up all day. We would fire upon them, then attempt to rush the store only to be driven back. We threw firebrands upon the roof, and even large stones, but they repulsed us. Finally, it came on evening, and we withdrew a little out of range. Some went to burn and pillage the remaining houses and buildings.

"The next morning, we began our attack anew. Fire Stick, Flaming Arrow, Bone-in-Nose, and I could do little with our bows. We helped with reloading the guns of the others once they taught us how. Fire Stick was getting tired of not playing a warrior's role in this fight, but I could see nothing we could do to change that. I knew the anger within him was building. I turned to him to counsel patience, and he was no longer beside me. The rage consumed him, and he rushed the store, his ax raised, a great war-whoop ringing forth. He only got fifteen paces or so across the open ground in front of the Coe Store before a single shot among many cut him down with the wound you have seen. I don't know what came over me, but I was out of my hiding place and running to his side. I felt the bullet graze my head and didn't even know then it had taken part of my ear. I knelt beside Fire Stick, who was wounded bad, and began dragging him back to safety. A second hail of bullets and one caught me in the arm. I just kept dragging. Finally, I reached the brush and my tree, now mostly denuded of bark, before a third round of balls hit the bush and tree above me.

"At that point, I thought of nothing except getting away. Flaming Arrow and Bone-in-Nose said they would stay, cross the river at night, and walk home. I hope they made it, but it will take some days for them to sneak around The Dalles. I dragged Fire Stick back to where we had hidden the canoe. Along the way, I do not even remember where, I found some cloths for bandaging. I lay Fire Stick in the bottom of the canoe and paddled out into the current. All I could think of was returning home. When I reached the Cascades, I just kept going. Either I would make it through the rapids or I would not. I remember hitting a couple of rocks, and there is that one place where the river is split by a huge boulder. I had trouble there, hit the rock and bashed in the side of the canoe and shipped some water. But the water is deep this year, and I made it through. Just below the Cascades, I saw a group of The People, forty or so guarding a narrow causeway, the only path upriver. I was looking at them when I saw the whiteman's soldiers at the downriver end. Neither could advance. Just then, they saw me and turned their rifles upon me. I dove onto the bottom of the canoe and covered Fire Stick with my body. That is when I got all the splinters in my ass. I passed them and then just let the boat drift downriver with the current. A steamboat full of soldiers headed upstream, but they were out in the main channel. I must have passed out because the next thing I remember clearly was being carried from the canoe into the longhouse."

Drifting Smoke stopped suddenly with his tale. There was not a sound in the longhouse except the soft crackling of the fire and the breathing of some ninety people. This swirl of silence drifted around the room and eventually followed the smoke through the vent in the roof.

"Thank you for your tale, Drifting Smoke," *Tyee* Running Blade said.

"I can say one thing more, please," said Drifting Smoke. "My experience with this raid upon the whitemans has taught me this sad lesson. There is no way that The People, and by The People I mean all of us natives, every one of us, can prevail over the whitemans. There are not enough of us to even start such a war. Such a war will only end in death. I am saddened to the bone to say this, but it is truth as I see it."

GRIEF
AND HEALING

CHAPTER 21
MARCH 29 TO APRIL, 1856

THE LONGHOUSE WAS silent for a few minutes as the clan digested Drifting Smoke's story and his final assessment. When there began to be murmurings of talk, it was quiet talk. Among the younger Chinook, there seemed to be disagreement with his final assessment. "Did we not strike the whitemans a mighty blow?" and "The whitemans will pay attention to us now." Among the elder, cooler heads there was quiet, sad agreement and little talk at all.

"I will speak now," said the *Tyee*. The gravity of his presence drew them like the sun draws the planets. The sough of talk subsided.

He looked about this group, the Bent Creek Clan of the Chinook that had been his charge to lead and protect these many years. The years of care had taken their toll upon him in wrinkles and graying hair, but they also lent him a kind of strength of purpose. A strength one could sense was wearing thin in places but would last him the rest of his life.

He nodded respect toward Drifting Smoke. "First, I want to thank Drifting Smoke for his detailed and accurate report on the whiteman's camp. You were in the midst of the fight yet stayed cool and fought bravely. You rescued your friend and our clan member at great risk to yourself. You are to be commended, Drifting Smoke. Second, all four of you have brought honor upon the Bent Creek Clan by your actions. History shall not record that we shied away from this action against the *cultus* whitemans and their taking of our lands." He looked about the longhouse, proud of his people. All looked at him, elders and young alike, with a look that implied faith in his leadership.

"Although I was only a young child when the Lewis and the Clark first came down this river some fifty-one summers ago, I do remember what it was like then. The Chinook were one of the richest trading tribes any had ever seen. We controlled the *Wimahl* from its great mouth up to the Celilo Falls. We traded in goods from the coast, from the far northern lands, to the far south. The fur trade and the trade from the Nez Perce and all the plains people passed through our hands. We were great in our numbers and great in our trading power. The Chinook Jargon, which we speak in trade, is used by tens of thousands of people, whitemans and The People alike. In my lifetime, I have seen the *cultus* whitemans first bring more trade, which we welcomed. They brought disease which emptied four of every five huts. They brought settlers who we helped, and we tried to accommodate them. Lastly, they have swarmed like flies upon the dead carcasses of salmon until you cannot see the sky. Now they force us to move from our homes to a new place. We will be the Chinook of Bent Creek no longer. We cannot stop the whitemans. But I am glad you have struck this blow against them, my friends Drifting Smoke and Fire Stick and Flaming Arrow and Bone-in-Nose. We may have to move. We will make this new place, Warm Springs, our home. We may change, but we will be the Bent Creek Clan in our hearts, and we will mold this Warm Springs on the Deschutes River to fit us. The whitemans will long remember this day. It will be remembered with a whiteman's date, but we will remember it in our own history as well. They will write of it as being an unprovoked attack. But we will remember the truth of it. And they will still write of it in a hundred years' time."

Two Blankets stayed with Fire Stick through the night, accompanied by Fox Tail and Sweet-Pollen-Flower. One or another of the three would stay awake while the other two lay down on the floor and pulled a fur over them and slept. At the moment, Sweet-Pollen-Flower lay in disturbed sleep, and Two Blankets lay with her, just hugging her. There was not any real way to comfort either of them. They both knew deep down that this was a death watch, but they still wanted to be with him.

Fox Tail sat, touching Fire Stick's face, her tears flowing freely. "My brave and foolish warrior, Fire Stick, I am so proud to have been wife to you, even so short a time. I wanted, at first, for you to stop teasing me so much. It irritated me so much. I never really told you that. Now I just want to be your Burr-Up-My-Ass a little longer."

Stinging Nettle relieved Two Blankets at dawn. She checked on Fire Stick first, carefully pulling off the poultice of Old Man's Beard and honey. He was still fevered, and his breath rattled with the liquid in his lungs. The wound was inflamed, and the stink of infection seeped from it with the yellow pus. "Go home for a few hours, Nika," she said.

"Yes, Stinging Nettle. But I want to be here when—"

Stinging Nettle hugged her. "You are a brave and honest friend. He still has a few hours left, but I do not think he will last the day. If he does, then his time will come tonight. Go, put in an appearance for your husband, Marshall Johnston, then come back. You belong here, with us."

Two Blankets walked through the mists toward Marshall's longhouse. She no longer thought of it as hers, which was sad as she recalled the stolen hours she had spent there with Standing Bear. Over the river, the morning mists were rising. It would soon clear and be a fine day, but not a fine day for her.

When she reached the hut, she girded herself, then entered. Marshall was still asleep on his pallet, and the room stank of unwashed flesh, half-eaten food, and whiskey. She took the bucket and egg basket and went out to feed the chickens. They clucked about her as she scattered grain and picked up eggs. She knew Marshall had not gathered any in several days for these were mostly rotten. Throwing the rotten eggs into the midden pile, she reentered the hut. She marked the egg count on Marshall's record paper and began to tidy up. Every moment was a painful one away from the real and sad events taking place just two hundred fifty paces downriver in the *Tyee's* longhouse. That was where she wanted to be, among her friends and family.

It stopped her, this thought. They are my friends and my true family. What will I do when they are gone? She longed to go with them, desperately needed that communal family. She knew she could not. The one I long for most, the one I need just to hold me, is Standing Bear.

She wiped the tears from her eyes and built the fire back up. Slicing potatoes thin, she put the pan of them onto the fire to begin cooking. In another pan, she placed thick slices of bacon and started it sizzling. Meanwhile, she gathered up all the empty whiskey bottles and put them in a wooden crate to trade later. Marshall was beginning to stir from his drink induced sleep and finally sat up rubbing his eyes.

"There you are. Where you been these last couple days? Not caring for your husband like you ought to, I know that."

"Good morning, husband Marshall. You know where I have been, caring for the injured in the attack at the Cascades." She turned the potatoes, poured a little water over them, and covered them to steam.

"You mean the god damn massacre of innocents at the Cascades, don't you? Because that is what it was."

"The clan has a different view, husband. They look upon it as an attempt to drive out those who have taken their land." She broke three eggs into the bacon pan.

"Well, I warned them is what I did. When the steamboat came upriver, I paddled out and told that Lieutenant Sheridan you savages was coming. Likely that saved a whole lot of people because of my warning."

Two Blankets pulled the pans from the fire and dished potatoes, bacon, and eggs up for Marshall. She found a dirty fork and handed the plate to him. Sitting back on her heels she plucked a slab of bacon from the pan and absently ate it. Usually, she liked the bacon. Today it just tasted like grease and bitterness. She threw the piece back into the pan.

She turned on him. "Apparently, husband Marshall, your warning didn't do any good at all. Or perhaps they just didn't believe. Our warriors walked straight through the *cultus* whiteman's village, and no one paid any attention. Even two days later when they attacked, the whitemans were completely surprised."

"The hell you say," Marshall said, spitting out a hard piece of bacon rind onto the floor. "Son of a bitch."

"I have to go back to the *Tyee* Running Blade's longhouse now. I hope, husband Marshall, you have everything you need." Two Blankets rose and walked from the hut. She still found some things she could do with pride, and she walked with pride.

"Son of a bitch. They didn't pay any attention," was the last she heard as the door flap closed.

Two Blankets hurried back to the *Tyee's* longhouse. She didn't know exactly why, only that she felt she must. When she got there, she saw that Fire Stick was sitting up and conscious for the first time.

Approaching his sleeping pallet, she caught Stinging Nettle's eye. "Is he—"

"Better? No, I do not think so. I think it is taking a tremendous effort on his part. His last effort, I am afraid."

Bone Rattler was there, as well, bearing witness to what Fire Stick said.

"So, Burr-up-my-Ass, it was a great battle, was it not?"

"It was, Fire Stick, so Drifting Smoke tells us. Your bravery has brought honor upon the Bent Creek Clan. So, the *Tyee* Running Blade says as well. The whitemans will remember that day and the men you killed."

"I know I shouldn't have charged the store, but I got so damned tired of hiding behind that tree being showered with bark. I finally just got up and charged the *cultus* bastards."

"You are ever my brave warrior," Sweet-Pollen-Flower said.

"Now, as to my burial," he said.

"Oh, please don't say that, Fire Stick." Two Blankets saw the cloth Fox Tail was using to clean Fire Stick's lips. It was pink with blood.

"My two loving wives," he extended his arms, and Sweet-Pollen-Flower and Fox Tail joined him on his furs. "No warrior was ever more blessed with such."

Sweet-Pollen-Flower sniffed back her tears. "How do you want to be buried, warrior Fire Stick?"

"I had never thought about it before, but I have had some time. I want you to use the canoe we took for the battle."

"But it is damaged. Surely you deserve better," Sweet-Pollen-Flower said.

"It is damaged from our attack. I want to be buried in it exactly as it is now, with broken planks and bullet hole, as a tribute to what we did."

"It shall be done as you ask, Fire Stick," Fox Tail said.

"I want to be buried in the new place, in Warm Springs." This brought a series of surprised exclamations from those listening.

"So," Bone Rattler said, "you do not want your place in the trees with your father and grandfather to keep you company?"

"No, I do for now. Fox Tail will tell you I was ever one for new adventures. Someone has to be first to have his canoe lifted above the prairie at Warm Springs. Let it be me, and I will welcome all those who come after me. And I will also be close to my beloveds, Sweet-Pollen-Flower and Fox Tail."

"It shall be done as you wish," Bone Rattler said. "We shall first raise you in the trees here at Bent Creek, and then we will take your body and canoe to Warm Springs and post you high there for everyone to see that we honor you."

Fire Stick leaned back. "Now I may rest easy with my death. Come here my loves and be with me in my last minutes. I would feel your bodies close to mine."

He lay back on his sleeping furs, and Sweet-Pollen-Flower lay her head upon his stomach where she could feel his troubled breath easing in and out. Fire Stick rested his left arm across her shoulders, his hand at the nape of her neck softly stroking her long black hair. Fox Tail tucked under his right arm, her head upon Fire Stick's shoulder where she could just look at him.

Fire Stick closed his eyes. "Now it is not so bad. I will wait for you."

Bone Rattler began a low chant to ease his passing into the spirit world. "Spirits of the world beyond please welcome our brother, Fire Stick. He brought honor to the Bent Creek Clan while alive and now brings that honor to you, ancestors of the Bent Creek Clan." The rest of the clan present and awake took up the chant in low voices. "Spirits of the world beyond please welcome our brother Fire Stick. He has brought honor to the Bent Creek Clan while alive and now brings that honor to you, ancestors of the Bent Creek Clan."

The rhythmic cadence soon had everyone in its grasp, from the smallest child who only nodded to the beat of it, to the eldest who remembered many of those passed ancestor spirits in their chanting. After about an hour, Fire Stick's breathing slowed. He did not suddenly sit up, nor speak any last dramatic words. His breathing just slowed each time, taking a little longer to inhale again. Finally, it stopped, and he inhaled no more.

Some there felt only the silence of his passing. A few, including Two Blankets, would later swear to seeing a wisp of the gold of his humor and red of his bravery twine about itself and rise above his body like smoke.

One round-head child of four, called Sees-What-No-One-Else-Sees by his mother, broke the silence, "Do you see him? He rises from his body and drifts to the smoke hole. He waved at me. Now he is gone."

Bone Rattler turned and noted the child with a nod. "Fire Stick is with the spirits now. Take his empty body to Stinging Nettle's longhouse, and I will prepare it for the raising into the branches. We fast and cleanse for three days, then we will raise him." Four warriors gently lifted Fire Stick and carried him out. Death was a business to be treated with the respect of ritual, and this they honored.

A few repaired immediately to the sweat lodges, and most sat silent where they were remembering Fire Stick and his every joke, bad and good, his every act. These they fixed into their memories. He would not soon, if ever, be forgotten.

Two Blankets followed the body, she did not know why. She knew she would not go back to Marshall Johnson's Landing until after the raising of the body. Bone Rattler and Stinging Nettle were there, beginning to strip the body of his clothes. Two Blankets took over that task and brushed off his blood-stained cloak and folded it. She removed his moccasins. They bathed him with herb infused water until his battered empty body was perfectly clean. The wound Stinging Nettle probed until she found the minie ball and removed it.

"We don't want any *cultus* whiteman's device in the sacred grove," she said by way of explanation. She repacked the wound with sweet-smelling herbs and cleansed around it.

Bone Rattler opened Fire Stick's mouth and cleaned it of blood and spittle. At last, they were finished with their preparations and began to dress him in his spirit robes. A white elkhide cape draped him to his feet, and moccasins encased his feet. These both were worked with care and carried intricate beadwork. They brushed and plaited his hair away from his proud, sloped forehead and bound each plait with dentalium shells.

Bone Rattler announced. "That is enough for this night. Go, Stinging Nettle and *mistshimus*, to the sweat lodge and cleanse yourselves well of this life and Fire Stick's death. Tomorrow we will begin the preparation for his spirit voyage. I will watch the body this night."

Stinging Nettle turned to Two Blankets. "Come, Nika, we will go to the moon cycle hut."

When Two Blankets left the sweat bath in the morning, she passed Fox Tail and Sweet-Pollen-Flower in the midst of their own preparations for the raising of Fire Stick into the branches. Both had shaved their heads, as was proper for the wives of a deceased warrior. They were chanting the pre-internment ritual together and seemed almost incandescent already. Another two days of cleansing and fasting and they would be spirit-like themselves.

She cast an eye toward Marshall's longhouse, and all she could see was him going about his tasks as usual. No doubt, he was angry at her absence. Also, he was certain to be angry at the way the "savages" in the Bent Creek Clan were treating him. She did not care about this either. If she had a choice, she wouldn't be going back to him. At present, she could see no other way.

Best to focus on today, and this moment only, as Fox Tail and Sweet-Pollen-Flower do. They have lost a husband. That is a great loss. I merely have a bad husband.

She continued to Stinging Nettle's, where Bone Rattler sat quietly chanting over Fire Stick's body. She took up the chant, and in a few minutes, there was only the chant, the herbs burning over the body, and Fire Stick's resting corpse. Bone Rattler got up quietly and went for her own cleanse in the moon cycle hut. The sun moved across the sky. When it had moved three or four hands, Stinging Nettle sat down beside Two Blankets and took up the chant. After a two fingers of sun time, when they were in perfect synchrony, Two Blankets rose and left the hut first to relieve herself and then to take a small amount of food in the *Tyee's* longhouse.

No one spoke unless it was absolutely necessary. All were intent upon the coming raising into the trees. The canoe that Fire Stick and the others had departed in, in such high spirits only two hands of days before, was pulled up on the beach. Several round-head warriors and a couple of title born were working over it inch by inch. Per Fire Stick's request, they left the damage done by the *cultus* whiteman's bullets and the broken planks from the run down the Cascades as they were. That did not stop them from cleaning every bit of debris from it from stem to stern and touching up the design painted on the bow. No speech came from that group either. None of the usual joking camaraderie Two Blanket had come to expect from any work group.

At some point during this process, Flaming Arrow and Bone-in-Nose had returned, exhausted from having to walk the entire journey and possessing some bruises and light cuts from the battle but not significantly damaged. They met with the *Tyee*, then proceeded to communal tasks appropriate to them. Both appeared saddened by the news of Fire Stick's death and vowed he should not be forgotten.

For three days and nights, this new rhythm acted upon the Bent Creek Clan. Sometimes Two Blankets could hear the wail of Fox Tail or Sweet-Pollen-Flower as they grieved. On the evening of the third day, the canoe was carried with great ceremony and the soft beating of a drum up from the beach to Stinging Nettle's hut. Four of the elders entered and carried out Fire Stick's body and placed him solemnly into the canoe. Stinging Nettle carried the chant now. As the people filed past, they left gifts for the spirit of Fire Stick. Many cut a forelock of hair and placed it into the canoe. Stinging Nettle cut a plait of her own hair, as did Bone Rattler. Each took up the chant, as they laid down their gifts whether it be a lock of hair, a shell, a dentalium bracelet or choker, a special dish of Fire Stick's favorite food, or any of the other myriad gifts. Fox Tail and Sweet-Pollen-Flower laid their shaven locks within, carefully braided into many plaits, each plait bound with a dentalium shell. Finally, it was the *mistshimus'* turn, and Two Blankets was not surprised to find them no less generous. They, of course, had no property, but that did not stop them from cutting a lock of hair and decorating that gift with twined wildflowers. Two Blankets herself had braided her hair tight and cut a braid off at the scalp and laid it across Fire Stick's folded hands. She had nothing else to give except her glass from Marshall's, and a *cultus* whiteman's gift did not seem appropriate.

I can only give you, this spirit of Fire Stick. You were one who was responsible for taking me from my family and my tribe, the *Nimi'ipuu*. For many years I hated you for this act upon me. Now you are gone. I can only forgive you this action. I hope your spirit will accept my tiny forgiveness.

She, too, joined in the chanting. The *Tyee* Running Blade was last in the line, and he cut one of his braids of waist-length, gray hair and laid it across Fire Stick's body. His deep voice also joined in the chant as eight warriors, title born and round-head, picked up the canoe and led the procession in the direction of the Sacred Grove.

When they reached the Sacred Grove, Bone Rattler turned to the group. "All will strip naked who enter this grove to raise this warrior, Fire Stick, into the trees. Put all clothes and jewelry aside and enter as the gods made you." She proceeded to remove her garments, as did the others. Two Blankets had not been allowed into the grove before but proceeded as though Bone Rattler's remarks referred to her as well. The other *mistshimus* looked about, then, doing as she did, removed their capes and moccasins. Soon the whole Bent Creek Clan stood naked and chanting, standing still within the Sacred Grove before the place of the raising of the dead.

Now that Bone Rattler's cape was removed, Two Blankets saw she was painted from head to foot in a whitish-gray ash of a light burning wood. On top of this were stripes of red and black zig-zagging down her body. She appeared as almost a ghost herself. Next to her stood the *Tyee* Running Blade, also totally painted but with different designs. As she looked about, she saw that all the title borne were similarly painted. The round-heads had less dramatic body paint, but still had their faces painted. Only the *mistshimus* were unpainted as they did not have the property rights to a design nor own any paint.

Still, they were to be allowed to enter the Sacred Grove. Following the canoe bearers, who seemed to bend and lift as one organism, they walked slowly, all the while chanting, into the Grove. Reaching the section reserved for title born warriors, Two Blankets saw the frame upon which the canoe was to be lifted. It consisted of four forked posts driven securely into the ground, crossed by two beams, one to the fore and one aft. Normally, she knew, holes would be cut in the bottom of the canoe for a raising like this. Not this time. The canoe was whole, presumably because it was to be moved upriver in another two months. With all the ceremony due to a warrior killed in battle, the canoe was slowly raised over the bearer's heads, then passed over the first beam. Without a pause, the first two bearers on the stern portion passed under the beam and took up their burden again. Slowly, in this manner, the canoe slid, as easily as it would into water, along the path that led to its final resting place. A smaller canoe was inverted and placed over Fire Stick's body.

Two Blankets did not see any spirits, but it seemed to her that they would be pleased by the reverence of the whole tribe standing naked in a surround about Fire Stick's canoe-borne body. When this was done, four small banked fires were lit in each of the cardinal directions—North, South, East and West. Pungent herbs were sprinkled upon these by Bone Rattler, Stinging Nettle, and two other elders. Each direction received a different herb. Two Blankets could smell one as acrid, another as soothing, another fiery, the fourth as an almost decayed fruity smell.

Finally, the chanting which had carried on for three days, until it had a life and breath of its own, ceased. The eerie silence crept in behind it and took possession of the tribe. The clan crept away, making as little noise as possible. A baby cried out once and was quickly "shushed" by her mother. They reached their clothes and put them on in silence. They left the area in silence. Two Blankets knew this strange calm and quiet could not last, but no one wanted to be the one to break it. All wanted to preserve it as long as possible.

It was a kind of peace and balance which, especially for Two Blankets, could not last as she headed for Marshall Johnston's longhouse and a man who would never comprehend meaning at this depth.

R. L. ADARE HAS been writing since he was a teenager. Taking a major in linguistics at university, his interest in anthropology and language development has frequently played a part in his writing. While studying linguistics he also took a minor in German, so he could read Hesse in the original as well as obtain a teaching credential. He has taught for ten years after having been an accountant for thirty-five. Along the way, he and his wife owned a kite shop on the Oregon coast for ten years and lived on a thirty-six-foot sailboat for ten years, which they sailed down the coast from Seattle to Monterey.

Among his favorite thousand authors are Zane Grey, Herman Hesse, D. H. Lawrence, C. J. Cherryh, Lawrence Durrell, Ursula Le Guin, Anne McCaffrey, Kurt Vonnegut, Jacqueline Cleary, and Diana Gabaldon.

He has been published in *Wings, Pass the Hemlock, The Whale Song Quarterly, Ariel Chart, The Wyrd, Saddlebag Dispatches* and *Cobra Lily*. He lives with his wife of 35 years and their manx cat, Pixie, in South-western Oregon.

www.facebook.com/RLAdare/